A DOUBLE-WIDE MURDER

He was stretched out across the kitchen floor, face-down, a pool of blood running away from me toward the back hallway. Big guy. Muscular. Wearing a white T-shirt and jeans, gray socks, and black high-tops. I tiptoed over to him, watching where I stepped, and squatted beside him. I pushed his tangled dark hair off his neck and put my fingers on his throat, feeling for a pulse. There wasn't one. He was dead.

I hurried back out through the door. John had the woman handcuffed behind her back. She was sitting in the shadowy driveway, crying, her body swaying, her head bowed. Her tangled blond hair hung down between her knees.

When he finished reading her rights out loud, I said, "There's a dead guy in there."

He raised his radio to his mouth and began to tell the dispatcher he needed the coroner, as the woman sitting on the driveway raised her dazed blue eyes to look at me, let go with a sob, and said, "Terry?"

Danny came running up behind me and skidded to a halt, staring at her. "Holy shit!" he said. "Marylou?"

LIGHTS OUT

A WORKING MAN'S MYSTERY

L. T. Fawkes

A SIGNET BOOK

SIGNET
Published by New American Library, a division of
Penguin Group (USA) Inc., 375 Hudson Street,
New York, New York 10014, U.S.A.
Penguin Books Ltd, 80 Strand,
London WC2R 0RL, England
Penguin Books Australia Ltd, 250 Camberwell Road,
Camberwell, Victoria 3124, Australia
Penguin Books Canada Ltd, 10 Alcorn Avenue,
Toronto, Ontario, Canada M4V 3B2
Penguin Books (N.Z.) Ltd, Cnr Rosedale and Airborne Roads,
Albany, Auckland 1310, New Zealand

Penguin Books Ltd, Registered Offices:
80 Strand, London WC2R 0RL, England

First published by Signet, an imprint of New American Library,
a division of Penguin Group (USA) Inc.

First Printing, February 2004
10 9 8 7 6 5 4 3 2 1

Copyright © Margo Pierce Dorksen, 2004
All rights reserved

 REGISTERED TRADEMARK—MARCA REGISTRADA

Printed in the United States of America

Without limiting the rights under copyright reserved above, no part of this
publication may be reproduced, stored in or introduced into a retrieval system, or transmitted, in any form, or by any means (electronic, mechanical,
photocopying, recording, or otherwise), without the prior written permission
of both the copyright owner and the above publisher of this book.

PUBLISHER'S NOTE
This is a work of fiction. Names, characters, places, and incidents either are
the product of the author's imagination or are used fictitiously, and any resem-
blance to actual persons, living or dead, business establishments, events, or
locales is entirely coincidental.

BOOKS ARE AVAILABLE AT QUANTITY DISCOUNTS WHEN USED TO PROMOTE
PRODUCTS OR SERVICES. FOR INFORMATION PLEASE WRITE TO PREMIUM MAR-
KETING DIVISION, PENGUIN GROUP (USA) INC., 375 HUDSON STREET, NEW YORK,
NEW YORK 10014.

If you purchased this book without a cover you should be aware that this
book is stolen property. It was reported as "unsold and destroyed" to the
publisher and neither the author nor the publisher has received any payment
for this "stripped book."

The scanning, uploading and distribution of this book via the Internet or via
any other means without the permission of the publisher is illegal and punish-
able by law. Please purchase only authorized electronic editions, and do not
participate in or encourage electronic piracy of copyrighted materials. Your
support of the author's rights is appreciated.

Thank you
Claire Zion,
John Paine,
and Carol Mann

Chapter 1

I was sitting in Brewster's one Friday morning in the middle of November, happily mauing my number four breakfast like a healthy growing boy. I was enjoying my friends' goofy small talk and watching the weather out Brewster's big front windows. Lightning ripped through black, boiling storm clouds, and sheets of cold, wicked rain slapped at the vehicles in the big parking lot.

Ah, late autumn in northeastern Ohio. Nothing else like it.

My name's Terry Saltz. I'm a carpenter. Breakfast at Brewster's every weekday morning is sort of a ritual for me and my friends. Eat. Shoot the shit. Get our natural juices flowing by ragging on each other before we head out in different directions to earn our daily pack of Marlboros. As I sipped my coffee and glanced around that particular morning, I was lazily speculating whether or not to go ahead with a fairly radical plan.

I was thinking about maybe getting a haircut.

My hair was long. I'd worn it long since I was thirteen. At first, it got long because my old man wasn't around to spot me the cost of a haircut, and I wasn't willing to hand my hard-earned paper-route money over to a barber. In those days, half the time I was using that paper-route money for food.

My hair grew down over my collar. Teachers started getting on me about it, and I liked being a bad boy.

When it got longer, the girl I'd been watching for a while suddenly got interested in me. Sometimes after school we'd go stand behind the middle-school building and she'd reach up to run her fingers through my long black hair and say how silky it was and how good it smelled.

After that, I was enthusiastic about three things: my girlfriend, my long hair, and what kind of shampoo and conditioner smelled best. No shit. I spent the better part of a year sniffing bottles up and down the shampoo aisle in the drugstore.

When I was fifteen, my older brother, P. J., got me and my best friend, Danny Gillespie, jobs as gofers for Red Perkins Construction. P. J. and most of the other carpenters who worked for Red wore their long, scraggly hair in ponytails, so me and Danny split a pair of leather shoelaces and tied ours back like theirs. That's how we'd had it ever since.

Only recently I'd been thinking about getting it cut. All that long black hair was a lot of trouble. That November morning, while I chewed my Texas toast and watched the rain, I was thinking how much easier it would be if I got it all chopped off.

The absolute last thing on my mind was my wife, Marylou, also known as the Bitch. Which, by that time, she was supposed to be my ex-wife. Except that the divorce she'd so cold-bloodedly initiated six months earlier while I was sitting brokenhearted and forlorn in jail somehow got canceled once I was out and on my feet again, in a new town, with new friends, new money, and a new outlook on life.

The talk around the table that morning turned to names. Gruf Ridolfi mentioned that if your initials spell a word, it makes you lucky all your life. Danny Gillespie piped up right away with the information that his initials spell DIG.

I looked at him. "*I?* What's your middle name?"

He got a look on his freckled face like he'd stepped in something. Which he had.

Bump Bellini grinned at him. "I can't even think of a name that starts with *I*."

Danny got busy stirring sugar into his third cup of coffee. He said, "Don't start with me. Everybody has a weird middle name."

John Garvey said, "Mine's Thomas."

Bump said, "Mine's Edward."

Gruf grinned. "Andrew."

I said, "William."

Gruf said, "William? So your initials are *TWS*? Ouch. Sorry, Terry."

I said, "*TWS* spells something. It spells *Twees*."

Bump said, "Nice try."

I said, "Hey, you know? Twees wouldn't be a bad nickname."

Bump groaned. "Here we go."

I said, "No. Really. You guys didn't like Muzzy for my nickname. So let's go with Twees."

I saw them all make eye contact. Four pairs of eyes making connections all around the table. Well, fuck 'em if they can't take a joke.

I said, "Yeah, I'm going with Twees from now on. That's what I wanna be called."

There was a heavy silence. Then Bump turned back to Danny with an evil gleam in his eye. "So where were we? Oh yeah. What's the *I* stand for?"

We all watched Danny and waited. He squirmed.

John poked him. "Well?" He was grinning.

Finally, Danny blurted out, "Okay, it's Ignatius. Happy now?"

I'd have to say we *were* pretty happy. Everybody howled.

And just at that point, Danny glanced toward the front door.

He said, "Uh-oh."

I followed his eyes, and there was the Bitch, bearing down on me like a mall surveyor. All up and down the table, my friends saw her coming and got the squirms. It looked like Danny, Gruf, Bump, and John had all suddenly gotten infested by some kind of specialized flea that only enjoyed the rich red blood of mid- to late-twenty-something males.

She walked down the side of the table and stopped behind me. An expensive cloud of Jessica McClintock perfume wrapped itself around my head. I dropped my fork and turned to look at her. She smiled down on me, but you could see that behind her eyes, lots was stirring.

She said, "Hi, Terry. Can I talk to you a minute?"

I said, "Shoot."

Her eyes flicked briefly around the table. "In private?"

In my brain, I said, Oh, shit. I looked mournfully at what was left of my breakfast, picked up my coffee cup and my cigarettes, and looked around. The only open table in the place was a booth right behind the pushed-together tables where me and my friends always sit. That was way too close for comfort, but what was I gonna do?

We slid in across from each other, and she nodded when Mary, the waitress who takes care of us every morning as if we're her own family, asked if she wanted coffee. Mary glanced at me and gently patted my shoulder. I noticed the slight rise in her sweet little eyebrows as she turned away.

She brought the Bitch a cup and topped me off. She said, "Don't you want your plate over here, hon?"

I shook my head. I wasn't hungry anymore.

There were a million thoughts flying around in my brain, but the main two were: How did the Bitch know where to find me? And what did she want? I wanted to say something to her like, Where did she get off bothering me during my leisure hours. Then I realized it wouldn't make any sense.

So then I thought, Okay, what I was really feeling was that she must have been spying on me to know where and when I ate breakfast. Because ever since I got out of jail and moved to Spencer, I'd been pretty careful not to let her know how to get in touch with me. I should demand to know where she got off doing that. But I didn't.

I thought about saying that I didn't want her coming around me anywhere, anytime, anymore. I didn't want to always be looking over my shoulder, thinking she might turn up here or there. But I didn't really want to say anything hurtful. That was more in her line, if you catch my drift.

I ended up not saying anything. I just sat there looking at her, waiting for her to start, while my friends sat at the next table with their ears sticking out. You could almost see their little pink lobes quivering, waiting to pick up every word.

Oh, jeez, look at that. Bump and Gruf were laughing. Danny, too. Now John was leaning over to Danny. Yeah, Danny had said something to make Bump and Gruf laugh and now he repeated it to John, and they were all laughing behind their hands.

I knew Danny's remark wasn't anything mean directed toward me. These friends of mine, they're the loyalest bunch of humanus erectus you could ever find anywhere. I doubted it was anything mean directed toward Marylou, either. What it was, it was just one of Danny's wry little comments on the situation in general. Danny can come up with some pretty good ones sometimes. But it wouldn't have been mean. Danny doesn't have a mean molecule in his body.

I looked at Marylou, sitting there with her big blond seventies mall hair and her two-fisted makeup covering up all her natural good looks. I lit a cigarette and waited. She took a sip of her coffee. Then she looked up at me through her heavy black mascara, combed out into what looked like millions and millions of long, long lashes.

She smiled like she was flirting with me and said, "You could at least act like you're glad to see me."

I didn't want to say anything hurtful to her, but I wasn't gonna sit there and lie, either.

I said, "Why? I'm not."

She poured it on, turning her head a little and batting those eyelashes. "Not even a little bit?" There was actually self-confidence in her voice.

"Not even a little bit," I said coldly. "What do you want?"

Mary was over at the guys' table with the coffeepot. She stopped by Bump, bent down to whisper something, and stayed bent down to hear the answer. It looked like he was whispering into a microphone hidden in the red carnation she had pinned on her green waitress dress. I swallowed a chuckle and turned my eyes back to the Bitch, who was busy pushing her cuticles back from her pearly white nail polish.

I said, "Marylou, say what you want and leave, so I can finish my breakfast in peace."

She gave me a hurt face and puckered her lips. "You don't have to be so grumpy."

I drummed my fingers and waited.

She drew breath and said, "Okay. I want you to help me move."

I thought about hauling her out of the booth, pointing her toward the door, and giving her a gentle shove, saying, There. You're moving. Happy now?

Instead I said, "Move. To where?"

But I already knew to where. A few months earlier, she'd been in Carlo's, the little pizza place where I worked nights as a driver, and she'd told Debby the waitress that she was going to sell our mobile home down in the southern part of the county and move into a town house here in Spencer. I'd been horrified at the news.

She said, "Green Meadow Town Houses."

There it was. It was really gonna happen. Not only that, but she wanted me to help her do it. I got pissed.

I said, "I'm not gonna help you move up here. I don't want you up here. Find yourself another sucker."

I reached to pick up my cigarettes and go back to my place at the table, but she put her hand on mine.

She said, "You have to help me."

"No, I don't. Get some of your friends to help you."

"You're my friend."

"No, I'm not."

"But I love you."

"That's your problem."

You're probably thinking, Why does this guy have to be such a hard-ass? Would it kill him to help the poor girl move?

If you're thinking that, Chief, it's because you don't understand women. Or at least, you don't understand *this* woman. Neither did I, back when she and I were together. But I'd learned a lot about women since then, and I knew for a fact that she wasn't here about moving. She could get plenty of help with moving.

She was here because she wanted me and her to get back together. The moving was her excuse. She figured she'd get me to help her move, and she'd wear some Daisy Dukes or something. Then the whole time during the move, she'd keep brushing against me, keep posing and giggling, keep saying how much she missed me. Keep saying things about how nice the town house was and didn't I think I'd like to live there with her? Look, we could get a recliner and put it right there in front of the TV for me. Wouldn't that be nice?

I could see it all happening right before my eyes. And it would've worked once. But not now.

She tried to work up a tear. She even got a slight tremble going in her lower lip.

She said, "You loved me once. It's not my fault if your feelings changed."

Making a conscious effort to keep my voice soft and calm, I said, "Oh, you're wrong there. It's entirely your fault that my feelings changed."

She looked away. "Anyway. We're still married. You have to help me."

This made me laugh. "We're not married anymore. Our marriage was over the day I got your divorce papers in jail."

"But—"

I interrupted, making my voice even quieter. "But there's still a piece of paper in a file cabinet somewhere that says we are married?" I shook my head. "It doesn't mean squat to me. We're not married anymore. Plain and simple."

She looked down into her coffee cup.

I said, "And as far as that piece of paper goes, I don't care anything about it. It can sit in that file drawer until hell freezes over, for all I care. If it bothers you, you go pay a lawyer to make it disappear."

She said, almost whispering, "I don't understand your attitude, Terry. You make it sound like you hate me."

I said, "I don't hate you. I don't feel anything for you at all, except I want you to stay out of my life. Starting now."

Then I did pick up my coffee cup and my cigarettes and move back to my place at the table with my friends. They were looking at me curiously.

I stole a glance at Mary. I studied her kind face like it was my own conscience, but I couldn't tell whether she looked sympathetic or disapproving.

Well, whatever. I'd explain it to her later if she didn't understand. Because I was pretty sure I felt great. I'd stood up to the strongest of the old forces that had led me down a self-destructive path that ended in a jail cell, and I'd said no—loud and clear.

Mary came over with the coffeepot. "More coffee, Terry?" she asked softly.

"Thanks, yeah. Top it off."

I heard a little rustling sound behind me. In peripheral vision I saw a figure moving toward the front door. I turned to watch the Bitch go. Her short little black skirt bounced side to side like windshield wipers as she walked away.

All of a sudden, everybody was moving and coughing and talking at once. I looked around, waiting to hear what they thought.

A strand of long, golden hair had escaped from Bump Bellini's ponytail. He tucked it back behind his ear and grinned at me. "Whew. I guess you told her."

Daniel Ignatius Gillespie gave me a high five. He was laughing. "No offense, dude, but I really didn't think you had the balls."

They were all grinning and laughing. I started laughing, too. We all sat there, laughing like a bunch of idiots.

Everything would've been different if I'd helped the Bitch move that rainy November morning. Some stuff probably still would've happened, just in a different way. Some other stuff probably wouldn't have happened at all. If I were the kind of guy who sits around thinking about what might've been, I guess I could log some serious hours wondering about this. But I'm not, so I won't.

Chapter 2

It was getting to be about that time. After a few minutes, John, Danny, and Bump all took off. That left Gruf and me. We moved into the same booth where I'd just had my showdown with the Bitch, because the booth benches are considerably softer than the wood chairs at the tables. Mary topped us off for one final cup of coffee.

When I worked nights as a delivery driver at Carlo's Pizza, Gruf was my boss. He was Carlo's night manager. In the daytime, I guess you could say I'm Gruf's boss. We have a little carpentry business we call Now on Deck. I'm the carpenter and contractor. He's my "manual laborer," as we both like to say because we think it's funny.

After hearing me whine about paperwork, Gruf also stepped in to take care of the books for Now on Deck. He has a four-year college degree in accounting and was already doing the books for his dad's bar, Smitty's. That's where the two of us were currently working days. We were doing a major renovation job on Smitty's Bar.

That morning in Brewster's, Gruf stubbed out his cigarette and drained the last of his coffee. Then he ran his fingers through his glossy black DA. He fixed his ice-blue eyes on me and smiled. "Okay. Ready to go?"

I said, "I'll meet you over there. I'm gonna go get my hair cut off."

He raised his eyebrows at me. "Okay. See ya."

Forty-five minutes later I walked into Smitty's Bar through the beat-up old back door. It feels funny walking in there before the place is open. You feel like a burglar or something, walking in when the beer signs and spotlights are turned off and the bar's all dark and shadowy. All the action that time of day is in the kitchen.

The only two people in the place at that hour of the morning, besides Gruf, were Gruf's dad, Smitty Ridolfi, and his day cook, a skinny, geeky guy named Benny Jepson. Benny wears his black-rimmed glasses adhesive-taped together across the bridge of his nose and is always on the lookout for a chance to talk about the Internet.

Smitty and Benny were in the kitchen, working briskly and quietly. Benny was making hamburger patties and Smitty was tearing up heads of lettuce into a big, white plastic tub. Smitty looks exactly like Gruf, only older. He's a tall guy with a lean, strong face. He wears his snow-white hair in the same long, wavy DA and he's got the same ice-blue eyes.

Benny looked up and saw me standing in the doorway. He wrinkled his nose to adjust the way his glasses were riding and said, "Holy shit, Terry. What happened to you?"

I ran a self-conscious hand over my bald-feeling head. It wasn't bald *looking,* though. I'd told the girl to cut it just long enough so none of my scalp showed through. When I looked in the mirror, I didn't like my mustache anymore, either, so I had her shave that off, too. My head felt so weird I didn't think I'd ever get used to it. It was like reaching up to feel my hair and finding somebody's short-haired dog there instead.

"Got a little trim," I said, grinning. "And call me Twees. It's my new nickname."

Benny got a puzzled look on his face.

Smitty looked me over. His grin made papery wrinkles at the corners of his blue eyes. "I bet you felt every drop of that cold rain out there."

I laughed and nodded. It had already occurred to me that maybe I should've waited until the warm days of spring to make such a drastic change. I could already see that I was going to need a hat for the first time in my life. And I'd already started to wonder what kind of hat wouldn't make me look like a total dweeb.

I said, "Where's Gruf? Over in the New Part?"

They both said, "Yeah."

I walked past the dark bar, turned right, walked through the big darkened hall where the three pool tables were, and approached the double doorway to what we were now calling the New Part.

The New Part had been, until recently, a huge, unused, closed-off mess known as the Old Part. Once we had it renovated and open, it would double the size of Smitty's Bar.

The back section of the New Part was now a brand-new, state-of-the-art, high-efficiency commercial kitchen, with every shiny stainless-steel appliance a restaurant chef could ever dream of. Gruf and I had stripped the old room down to its carcass and rebuilt it, painted it white, installed the stainless-steel cabinets, put up the stainless-steel shelving, installed the appliances with the occasional help of the manufacturers' techs, and laid the shiny white tile during an intense three weeks in October.

Then we went to work on the rest of the New Part. We cleaned out the decades of junk that had accumulated there and stripped the structure down to its skeleton. We tore out the shitty old plywood flooring down to the shitty old subfloor. We tore out the cheap old paneling and the raunchy old ceiling. As soon as we finished building the new waitress station, we planned to turn the entire room into a large formal dining room, with wainscoted walls, thick carpeting, brass lighting fixtures, heavy oak booths and tables, and sexy captain's chairs.

I should go back a ways and explain how all this craziness got started. See, at first Gruf just wanted to persuade Smitty to let us build a large deck onto the back of the building, with an outdoor waitress station that looked like a gazebo and wide stairs leading down into a large three-court volleyball pit.

During the time that Smitty was considering that idea, Kenny Carlo decided to start franchising his pizza stores. The first one sold was Carlo's—Spencer, since it had the biggest volume. The couple that bought it were currently being trained for the takeover at the home store in Fairfield.

When Smitty heard that news, he put his cards on the table. Once the new owners took over Carlo's—Spencer, he wanted Gruf to quit Carlo's and take over running the bar so he could retire. Gruf agreed, so Smitty gave the go-ahead on the deck and volleyball pits.

Then the two of them started talking about the future of Smitty's Bar in general. They had a bunch of late-night heart-to-hearts. Gruf had a lot of big ideas. Smitty listened. Eventually, Smitty agreed to go large.

Gruf and I were still working nights at Carlo's while we waited for the new owners to come in. The plan was, we'd help the new owners get settled and help them train a new set of employees. Then we'd make the jump to Smitty's, taking most of the old Carlo's employees with us.

That morning I stood in the double doorway and looked back toward the brightly lit area where we were building the new waitress station. Gruf was already hard at work. I watched as he marked his cutting line on a piece of drywall. He made his last measurement, marked it quickly with his pencil, and tucked the pencil behind his ear.

I said, "Jeez, you look like an old pro doing that.

You look like you've been hanging drywall for twenty years."

He'd only been my "manual laborer" for a few months, but he was picking everything up really fast. I took a lot of pride in how fast he was learning.

He walked around me, checking out the haircut. When he got back in front of me, he nodded. "I like it. Looks good."

"It feels freaky. Gonna take a while to get used to. Plus, I'm gonna hafta wear a hat when the weather's cold. What the fuck kind of hat am I gonna wear?"

He said, "Get yourself one of those black knit caps. Those things look cool. You'll look like a guy that works on the lakes."

Well, there ya go. I nodded and looked around. "Where'd we hide the radio?"

He glanced around, too. "It might be back in the kitchen."

I nodded. Smitty sometimes stuck it back on a counter in the new kitchen to prevent one of the bar-flies from walking out with it. I found it sitting back there, brought it out, and turned it on, and we got to work drywalling the divider that would close off the waitress station from the dining room.

Once the divider was up, we leveled that section of floor by belt sanding the humps and shimming the outer joists. Then we laid five-eighths plywood and did the prep work for the tile before we broke for lunch.

We washed up in the kitchen sinks, took a minute to look over what we'd accomplished so far that morning, and walked out to the bar. Now it looked more like Smitty's, with the lights on and the barflies hovering over their beer mugs.

I made a quick call to the lumberyard for delivery of the plywood for the dining-room floor. Then I slid onto my usual bar stool next to Gruf. Our French dips were sitting on the bar waiting for us, along with my iced tea and Gruf's High Life.

We ate in silence for a while. I began to look up and around while I chewed. Now that I'd put in so many hours working in Smitty's, I knew most of the regulars by sight, if not by name. The unemployed and disabled ones were there every day. Today almost all the other regulars were there, too, since most of them were laborers and it was raining.

I began to notice something unusual. Normally, most of them sat alone, quietly drinking and smoking, staring off into space. But today, I noticed they were sitting in twos and threes and talking quietly. Now and then, one of them would slide off his stool, walk up to somebody else, and have a few words. I noticed they didn't look too happy. I also noticed that more than one of them glanced our way as they talked. I began to wonder what was on their minds.

After lunch, Gruf and I laid the tile in the waitress station and rolled it good. Then we moved the front pool table out of the way and went out back to wait for the lumberyard truck. The cold rain was beginning to clear off, but the parking lot had standing puddles, so we dragged out a couple of pallets and set them near the back door to take the plywood.

The truck came after about ten minutes. The driver off-loaded the plywood with a winch, I wrote him a check, and we carried in the first of the plywood sheets. We were starting back for the second load when two guys I didn't know came in carrying the next sheets. Gruf and I backed up against the wall so they could pass. I looked after them in amazement and turned back to the door in time to see the next two guys coming. These two I recognized as regulars.

Out by the stack two more guys were loading up. I looked at Gruf. He was grinning. "Looks like we got us some volunteers."

Needless to say, with eight guys working, it didn't take long to get the stack carried inside. Gruf and I brought in the last sheet. The other six guys were standing in the dining room, looking around squinty-eyed and critical. Smitty had walked back, too.

I said, "Thanks for the help, guys." I caught Smitty's eye. "Next round's on me."

Smitty winked at me. "Next round's on the house. Come on, boys. Let's get outa the way."

We got busy tearing out the old subfloor. After a lot of tedious shit we got the joists level and were able to begin laying the plywood. We were about half-finished when I happened to glance around toward the double doorway leading back into the bar. One of the barflies was standing there. He wasn't one of the ones who'd helped us, but I'd seen him around almost every time I'd been in Smitty's. Judging by his wet hair and rosy cheeks, I guessed he'd just walked in.

He's kind of a blurry-looking guy, average height, midforties, long brown hair parted wide to the side, skinny, droopy shoulders. His fuzzy green eyes watched us from under his raggedy brown eyebrows with the expressionless stare of the acid burnout.

Gruf saw me looking, turned around, and smiled at the guy. "Hey, Mule. Whad'ya think?"

Mule's smile was sweet. Shy. He gave Gruf a tentative grin and took a baby step into the room, looking around.

Mule said, "Sure looks different." He gave out with a nervous little chuckle.

We both joined him in looking around the place, nodding. I said, "That's for sure."

Mule nodded. "That's for sure." He produced another little chuckle and took another tentative shuffle step into the room.

A second guy appeared behind Mule. I knew this one's name. He's called Tiny. He's huge, taller than Gruf and me, even. We're all tall. Gruf, Danny, Bump, and me. We range between six-four and six-six. The only one who isn't tall is John Garvey. He's a brawny five-eleven.

But Tiny is enormous, and he's a very tough-looking guy. Which I had made every effort to stay out of his way, because he's so big he looks like he could kill a guy with a careless swat. He has long, greasy, sand-colored hair, always has a few days' beard on his wide face, and has the same vacant burnout expression in his eyes as Mule. That day he also had the same rosy just-came-in-from-outside cheeks.

Under their dirty Carhartt jackets, they both wore ratty old faded flannel shirts randomly buttoned over gray T-shirts, filthy Carhartt pants, and knee-high green rubber boots. I remembered somebody saying that Tiny installed septic systems. A bunch of Ohio Lottery instant tickets were sticking up out of Mule's jacket pocket.

Gruf said, "Hey, Tiny. How the hell are ya?"

Tiny didn't smile or hardly move beyond the tightest possible nod. His eyes darted around the room like bright lights were flashing at him.

Mule glanced over his shoulder at Tiny and said, "It sure looks different."

Tiny's eyes brushed across Mule and went back to darting around the room.

Gruf cocked his head and studied them. Then he said, "Come on back and have a look at the new kitchen."

He picked up his Coke and led the way through the kitchen doorway. Mule and Tiny came across the new floor toward me like they were afraid it might cave in on them or something. For that matter, as big as Tiny was, this actually could've happened to him before.

As they passed me, Tiny gave the top of my head a rough open-palmed noogy and said, "Shouldn'ta cut it."

I opened my mouth to agree with him. Big as Tiny is, offhand I can't think of anything I would ever *dis*-agree with him about. But by that time he was already in the kitchen and I realized no answer was required.

I set my nail gun on the counter frame, picked up my iced tea, and followed them.

I wondered why Gruf had turned on the exhaust fan, which operates with an efficient, state-of-the-art whisper. Not like the deafening, rattling exhaust fan in the kitchen over at Carlo's. When I saw Gruf's hands go to the back pocket of his jeans, I knew why. He was going to burn a bowl with the boys.

I leaned on the nearest available counter to watch. I was curious what Mule and especially Tiny would be like when they got high.

I leaned back against the counter because I don't do the weed anymore. I don't do the weed and I don't do the booze, because overindulgence in those two recreational activities a year or so ago were what caused me to go nuts in a bar one night, trash the place, pound on a few guys, and land in jail. For me, jail was an effective wake-up call. I've been sober as a judge ever since.

The bowl went around once. Then Gruf tamped it down and relit it. He said casually, "So. Whadda you guys think about the changes around here?"

They both stared at Gruf's hands as he got the bowl going again. The bowl went around another circuit. As Tiny passed it back to Gruf, he said in a low mumble, "Somma the guys wanna know what it's gonna be like."

Mule shifted uneasily in his worn, out-turned work boots, and I remembered all the whispered conferences around the bar during lunch. I began to realize that this was some kind of unofficial barfly delegation, and now I saw that Gruf was aware of it. I drank a slug of my iced tea and watched them with even more interest.

Gruf shrugged. "Bigger. Newer."

He sucked on the bowl a couple of times and handed it to Mule, who took a deep draw with his eyes squeezed tightly closed and passed it to Tiny. Tiny made a production of tamping it down with a split, dirty thumbnail and relighting it. He took a couple of deep draws and handed it back to Gruf.

Tiny mumbled, "Somma the guys wanna know if it's still gonna be their bar."

Gruf looked at him closely, reading between the lines, took a draw, and passed the bowl to Mule.

Mule sucked deeply. Still holding the bowl, he said, "Listen to this. This was the funniest thing. One time, me and my one brother Robert cut school and we were down by the tracks behind the feed and grain? Remember where the train tracks used to be, down behind the feed and grain? And Robert, he goes—"

Tiny put one heavy hand on Mule's shoulder and reached for the bowl with the other. He said, "Not now, Mule."

Gruf said, "What're you saying? Some of the regulars are worried the bar's gonna get too fancy?"

Tiny nodded, taking a drag. "Fuckin' yuppies in here, actin' all stupid."

Gruf said slowly, "Well, I hope all the boys know this'll always be their bar. Fuck, they've been supporting the place for all these years."

Tiny passed the bowl to Gruf and said, "Hard for a man to relax and enjoy his beer if there's a bunch a fuckin' yuppies all flyin' around actin' all stupid."

Gruf nodded and took a deep draw. "I see what you mean," he said, nodding. "Yeah, I see your point. Listen. Lemme think about this. I'll come up with something. Okay?"

Tiny cocked his head and gave Gruf a suspicious look. Gruf reached over and punched Tiny's arm.

I almost shit.

But Tiny grinned at him.

Gruf said, "You tell the boys to give me a few days to think about this. And tell 'em not to worry. I'll take care of them. Okay? Tiny?"

Tiny nodded, shook Gruf's hand, and elbowed Mule. Mule staggered sideways.

Tiny said, "Tell Gruf thanks for the bowl."

Mule grinned shyly and said, "Thanks for the bowl."

Tiny was already shuffling back out toward the bar.

Mule started after him. Then he stopped and looked up at my head. "Shouldn'ta cut your hair."

He didn't wait for my reaction. He just hurried out after Tiny.

When they were gone, Gruf grinned at me. "The regulars are getting their shorts in a twist. This is trouble."

It did seem like trouble at the time. But everything's relative. The problem with the regulars at Smitty's was just a little crease that needed smoothing out. The real trouble was lurking right around the corner.

Chapter 3

I've always been the type of person who's asleep when his head hits the pillow, and I'm a sound sleeper. But that Saturday morning the sharp crack of the first gunshot flipped me over on my back and popped my eyes wide open. The second and third shots, which came close together, sat me straight up in bed. I looked at my alarm clock. It was four thirty.

I knew right away they were gunshots, and I knew they were fairly close. I jumped out of bed and ran through the living room of the double-wide trailer that I share with Danny and John, unlocked the front door, and ran down our short driveway and into the street.

Everything looked dark and wet, quiet and deserted. I could see my breath, white smoke in the dark air. I looked up the street, then down, and saw nothing but empty cars parked here and there along the narrow berms. Puddles left from the rain reflected the yellow glow of the streetlights on the black pavement.

I heard a car engine start up somewhere. Dogs began to bark all up and down the street. As lights came on in trailers all around me, I heard another car engine start. I looked in every direction, but there was nothing moving anywhere that I could see.

I heard a noise behind me and spun around. John Garvey, who shares the trailer with me and Danny, was hopping down the dark driveway toward me, trying to get his cop pants pulled up and zipped under his gun belt. John's an Indiana farm boy who'd gradu-

ated from Ohio Highway Patrol School only a few
months earlier. He had his cop shirt on but not buttoned, and he was barefoot. He looked at me critically.
I was standing there in a T-shirt and red plaid boxers.

I can't help mentioning that I hate plaid boxers. I'm
a white briefs man. But I hate to shop, so while we
were together, the Bitch was in charge of buying my
underwear. She bought me plaid boxers all during our
marriage. I had a drawerful of the hideous things and,
until I got around to going to the mall, I was stuck
with them.

"Where'd the shots come from?" John asked me
quietly.

I shrugged. "I couldn't tell."

He pulled a little radio from his gun belt and began
to talk into it quietly as he clipped it to his lapel. "This
is Garvey. I've got shots fired, Chandler's Trailer Park,
middle block of Sumner Court."

His voice was steady and calm and I admired him
for it, since I knew for a fact the most serious offense
he'd handled so far as a first responder was a traffic
violation. John was a rookie on the Spencer PD, only
a few months into his six-month probationary period.

The voice of the female dispatcher came through
the speaker all buzzy. I couldn't understand what she
said after, "Copy. Shots fired."

John signaled me to start walking down the street.
He turned and began to walk in the other direction.

Doors were open and coming open in trailers here
and there. Ahead of me, a bare-chested guy in a pair
of cutoffs came walking out to the street.

I said, "Where'd the shots come from?"

He shook his head. "Maybe up that way, but I'm
not sure."

I turned back toward John. The dispatcher's voice
buzzed through the radio again, and this time I made
out, "Bushnell responding."

That meant Alan Bushnell was on his way. Sergeant

Alan Bushnell's a big guy with gray hair that grows down over his collar. Apparently there isn't anybody on the Spencer PD who wants to stand up and tell him to cut it. He wears wire-rim glasses. When he's being a hard-ass, which seems to be most of the time, I've noticed that he takes them off and polishes the right lens. I've never seen him polish the left lens. I guess he expects the left lens to take care of itself.

Alan's been best friends with Smitty Ridolfi since they were in kindergarten. Sometimes Alan and I are friendly; sometimes we aren't, depending what day it is. I can tell you this for sure: Don't call Alan "General." He doesn't see the humor.

I walked back toward John. I caught up with him quickly, since he paused to shine his flashlight up each driveway he passed. Now there were quite a few people, mainly men, out in the street, looking around and talking to each other in quiet, excited voices. John reached a little knot of them just as I caught up with him.

John was trying to button his shirt and hold on to his flashlight at the same time. I took the flashlight from him and he finished buttoning.

He said, "Could any of you guys tell where the shots came from?"

One guy pointed up the street, one pointed down the street, and everyone else laughed nervously.

I said, "Hold on." I pointed to the guy who said up the street. "Which trailer's yours?"

He pointed down the street. "The green one. With the light on."

I said to the other guy, "You?"

He pointed at the trailer across the street from where we stood. John and I glanced at each other. Then we ran down the street to a drive halfway between the two designated trailers. The lights were already on inside the trailer and the door was opening as John reached to knock.

John said, "Everybody okay in there?"

The woman said, "What was that?"

John said, "I believe it was gunshots, ma'am. Could you tell where it came from?"

She pointed through her backyard. "Back there."

John and I ran through her backyard and into the backyard of the trailer behind hers. Both of us were barefoot, so we slipped and slid in the cold mud. Just as we came up on the back corner of the trailer, there was a loud crash from the vicinity of its little side porch. We ran toward the noise.

John's flashlight beam picked up the shape of a tall, slender woman standing in the shadowy driveway, weaving drunkenly, her back to us. She was wearing a white T-shirt that was way too big for her and nothing else, as far as I could tell. Her arms hung limply at her sides. A gun dangled from her right hand.

John drew his gun and leveled it at her. He yelled, "Police. Freeze. Drop the weapon."

The woman just stood there weaving.

John yelled, "Drop the weapon. Now."

Almost in slow motion, the woman's fingers opened and the gun slid onto the wet cement of the driveway with a sharp metallic crack.

John yelled, "Take three steps to your right."

She obeyed, slowly and unsteadily.

He said, "Three more steps, right up to the trailer wall. Put your hands on the trailer. High on the trailer. Now."

She did as she was told, but sluggishly. It looked like her knees wanted to fold.

John brought his radio up to his mouth. "This is Garvey. Suspect in custody, middle block of Haskins."

The dispatcher said, "Copy, Garvey. Do you need an ambulance?"

John said, "I don't know yet. Hold on."

He approached the woman cautiously, pulling handcuffs off his belt. I hurried toward the porch, dodging the shards and dirt from the flowerpot she'd apparently knocked off the porch as she'd come down the steps. I ran up the steps, stretched my T-shirt over my hand to turn the handle on the screen door, and stepped into the dark trailer on muddy tiptoes.

I looked around and couldn't see anything. There was light streaming into the trailer from the streetlight outside, so eventually my eyes would have adjusted and I'd have been able to see, but I didn't wanna wait for that. I wanted light right now.

Figuring the trailer was probably laid out like the other ones I'd known, I ran my T-shirt-covered hand over the wall to the right of the door and found the light switch. Bright light blinded me for a second. There was no furniture in the living room and nothing on the walls. I scanned the empty living room toward the kitchen.

He was stretched out across the kitchen floor, facedown, a pool of blood running away from me toward the back hallway. Big guy. Muscular. Wearing a white T-shirt and jeans, gray socks, and black high-tops. I tiptoed over to him, watching where I stepped, and squatted beside him. I pushed his tangled dark hair off his neck and put my fingers on his throat, feeling for a pulse. There wasn't one. He was dead.

I hurried back out through the door. John had the woman handcuffed behind her back. She was sitting in the shadowy driveway, crying, her body swaying, her head bowed. Her tangled blond hair hung down between her knees.

When he finished reading her rights out loud, I said, "There's a dead guy in there."

He raised the radio to his mouth and began to tell the dispatcher he needed the coroner, as the woman sitting on the driveway raised her dazed blue eyes to look at me, let go with a sob, and said, "Terry?"

Danny came running up behind me and skidded to a halt, staring at her. "Holy shit!" he said. "Marylou?"

He sounded as stunned as I felt. I couldn't believe my eyes.

I stared at her. I thought she was drunk. There are a few things that happen to ol' Marylou on those rare occasions when she gets drunk. First, her eyelids begin to droop. Her eyelids are like a sobriety meter. The drunker she is, the lower they ride. At that moment, they were fluttering about one degree above lights out.

Another thing is, she gets weepy. The drunker she is, the weepier she is. And she also gets sleepy. It doesn't matter where she is, as soon as she hits a certain level, all she can think about is stretching out and going to sleep.

So even as John started apologizing to me for not realizing it was Marylou, because she'd been hanging her head and he'd been more concerned with getting her handcuffed and under control than getting a look at her face, there's ol' Marylou letting out with another sob, trying to roll over onto her side and go to sleep in a puddle on the cement.

I was about to reach down and pull her up off the wet driveway when she twisted her body and her T-shirt rode up and I saw her naked butt cheek sticking out. That's the other thing that happens to Marylou when she's drunk. She wants to get naked.

"Dammit, Marylou." I was disgusted with her. "Where's your fucking clothes?" I guess it might seem odd that I was more concerned with her bare ass than I was that she might have just killed a guy. But the thing is, I never for a second thought she was the one who had fired that gun.

She mumbled something in a sobbing little voice, but I couldn't understand her. I took hold of her shoulders and lifted her onto her feet, tugging her T-shirt down over her key areas. Then I held her up in front of me. I quickly ran my eyes over her, looking for blood, making sure she hadn't been hit, too.

"Let's try this again. Where's your clothes?"

"Huh?" She scrunched up her face at me, like I was speaking in a foreign language or something.

Danny said, "I'll go find 'em. Was she in this trailer?"

He'd come running up after everything was all over. He didn't even know yet that she'd been carrying the gun or that there was a dead guy inside.

John said, "Hold on, Danny. You'll have to wait until Alan gets here. That trailer's a crime scene now."

Marylou turned her head to look at him. "Huh?"

John said, "Marylou, tell us what happened."

She was shaking her head. "I wanna go to sleep."

John said, "In a little bit. Right now we need to know what happened."

She said, "About what?"

I said, "Who's the guy in there, Marylou?"

She said, "What guy?"

I said, "The *dead* guy in the *trailer*." and immediately regretted losing my temper with her because I knew by this time it was useless to ask her anything. The waterworks started up all over again.

John said, "Marylou, who fired the gun?"

She blinked at him, hiccuping with sobs. "Huh?"

When Alan arrived a few seconds later, he didn't take long to figure out we weren't going to get anything coherent out of Marylou until she'd had a few cups of coffee, at the very least. Once he'd satisfied himself that the guy in the trailer was dead, he got a blanket out of his cruiser, wrapped Marylou in it, and put her in the backseat, where she promptly rolled over and passed out.

By that time other cars were rolling up. Alan and John disappeared inside the trailer, along with everybody else.

Danny and I walked out to the street and leaned on the hood of Alan's car. Little knots of trailer-park residents were standing here and there, up and down the street, smoking and talking in quiet, excited voices. I started to feel the cold night air for the first time.

Every time I shuffled my bare feet, cold mud squished between my toes.

Danny pulled a pack of cigarettes out of his shirt pocket—he'd taken the time to throw on a flannel, jeans, and his high-tops—and tapped me out one. His long, reddish gold hair was loose and wild in the wind. The same strand kept blowing across his face. He looked like a big freckled Jesus standing there.

I told him about the gun.

He whistled softly. "You don't think she did it, do ya?"

I shook my head. "No way. She doesn't get violent when she's drunk. She gets a lot of other things, but not violent."

"Then how'd she get the gun?"

I shrugged. "Musta picked it up or something."

"I don't know how you can be so sure—"

"Trust me. I know the Bitch."

He looked up the street. "It looks like she did it. The cops'll think she did it."

I said, "I'm not worried about that. They have tests they can do to tell if she fired a gun. The tests'll show she didn't do it."

One thing about spending some time in jail, listening to the other guys talk, was that I'd learned a little bit about crime.

He said, "Oh. That's good, then."

I said, "Yeah."

We smoked silently for a while. We started seeing flashes go off inside the trailer as a police photographer recorded the scene.

Danny said, "Wait a minute. If she didn't do it, that means she was inside that trailer when the murderer was."

I shrugged. "Maybe. We didn't actually see her inside the trailer. She was in the driveway when we first caught sight of her."

One of the little knots of people began to move

toward us. The woman was reluctant and kept a tight grip on the arm of the man she was with, but the other guy encouraged them to come on. As they passed under the streetlight I could see they were all young like us, somewhere in their twenties. The two guys were average height and build. The girl was a plump little brunette.

The bolder of the guys lit a smoke as they joined us. They formed a little circle with us and he took a long draw. Nobody spoke for a while. The three of them were jittery and jumpy.

Then the bold guy said, "What a night, huh?" He let go a sleepy-voiced, nervous chuckle.

Danny and I nodded wordlessly.

The guy rubbed the brown scruff on his chin. "Well, fuck it. I'm glad this is Saturday. Be able to just sleep all day, huh?"

Danny and I both nodded like we agreed with him, even though we were both planning to work that Saturday. So was John. It was gonna be a long day.

The girl had a high little scared voice. "Is someone dead in there?"

I nodded. "Think so."

She shivered and turned to her boyfriend or husband or whoever he was. "I *told* you to call the cops. I *told* you someone was gonna get killed."

He said tiredly, "Oh, jeez, Janice. This had nothing to do with the fight. That was up the street. Across from us."

Danny and I said together, "What fight?"

The guy stuck out his hand and said, "Frankie Abbott."

Danny and me both told who we were and shook the guy's hand.

Then the other guy, the bold one, stuck out his hand and we formally met Will Nazinski.

Danny said again, "What fight?"

Frankie laughed nervously. "Some of the neighbors

were really going at it for a while before we heard
the shots. They were throwing stuff at each other and
screaming bloody murder. But that was up there." He
jerked his thumb. "And they must have settled down
when they heard the shots. Right, Janice? Nothing
going on in there now. Nothing to do with this."

She said, "Still . . ."

Frankie gave me a look that was supposed to mean,
Women. Can't live with 'em . . .

Danny said, "Still, it could have had something to
do with this."

Frankie shook his head. "I promise you, it didn't.
Those two up there go at it like that all the time. Next
day, to look at 'em, you'd swear nothing happened."

He shot Janice a look. She shrugged. He said,
"Anyway, that's a blonde lying there in the cop car.
The woman up there"—he jerked his thumb—"she's
got brown hair. Nothing to do with anything."

We smoked on. I was just bending over to scrub
out my cigarette butt when John came walking down
the driveway toward us. He stood looking up at me
and Danny, back and forth. John's not a short guy.
He stands around five-eleven. He just seemed short
because he was standing between me and Danny. He
ran a hand over his brown buzz cut.

He said, "They cut me loose, since I'm technically
off duty. Come on. We may as well go home and try
to get some sleep."

We said good night to Will, Frankie, and Janice and
began to walk back up the driveway and slog through
the backyards toward our trailer.

I stopped walking and said, "Hey. Did you find
Marylou's clothes and shoes in there anywhere?"

John shook his head. "Sorry. The trailer's empty. I
even looked in the closets and cabinets. Nothing but
a six-pack of beer on the kitchen counter."

I said, "Shit."

We went on walking.

Danny said, "Who was the guy?"

John shook his head. "No idea. We didn't find any ID on him. We don't even know yet whose trailer it is."

Danny said, "Once Marylou sleeps it off, she'll be able to explain a lot of it, huh? Hell, she musta been a witness."

I said, "She mighta been a witness, but she won't be able to tell anybody anything."

We'd reached our own driveway. John stopped and stared at me. "Why not?"

I said, "She's not gonna remember anything that happened tonight. She was too drunk. She was in blackout."

Chapter 4

By the time I washed the mud off and fell back into bed, it was five thirty. I closed my eyes and tried to go to sleep, but after a while it became pretty clear that wasn't gonna happen. Five minutes before my alarm was due to go off, I rolled out of bed and went to stand under a hot shower.

After the shower, I wiped the steam off the bathroom mirror and yelled, *"Gah!"* because I didn't recognize myself. I thought I was looking at some other guy. A tired-looking guy with all his hair cut off.

All I wanted in this life on that crisp, sunny Saturday morning was a cup of hot, fresh coffee, but I wasn't expecting to have it handed to me on the sidewalk outside Brewster's. Alan Bushnell was standing there waiting for me with two Styrofoam cups in his hands. Steam hung above the cups in the chilly autumn air. The deep lines in Alan's face showed what kind of fun he'd been having.

"You guys go on in," he told Danny and John. "I need to ask Terry a few questions in private." He waited until the door had closed behind them, then handed me my cup of coffee. "I guess you probably need this."

I nodded and drank. It wasn't sweetened as much as I like, but I wasn't gonna nitpick. Through Brewster's big front window, I could see Danny and John pulling out chairs and sitting at our usual table. I saw that Gruf and Smitty were already seated. Bump was there, and Nelma Wolfert was there that morning, too. Bump saw me looking and gave me a nod.

I turned back to Alan. "How'd you even know we'd be here on a Saturday morning?"

"Mary's working, isn't she? That means you guys'll be here. Got a haircut, huh?"

I just shrugged.

"Terry." He leaned closer, even though there wasn't anyone around. "Does Marylou have a drug habit, if you know?"

I blinked at him. "Fuck, no. She'd never touch the stuff. She'll overdo the alcohol once in a while, yeah, but nothing else. Hell, she doesn't even smoke. She's a fitness freak."

He nodded.

I said, "What makes you ask that?"

"After you guys went home, I went out to check on her. She was passed out in the back of my car."

"Yeah."

"Well, it occurred to me she might need medical attention. I sent one of the boys to take her down to the hospital. Get her looked at."

"Yeah? Is she okay?"

He nodded. "Well, yeah. I mean, she will be. They tested her hands and her T-shirt for gunpowder residue. Negative."

I nodded.

"They drew some blood, put her on a saline drip, or whatever. The tests showed she'd been drinking alcohol. She was also pretty cranked on some kind of controlled substance. But they said she didn't show any of the typical signs of a chronic user."

I just looked at him.

He said, "So what I want to know is how drugs got in her system."

"I can tell you how they *didn't* get there. She didn't put 'em there herself."

He nodded. "You're pretty sure about that."

"I'm positive about that."

"All right. So somehow, she ingested drugs without being aware she was doing it."

"What was she on?"

He said, "Don't know yet. They're running tests." He cleared his throat. "Uh . . ."

"What?"

"After she'd been on the saline drip for a while, she started to come around. She's upset. She has some, uh, discomfort."

"Yeah?"

"Well . . ."

"What?"

"She had sexual relations. Only she says she never consented to any sexual relations."

"What're you saying?"

He put a hand on my shoulder. "I'm saying, they did a rape kit on her. Sometime last night, apparently, she was raped."

I pulled a smoke out of the pack in my jacket pocket and lit it with my free hand. I took a deep draw and blew it out. "Shit."

He said, "I'm telling you this because I want you to hear it from me, man-to-man. Not some other way."

I nodded. "I appreciate it."

"They're testing the guy. The dead guy. See if it was him."

I nodded and sipped my coffee.

"Listen, Terry. It goes without saying. I don't want you to go poking your nose in this. You and your buddies. Not like last time. Got it? It's *our* job. You stay out of it."

He was still pretty sore about the way Bump, Gruf, Danny, John, and I got involved in the effort to find out who had killed our pizza driver several months earlier. Except he still didn't know John had been in on it with us. We kept John's participation quiet, since we were afraid it'd get him in trouble in the department, him being the new guy and all.

I just dipped my head at Alan. It wasn't a yes and it wasn't a no. There was a long silence.

After a while, he took a deep breath and said, "Well, I don't know about you, but I could do with some breakfast."

He took me by the arm and turned me toward Brewster's front door, but I stopped before we reached it. "Alan?"

"What."

"The dead guy. Who was he? What was his name?"

He gave me a cop frown. "Why?"

I shrugged.

"You just never mind who he was. This is police business."

I shrugged. "Whatever."

When we walked inside, Mary was already pouring coffee into the cup where I usually sit. Mary generally only works weekdays, but she was working that weekend to make up for some vacation time she'd taken earlier in the month. That was why we were all there. If Mary's waitressing, you gotta know we'll all be there eating.

It looked like she'd been waiting for us. She probably had. They'd probably all been watching me and Alan talk through Brewster's big front windows while Danny and John filled them in on what had happened the previous night.

Mary moved around to the place where Alan usually sits when he joins us for breakfast. She poured coffee into the cup that was already there. I saw that he'd been sitting at the table earlier. His folded newspaper was tucked under the saucer.

Mary said, "I went ahead and put in your breakfast orders, you two, since you both always order the same thing, anyway. You got a haircut, huh, Terry? I like it."

I smiled at her and said thanks.

She said, "You're welcome. It'll be right up," and hurried back toward the kitchen.

I was surprised that Nelma Wolfert was there that

morning, too. She likes to come in for breakfast a few times a week, but she never comes in on a Saturday. I realized she must've heard about what'd happened and come in for the details.

Nelma's about the best person who ever lived. She's a large, wise, sixtyish, orange-haired, big-voiced lady who started out being my probation officer and ended up being my friend. She's related to Alan Bushnell in some way that I still haven't quite pinned down, and she's known Bump since he was fourteen.

She greeted us with her cheery good mornings. Then she waited to see if anyone had anything to say about the murder. When nobody spoke up, she launched right into hearty conversation.

"Well, I finally saw *Natural Born Killers* last night. Rented the video. I'd been wanting to see that movie for the longest time. Wow. What a movie. Who's seen it?"

Bump said he'd seen it and they began to discuss it, but Bump was giving me sideways glances every few minutes. All of them were doing it—Bump, John, Danny, Gruf. Glancing my way every few minutes, but unable to say anything with Alan sitting at the far end of the table with his newspaper in his face. We had some talking to do, but we were gonna have to wait.

Almost right away, Mary came out carrying a tray with half the orders. A girl followed behind her with the other half. Mary set my plate down in front of me, and I got busy salting my eggs and spreading strawberry jam on my Texas toast.

Everybody was still talking about movies. They'd covered the subject of *Natural Born Killers* and were now on *Pulp Fiction*. All of them were talking about *Pulp Fiction* except me. And Alan. Alan was down at the other end of our pushed-together tables, eating behind his newspaper. When everybody was finished eating, Mary and her helper cleared away the dirty dishes, but no one left. Everybody was hanging around overly long. Lingering.

Finally, reluctantly, Nelma said she had to be on her way. She gathered up her stuff and left. John left with her.

Then Danny got up. He put a hand on my shoulder as he walked past me and leaned down. "Give me a call later on my cell phone."

Alan looked around the edge of his newspaper.

Danny added, "About those shingles."

Alan went back to his reading.

I said, "Yup."

That left Alan, still buried behind his newspaper, and Bump, Gruf, and me. It was pretty obvious now that Alan wasn't going anywhere until we had all cleared out.

I sipped my coffee, feeling sorry for him. I knew all he wanted to do after working a tough third shift was go home to bed, but here he was trying to keep us from hatching a plan to jump into his investigation with both feet. Or all of our feet. Or whatever.

I said to Gruf, "Well, let's go to work."

Alan looked relieved. "Guess I'll get out of here, too."

We tucked Mary's tips under our coffee cups and moved up to the register to pay.

Out in the parking lot, Bump paused at the door to his truck, looked back my way, and nodded. Alan didn't climb into his police cruiser until we were all pulling away. He probably felt pretty helpless as he watched us go.

Bump drove around the block by way of Oak Street and pulled into the back parking lot of Smitty's Bar as Gruf and I were walking in the back door. We stepped into the back hall to wait for him because there was a cold wind blowing. The three of us said a quick hello to Smitty and Benny. Then we walked back to the new kitchen. Gruf turned on the lights and Bump lit a smoke.

I said, "How much do you guys know about this so far?"

Bump said, "Just that there was a dead guy in the trailer, three shots fired, Marylou drunk and half-naked in the driveway, carrying the gun."

I said, "Okay. The rest of it is, somebody slipped Marylou some kind of drug last night and raped her. They're testing the dead guy to see if it was him."

Bump and Gruf both said, "Shit."

Bump said, "Did Marylou shoot him?"

I said, "No. They tested her for gunpowder residue, but I coulda saved them the trouble. Marylou's a lot of things, but she's not violent."

Gruf pulled a little notebook out of his shirt pocket and pulled the cap off his pen. All of us were carrying around little notebooks tucked in our pockets by that time. Bump got the habit started. Except that morning my own little notebook was sitting forgotten on my new oak dresser, right in front of my souvenir Niagara Falls cedar-barrel coin bank.

Bump said, "Where do we start?"

I had to laugh. He didn't ask, Are we gonna do anything? He asked, What are we gonna do first? And Gruf was ready with his notebook. You gotta love these guys.

I said, "Alan's still mad about last time. He wouldn't even tell me the dead guy's name. I wanna know his name, and I wanna know if that's his trailer or if it belongs to somebody else."

Bump said, "I'm on it. But first I'm gonna go down to the hospital. Check on Marylou."

I glanced at the wall clock. Bump was a day driver at Carlo's Pizza. It was only eight thirty and Carlo's didn't open until eleven, so he had enough time.

I said, "They don't have morning visiting hours, do they?"

He snorted. "Visiting hours are for pussies. See ya later."

As he walked out, Gruf pointed to the wall phone and said, "Dial Danny's cell phone?"

I just grinned at him. Once he had Danny on the line for me, I told him about my talk with Alan. Danny said if anything came up, call him. I said we'd see him later at Carlo's.

Chapter 5

We cranked the radio and spent the morning laying the electrical lines for the waitress station. When we broke for lunch, Gruf called to see if we could get the building inspector over to take his look, because we wanted to start installing the heavy stainless-steel under-counter cabinets in the waitress station that afternoon.

We were just lighting smokes after lunch when we were surprised to see Kenny Carlo walk in the front door. Kenny owns the Carlo's Pizza chain. I don't normally have much to say to the Kenny Carlo types of this world. Rich, businessman-type guys. But I got to know Kenny some while we built him a pool house and deck, and I ended up liking the guy. He's pretty cool.

He's average height, slender, as tan in November as he had been all summer. That day he was wearing a pair of gray jeans and a white windbreaker over a white Carlo's T-shirt. He said hi and swung a leg over the stool next to Gruf. Smitty, who'd been down at the end of the bar talking to some of the regulars, moved toward us.

I leaned forward around Gruf and said, "Fuck you doin' here, Kenny?"

He leaned forward and grinned at me. "Nice haircut. I had to stop over at the store to talk to Barb. Thought I'd swing by and touch base with you guys, too."

Gruf said, "Kenny, I don't think you've ever met my dad, Smitty. Dad, Kenny Carlo."

The two men shook hands across the bar and sized each other up in a way I thought was interesting. You know, the boss and the proud father type of thing?

Kenny threw an arm around Gruf's shoulders and said, "Quite a kid you got here."

Smitty smiled. "He'll do. What can I getcha?"

Kenny said, "You got any of that—whadda they call that? Red Dog? I've been meaning to try that."

Smitty took a few steps down the bar and slid open a cooler lid. He pulled out a bottle of Red Dog, popped the cap with his thumb, and poured it down the side of a frosted mug. He set the mug in front of Kenny and took a step back. Kenny reached for his wallet, but Smitty waved him off.

Kenny drank a slug. "Huh. Interesting." He looked over at us. "Gruf, I wanted to check in with you and Barb about the new owners coming in." Barb meant Barb Pannio, the day manager at Carlo's. "Just wanted to make sure you're all set for their first day Monday."

Gruf and I grinned at each other.

Kenny said, "I told Barb the store looks pretty good. But keep your crews working so the store gleams from top to bottom when they walk in."

Gruf nodded.

"And if any of your employees have a problem with the new people, let them know I'll find places for them in one of the other stores. I don't want anyone to be screwed because of this change."

Gruf said, "That's pretty decent. I'll tell 'em. But remember I told you, once we have this place open and the new owners have their own employees trained, most of the Carlo's staff is coming over here with me."

Kenny nodded.

I said, "What are they like? The new owners?"

Kenny shrugged. "They seem nice enough. They seem to get along okay with everybody up in Fairfield. Course, you can never tell how someone's gonna be once they're in charge."

Gruf said, "That's true."

Kenny said, "So. How's the work coming here?" He looked at Smitty. "Big changes, huh? Quite an investment."

Smitty said, "The new kitchen's in. We'll walk back and have a look if you want to."

Kenny nodded.

Smitty said, "How'd your pool house and deck turn out? You happy with it?"

Kenny nodded and looked over at me. Gruf leaned back so we didn't have to talk around him. "I don't know if you know it yet, Terry, but I'm an anal-retentive perfectionist. Gruf knows. Huh, Gruf?"

Gruf nodded.

Kenny said, "I know a little about carpentry, and I went all over your work with a fine-tooth comb, looking for something to complain about."

I watched him sip his beer and waited.

He looked over at me. "And I can't find a thing. It's perfect. It's beautiful."

I grinned at him.

He said, "Really. You're an artist."

Now he was embarrassing me. I picked at a callus on my hand. I said, "Well. Thanks."

He said, "I've got some other jobs I want you guys to do. That's another reason I stopped over today. Three or four other jobs, actually. The first one is, my daughter and her husband bought an old century home out in Ladonia. It needs a lot of work, and a lot of it's gonna be tricky—duplicating old moldings, walls out of plumb, that kind of thing. I mean, you could run into about anything in that old place. Ever done any restoration work?"

I nodded. I love restoration work. The older the

structure, the better. A lot of guys really hate working on an old structure. But to me, there's something about seeing the old saw marks or hammer marks on the wood, the old nails or pegs, thinking about the guy that did the work originally, imagining his hands and his tools, seeing how he worked.

Kenny said, "Good. Because I want you guys to do the work on my daughter's house."

I said, "Sure."

We left it at that. When Kenny was finished with his beer, the four of us walked back to the New Part. Kenny about dropped his shorts when he saw the new kitchen. Being in the restaurant business himself, he knew what it cost the second he saw it. The building inspector walked in while Smitty and Kenny were examining the fancy new appliances.

Of course the building inspector, Evan Lustig, was an old friend of Smitty's. That's why he was willing to come over and do an inspection on a Saturday. Everybody in Spencer is old friends with everybody else in Spencer. He took a look at the lines in the waitress station, gave his nod, and walked back to the kitchen to shoot the shit with Smitty and Kenny Carlo. Gruf and I got back to work installing and leveling the under-counter cabinets.

Bump walked in just after two. He stopped off at the bar and got himself a Coke, then walked on back. Gruf and I were lying on the floor in the waitress station, installing shelves. We stood and stretched our backs.

I lit a cigarette and looked around for my iced tea. "So, Bump. Did you find out anything?"

He said, "The dead guy's name was Reese Tornow. He'd been working third shift as a clerk at Petey's. Only been there a month or so. Lived with a girl named Amy. Rented part of a house over on Washington." He gave us a smug smile. "I had his name before the cops did."

Gruf and I looked at each other. Gruf said, "How'd you do that?"

Bump grinned. "I was gonna drive over to Chandler's and have a look at the trailer, you know? On my way out, I stopped in Petey's for a pack of smokes. That one morning girl in there, Nancy? She was pretty upset."

I said, "Nancy. Is she the one with the headlights?"

Bump laughed and nodded. One of the morning girls at Petey's didn't usually wear a bra and had a chronic case of erect nipples. Guys stood in line at the register every morning craning their necks to get a better look. Some of them made comments like, "Nancy, you left your lights on." She didn't seem to mind.

I couldn't think what her face looked like, but I had a clear recollection of the front of her shirt.

Bump said, "She's pretty upset. It was hard to get it out of her, but it turns out her and her boyfriend live in Chandler's on Haskins Court, just up from where the murder happened. They were standing in the street when the cops brought out the body. She recognized the guy. She didn't say anything to the cops. She figured they already knew who he was."

Me and Gruf shook our heads.

Bump said, "Nancy pulled his employment application for me. He wrote on it he'd been in the Navy for nine years. Navy SEAL."

I said, "Navy SEAL? Those guys are like ninja warriors or something, aren't they?"

Gruf said, "Yeah. They do all that dangerous and surreptitious stuff, going in hostile territory and shit."

Bump nodded.

Gruf said, "Do the cops have his name now?"

Bump sipped his Coke and nodded. "I stopped back at Petey's on my way home from the hospital. The cops had just been there."

I said, "I hope Nancy didn't tell 'em she'd already had a long chat with you."

He shook his head. "Course not."

I took a drag on my cigarette. "You went to the hospital? Did you see the—Marylou?" Suddenly, it didn't seem right to call her the Bitch, after the night she'd had.

He nodded.

I said, "How's she doing?"

He said, "She's okay. Bummed out, understandably. She's scared."

Gruf said, "Scared?"

Bump said, "She's got it figured like this. Whoever killed Reese Tornow didn't realize she was there. He finds out now, thinks she's a witness, he's gonna come looking for her. She thinks she's gonna be next."

I said, "Did she see anything? Does she even remember anything?"

He shook his head. "Swirling colors and sound. Confusion. She doesn't even remember seeing *you* there. Anyway, I think she's right to be scared. They discharged her this morning. I've got her hidden."

That got my attention. "Hidden? What does that mean?"

He grinned. "I took her to my sister, Mike's, house. She's gonna stay at Mike's until this thing is over."

I didn't like that. I didn't like that at all. I'm gonna have to explain why. See, I had only ever seen Mike one time. It was while Gruf and me were building a deck for a guy named Bud Hanratty. Bud's a lawyer and he's like a second father to Bump, Mike, and their brother, who I hadn't met yet.

Well, anyway, we were at Bud's working on the deck one day and out comes Mike. She's the most beautiful girl I've ever seen in my life. I about shit when I found out later that she was Bump's sister. She's an emergency-room nurse at the Cleveland Clinic.

Ever since that day I first saw her, I haven't been able to get her out of my mind. If you could just see her, you'd know what I'm talking about. And now

Bump's telling me he's got my worst nightmare living with my dream girl. It was not good news, not in any specific way, but just on general principles. Gruf and Bump went on talking while I stood there pre-occupied.

Gruf said, "So if this Reese guy lived on Washington, who owns the trailer where he was murdered?"

Bump said, "I've got Bud Hanratty checking on that. He knows Jimmy Chandler. He's represented him a few times."

Gruf said, "Didn't that girl at Petey's, Nancy, didn't she know?"

Bump shook his head. "No. She said it's been empty since she's lived in Chandler's."

I was still hung up on the question of where Bump had taken Marylou. "But why stash Marylou at Mike's? All that does is put Mike in danger, if there is any danger in the first place."

Bump shook his head. "Staying with Mike and Ray is the safest place there is."

Ray. That was the first time I'd heard Bump's brother's name.

Bump said, "First of all, if anybody's looking for Marylou, they'd never think to look for her there. Second, even if they did find her there, those three dogs Mike and Ray have are better than a gang of body-guards. Third, Mike and Ray work opposite shifts, so one or the other of them will be there most of the time. Plus, their house is right next door to mine. If there's anything going on over there, and I'm home, I'll hear it. It's perfect."

I still didn't like it, but I couldn't find anything to argue about.

Bump lit a smoke. "We're still playing cards tomorrow night, right?"

We usually get together Sunday nights to play cards and enjoy one of John's home-cooked meals. Cooking is John's hobby. Eating his cooking is our hobby.

I said, "Oh, hail yeah."

Bump said, "What's John making?"

"No idea. Hey, the house on Washington—the dead guy's girlfriend. Amy, did you say?"

Bump nodded.

I said, "Did you get an address and phone number off the employment application?"

Bump said, "Got 'em right here."

Gruf copied the information down.

Bump said, "I've tried the number a few times. No answer."

I said, "I'll stop over there as soon as we're done here. See if I can talk to the girlfriend."

Chapter 6

The house on Washington where Reese Tornow had lived was a big old century home that had been split up into rental units. It was a lot like the house where Danny and I had shared the attic apartment, before we bought the trailer from Bump. The only lights I saw were on the first floor, toward the front. I knocked on the door at a little before four Saturday afternoon.

The woman who answered the door was short and heavy, maybe midthirties. She had her dark hair all teased up into big curls and wore big silver hoop earrings and a lot of makeup. She was wearing a tight black dress with sparkly things all over it. It looked like she was dressed up to go out to dinner or something.

I said, "Hi. I was stopping by to talk to Amy for a second? But I don't know which unit is hers."

The woman narrowed her eyes at me. "Amy Grodell?"

I smiled. Grodell, huh? That was easy. "Yeah. Amy Grodell. You know her?"

She said cautiously, "Well, I sort of knew her. She was only here a week and a half."

I said, "Oh, darn. You mean she doesn't live here anymore?"

She shook her head. "Just up and took off early this morning. Left half her stuff sitting up there."

I said, "Are you the landlady?"

She nodded.

Thinking fast, I said, "Well, is Reese here?"

She blinked at me. "Reese?"

I said, "Yeah. Her boyfriend, Reese. Is he still here?"

She said, "Oh, my God. You don't know?"

I widened my eyes, trying to look innocent, and shook my head. "Know what?"

Her eyes lit up. You could tell that this was a woman who loved to be the one who knew the juicy gossip. She said in a loud whisper, "Reese was *murdered* last night."

I acted like I was staggered by the news. "No."

She said, "*Yes.* The police were here this afternoon."

I said, "I can't believe it. Reese is dead? Poor Amy."

She nodded. We were both silent for a minute. Then she said, "And you know? I think Amy knew it was coming, too. She changed so much in the short little time she was here."

I said, "How do you mean?"

She said, "Well, a week ago last Wednesday, when they started moving her stuff in? She was like a giggly little girl. She was totally snowed. You could tell. She couldn't keep her hands off him."

"You said, when they started moving *her* stuff in."

She frowned. "Well, Reese already lived here. He'd been here more than a month. She moved in with him."

I said, "Oh. I didn't realize that."

"Of course, who wouldn't be excited, in her position? Here's this little plain Jane, old maid material if I ever saw it, setting up housekeeping with a hunk like that? Used to be a big, brave firefighter and all? And he was just as good-looking as those firefighters in that calendar, let me tell you."

I nodded encouragement.

"I was surprised they moved in on a Wednesday,

though. That was Reese's pool night. He played in the bar league. But I thought, well, maybe his team has a bye week or something."

I shrugged.

"The next day she was still so excited. They didn't have much, but she went over to the Love Bouquet and bought a bunch of flowers. It was so cute." She patted her big hair. "Well, I mean to tell you, she was a different person when I saw her Friday, that's for sure."

"Different how?"

"I was taking down my screens and putting up my storms? She comes walking across the grass looking ten years older. She looked all stressed and angry. She goes, 'Has anybody come around here asking about us? About Reese?' I'm like, 'No?' She goes, 'Are you sure?' Not, 'Hello, how are you today?' Just starts right in, like she's mad at me. Am I sure? I guess I know whether anyone's been asking questions or not. She was pretty rude."

"Like she was scared?"

"I guess you could say. Or angry. Anyway, she goes, 'Well, if anyone comes around asking about us, or about Reese, you say you don't know any Reese. Okay?' I'm thinking, I don't want any problems around here. If this Reese has got himself in some kind of trouble—"

I said, "I don't blame you."

She said, "You can't be too careful, this day and age."

I said, "It's a crazy world."

She said, "Don't I know it."

I shook my head sadly. "Whew. Reese and Amy. You think you know a person. So, did she stay like that? All scared or angry or whatever?"

"Please. She got worse. Paranoid. Like, a couple of times? I saw her drive by the house real slow, looking the place over. She drove on up the street and turned around in a driveway up there, before she came back to the driveway here. And she musta asked me ten times a day, 'Anybody come around?' She'd be up there at night when Reese was at work. He worked third shift at Pete's. I'd hear her moving around, but she'd have all the lights off. Good God. What a way to live. I'm glad she's gone."

I said, "What kind of a car did she drive?"

She pursed her lips, thinking. "One of those big ol' beaters, like a big ol' something or other. Faded red. Had a bad muffler. You could hear it a mile away. You could smell that exhaust. She left the motor running this morning. While she loaded her stuff in it? Gave me such a headache, that exhaust."

I said, "When was the last time you saw Reese?"

"Last night about midnight, I guess. I was just getting in, and he came walking out to his car. I thought he was leaving for work. You know he works third shift at Pete's."

I nodded. "Did you talk to him?"

She shook her head. "Well, I might've said hi or something. I think he just waved."

I said, "What kind of car did he drive?"

She said, "An old VW. Gray Beetle."

I sighed. "You think you know people." I thought over what she'd said for a second, then said, "So now you have to clean out all their crap, on top of everything else?"

She said, "Huh?"

"You said she only took half her stuff with her. So now you're stuck with the rest of it?"

She said, "Oh. Well, they're paid for the month. Maybe she's planning to come back for it. Anyway, it can sit up there until the end of the month. Then I'll figure out what to do with it."

I said, "Did the cops think it was important, how scared Amy was all week? When you talked to them this morning?"

She shook her head. "Oh, I didn't tell them any of that stuff. They're not interested in gossip."

I said, "Yeah. I guess you're right."

I hurried home. I had to shower and change and be at Carlo's before five because I was working that night. Danny came in from his roofing job while I was shaving. He leaned in the bathroom doorway while I brought him up to speed on the day's news.

When I was finished, he said, "I could go for a pizza. Think I'll go over to Carlo's when you do. Shoot the breeze with you guys till you go to work."

I nodded.

He said, "How's the work at the bar coming?"

"We're busting our asses. There's so much to do before Gruf can open the new dining room, and time's running out."

He nodded. After a while he said, "I kind of miss carpentering with you."

I said, "Those were some good times."

We were referring to when we worked together for Red Perkins Construction. Before he got disgusted with Red and went to work for Miller Roofing.

He said, "I don't mind roofing, but I miss carpentry."

I looked over at him. He was staring out my bed-room window.

I said, "You do?"

He nodded, but didn't look at me.

I thought about this. I wondered if he was hinting he wanted to come to work with Gruf and me.

I said, "Hey, Danny, do you ever think about leaving Miller's?"

He shrugged and nodded, but still didn't look at me, and now I knew that was exactly what he was thinking about. I was happy. Danny's a great carpenter and a lot of fun on a job.

I said, "Me and Gruf have jobs lined up out the wazoo. Anytime you wanna quit Miller and join us, it'd be cool."

He still didn't look at me, but I saw a line show up at the corner of his mouth and I knew he was trying not to grin. He said, "I'll give old man Miller my notice on Monday."

We got to Carlo's around a quarter of five. It was already dark out. Gruf and Bump were waiting out front, looking all serious. The parking lot was busy. Lots of cars were coming and going, their headlights winking in the cold, clear night.

I said, "Whassup?"

Bump said, "I talked to Marylou a little this afternoon. She and Mike were over my house using the hot tub."

I groaned silently, picturing Mike in that little silver thong bikini she'd been wearing when I saw her that time at Bud Hanratty's. I thought about her sitting in the hot tub I'd installed on the deck I'd built for Bump.

I said, "Yeah."

"Marylou wants to see you. Wants you to stop over."

"I don't think that's a good idea. Anyway, I don't know when I could. Everything's so busy. Tell her I'm glad she's okay."

Bump shrugged. "She got the results of the tests they ran on her. She was dosed with some of that date-rape drug. Fortunately for her, it was a smaller dose than they generally use. That stuff can kill ya. And Tornow isn't the one that raped her."

Gruf said, "What the fuck. If it wasn't him, then who was it?"

Bump said, "Terry, you know a pair of brothers named Stevenson?"

Danny and I looked at each other. I said, "Couple a sleazy weasels named Ricky and Ronny. Yeah, we know 'em. What about 'em?"

Bump said, "Dude, when Marylou came into Brewster's, asking you to help her move, she meant *that day*. Did she really think she could get you to drop everything and help her move *that day*, just like that?"

"Why do you think I call her the Bitch?"

They all chuckled.

Bump said, "Man. That's some world-class bitchery."

I said, "She's the best. But don't leave me hangin'. What about the Stevensons?"

He said, "After Marylou was in Brewster's that morning, she went back home. She had some girl-friends lined up to help her move. One of 'em was your sister-in-law."

I said, "P. J.'s wife? Marcy?"

He said, "Marcy. Right. I guess Marcy brought your brother's truck along. The three of them started car-rying stuff out of the trailer."

"Uh-huh."

"Then these Stevenson brothers—they live across the street?"

"Uh-huh."

"They noticed all the activity. They came walking over."

Danny nodded. "Course they did. They woulda smelled all that pussy. Woulda woke 'em out of a deep sleep."

Gruf and Bump laughed. I didn't.

Gruf said, "I'm starting to get a mental picture."

Danny said, "Take your mental picture, multiply by ten, you'll start to have the idea."

Bump said, "So they came walking over. Asked what was going on. Offered to help."

I said, "Marylou didn't let 'em, did she? Tell me she's not that stupid."

He said, "She *is* that stupid. They got it all done in about three trips using Marcy's truck and Ricky Stevenson's truck. When they were finished, they got some Kentucky Fried Chicken and had a little party in Marylou's new Green Meadows town house. The last thing Marylou remembers, Marcy and the other girl were leaving and Ronny Stevenson was in the kitchen, mixing up some kind of punch. This all came back to her this morning. Mike called me right away."

Gruf and Danny groaned.

I said, "Oh, shit."

Gruf said, "So, the cops don't know about this yet?"

Bump said, "Uh-uh."

Gruf stepped over and held the door for a family of early customers.

I stood there thinking. I was plenty steamed. When Marylou and I were together, I'd had to go around a time or two with the Stevensons. After the second time, they'd had it pretty clear in their minds that they needed to stay away from my wife. But once they heard we were quits, they musta thought she was fair game.

Bump said, "So, how do you wanna handle it?"

I said, "I wanna bring my tire iron down to the Stevenson brothers' trailer." And I wasn't kidding. Not at all.

Bump didn't say anything. Gruf looked at me. Suddenly nobody had anything to say. A kid in a souped-up royal blue Mustang cruised past us and turned down the exit driveway, his custom speakers thumping.

Bump's voice, when he spoke, was slow and precise. "If you go, I go with you."

Danny said, "Me, too. Goes without saying."

Gruf said, "Well, shit. Me, too."

This pissed me off. They were putting me in a bad position. Like, it was one thing for me to go down to the Stevensons' and bust some heads. But they were saying if I went, I was gonna be dragging them into it, too. I looked at Bump to see if he knew what he was doing. He looked away. He knew, all right.

Finally, I said, "You guys wouldn't like jail. So. We gotta get the cops over to the town house. They'll probably be able to find traces of the drug and the Stevensons' fingerprints all over everything. Then *they* can nail the Stevensons for what they did to Marylou."

Gruf said quietly, "Good decision."

I said, "Yeah. I guess."

I fumbled for my smokes in my jacket pocket and

the pack fell out of my hand onto the sidewalk. Gruf beat me to it, pulled one out of the pack, stuck it in my mouth, and lit it up for me. Then he slid the pack back into my pocket and patted it.

Bump said, "I'll tell John about the Stevensons tonight."

Danny said, "Come in and eat supper with me. After supper we'll go back to the trailer and we'll both tell him about it."

Bump said, "That's a plan."

"So, where does that leave us? The Stevensons are gonna be busted. Our part of it's over. All we gotta do is keep Marylou hidden."

Gruf looked at me.

Bump said, "It's not over all the way. We've still got a dead guy."

I shrugged. "None of us knew him. As long as we don't let anyone get to Marylou, we're done. Right?"

Bump said, "Come on. There's a dead guy, shot dead in your trailer park." He shrugged. "I think we stay in the game, is what I'm sayin'. Play the game awhile."

I looked at Gruf. "Bump wants to stay in."

Gruf grinned at me. "Course he does. So do I. So do you."

Danny said, "So do I. Goes without saying."

I laughed. "Okay."

Bump said, "Heh."

Debby's car came wheeling into the parking lot. We watched her park in a slot along the side of the building. As she walked toward us, she and Danny made eye contact and said hi to each other. Then she stopped in her tracks and stared at me.

She said, "I hate your hair. What the fuck were you thinking?"

That's Debby for ya. You never have to wonder where she stands on any given issue. Debby's a night waitress at Carlo's. She's a big, tough biker chick. She's attractive in a scary sort of way, with her severely layered black hair, her laughing, smart-ass dark eyes, and her big whiskey voice. She always wears enormous hoop earrings that bob around when she talks.

I laughed and said, "It'll grow on you."

She blinked, said, "Ew," and hurried on inside.

Danny said, "So, what do we do first?"

I said, "I guess we could try to find out more about Reese Tornow. How long had he been in Spencer? Where'd he come from? Where'd he hook up with this Amy chick? And how did he and Marylou get together?"

Bump said, "Okay. I can work on that. Here's something I've been wondering about. Petey's is right on the corner of Green Meadows and Third. So maybe that's how Marylou and Reese Tornow got hooked up. He works in Petey's, she stops in for cigarettes or pop or something."

I shook my head. "I can't figure it out. I can't figure out how either one of 'em ended up in an empty trailer in Chandler's."

Gruf said, "Jeez. It's almost five already. Terry and I have to go clock in."

Bump said, "Did you hear the news? The new owners are coming in here Monday."

Gruf nodded. "Yeah. Kenny came over to the bar to tell us. I've gotta find time tonight to call the second shift together and tell 'em."

I said, "What's their name, anyway? I don't think I've heard anybody say."

Gruf said, "Forman. Richard and Dawn Forman."

Danny said, "Is he a Dick, do you think?"

Bump chuckled. Gruf said, "I guess we're about to find out."

Chapter 7

Sunday morning, John was sitting at the kitchen table shining his cop shoes. I leaned over his wide shoulder and gazed at them. "Ooo. Purdy."

He said, "Are you guys going to Brewster's this morning?"

I heard the shower go on at John and Danny's end of the trailer. Danny was up, too. I said, "That'd be my guess."

"Good. Alan wants to meet us over there. I gotta call him. Tell him about half an hour?"

"Yeah. Why—"

"Danny and Bump stopped over here and told me about the Stevenson brothers last night. I called it in, and they said they'd get a crime team over to Marylou's town house right away. Then I guess somebody called Alan, because he called me an hour or so later and said he wants to meet us at Brewster's this morning. He wants to hear all about the Stevenson brothers."

I said, "You mean he's looking at them for Reese Tornow's murder? Because I don't think—"

He shrugged and reached for the phone. "He wants to hear about them." While he called Alan, I got a glass of water. The call only took a minute. As he reached to set the phone back on the base, he said, "Well, did you guys have a busy and productive day yesterday?"

I pulled out a chair and sat across from him, trying to look innocent. "Whatever do you mean?"

He gave me a look. When John thinks he's being played, he gets a look on that wide-jawed, all-American face of his that makes me want to giggle. I always half expect him to blurt out, "Nuh-uh," like a little kid would say. With that face of his, John could be a poster boy for the Marines or the Boy Scouts. His careful buzz cut and that firm jaw and those big, clear hazel eyes just shout 4-H or something.

He didn't actually grow up on a farm. He grew up in a suburb of Indianapolis. His dad's a chef at some big Indianapolis hotel. That's why John can cook like he does. But there are still farms on both sides of the family. To hear him tell it, he spent nearly every weekend and the better part of every summer on one granddaddy's farm or the other. I bet he was the best little boy that ever lived.

Anyway. He gave me that look and said, "Come on. I know you guys are all over this case. What have you got so far?"

I grinned at him and lit up a cigarette. "I'll show you mine if you show me yours."

He grimaced. "I was off yesterday. When I talked to Alan last night, he told me they're trying to find Reese Tornow's girlfriend, that Amy Grodell girl, and not having any luck. They think her family might be hiding her. But that's it as far as my news goes. I won't have anything else until tomorrow. Now it's your turn."

"Okay. Reese Tornow drove an old gray VW Beetle. Amy Grodell drives a beater car, faded red, bad muffler."

"Huh."

"And your guys missed something when they talked to the landlady on Washington. She didn't think they wanted to hear gossip. Amy Grodell saw trouble coming. She got all paranoid starting two days after she moved in with Reese."

He looked at me with his eyebrows raised. "No kidding? Huh."

"And when she moved out of the house on Washington, she only moved half their stuff. We're wondering if the half she left might be Reese's."

He pulled a little notebook out of his shirt pocket and made a note of that.

I said, "Tornow worked at Petey's. He wrote on the employment application that he was in the Navy nine years. Navy SEAL." He looked at me. "So I'm asking myself, what's a former Navy SEAL doing working third shift in a convenience store?"

He said, "Good question." He gave a final slap at the toe of the second shoe and put them side by side on the floor.

I said, "He also claimed to be a former firefighter, according to his landlady. Maybe he was a compulsive liar."

He straightened and shrugged. "Is Marylou still in the hospital?"

I groaned. "Bump took her over to his sister's house. She's gonna stay there until this thing gets settled."

He nodded.

I set my empty water glass on the counter by the sink as Danny came down the hall buttoning his flannel.

Alan was already at Brewster's when we walked in. He wasn't in uniform. He was in civvies. He looked like a regular guy in that flannel shirt and that old wrecked pair of jeans. Actually, he looked like one of us. But he watched us like a snake watching a bunch of rats.

We talked about the Stevenson brothers over breakfast. Bump told Alan everything Marylou had said, and I told him everything I knew about the two sleazeballs. Then Alan asked a bunch of questions.

When he seemed to be satisfied, I said, "John said a crime team went over to the town house last night?"

Alan nodded. "There were traces of something left

in the blender and a glass, so they took that into evidence, along with some empty beer cans, a bedsheet, and a couple of towels. They lifted a bunch of prints and compared them to the prints on file. . . .'' He looked at me. "I guess you already know both the Stevensons have records."

I nodded.

He said, "So once they matched the prints, they sent a car down to pick 'em up. They'll match up all the other prints and samples. Then they should be able to wrap it all up as soon as they get the lab reports back. I'll stop by the station after breakfast to see what's going on."

John said, "I'll go with you."

Alan nodded.

I said, "That's that, then. Cool."

As I finished my last cup of coffee, I was thinking how, on the surface, the mood around the breakfast table that morning had been fairly friendly. On the surface. But deeper down, things still felt heavy. Me and the guys talked to Alan, and we answered his questions, but we didn't talk among ourselves at all. We could still feel Alan's attitude, and nobody wanted to accidentally blurt out something he could jump all over.

When Mary handed me my breakfast check, there was a little note on the bottom. *Bump wants to talk to you.*

I looked over at him. He was watching me. We nodded courteously to each other.

He pushed away from the table and got an arm around Mary's waist as she hurried past him. He said, "Gotta go, sweetie. Later." She giggled and wiggled away from him.

Gruf and I left, too, with Danny, John, and Alan right behind us. Alan waited in the parking lot until we'd all pulled out. I wondered again what he thought he was accomplishing, keeping us from talking to each other at breakfast when the whole day and night stretched ahead of us, Alan-free.

Bump's truck came rolling down into the back parking lot at Smitty's Bar while Gruf and me were still climbing out of our vehicles. We stood there in the crisp morning air, puffing little white balls of breath around our heads, waiting for him to park.

As he walked up to us, I said, "What are you, now, Secret Agent Man or something? Sending notes on the bottom of the breakfast check?"

He laughed. "Alan's cracking me up, watching us like that. I figured, let's see what I can get away with."

We headed for the back door, laughing. Gruf pushed it open. He said, "You're an idiot, Bump. We're all fuckin' idiots."

We scuffed down the hall, stuck our heads in the kitchen door to say hi to Smitty and Benny, and headed for the New Part.

Gruf went back to the new kitchen for the radio. Bump said, "I've been asking around about Reese Tornow, but I'm drawing a blank. Nobody seems to have known the guy."

I said, "His landlady said he played in a Wednesday-night bar pool league."

Bump wrote that down in his notebook.

I said, "What I wanna know is, how did Marylou end up in that trailer?"

Bump said, "How are we ever gonna answer that question? She was unconscious, and the only other person who knows what happened is dead."

Gruf said, "There's gotta be a way to figure it out."

We all thought that over for a minute. Then I nodded, and then Gruf nodded.

Gruf said, "I'm getting some Coke. Anybody else?"

I said, "Iced tea."

Bump said, "Nothing for me. I gotta take off."

I said, "Let us know if anything comes up."

*   *   *

Gruf and I hit it hard all that day. We finished the cabinets, fitted on the countertops, installed the beverage-dispenser units, and connected all the feeder hoses. After a quick lunch, we painted the waitress station walls white and spent the rest of the day trimming everything out.

Sunday nights everybody comes over to our trailer. John cooks a big meal and then we play cards and shoot the shit. It's gotten to be a tradition. So that night at the trailer there was a big pot simmering on the stove, filling the air with the mouthwatering fragrance of chili. Danny was half-asleep in his La-Z-Boy, and there was a big piece of unfamiliar furniture sitting by the front door. I stopped in my tracks and stared at it.

"What the fuck is this?"

Danny struggled out of his La-Z-Boy and came to stand beside me. "It's a coat-tree. I got sick of always wondering where to throw my jacket."

I stared at the thing. It looked like it cost a fortune. It was a big oak structure almost as tall as the ceiling. There were brass coat hooks down both sides, a mirror in the middle, and a wide bench with a lift-up seat. Danny demonstrated that the hinges on the thing did, in fact, work. "See? There's even a place to stash gloves and hats. Whad'ya think?"

"It's awesome. Am I allowed to hang my shitty jacket on it?" I patted my pea-jacketed chest.

Danny grinned. "That's what it's there for."

I was just coming back out from taking my shower when someone began to pound on the front door. I opened it and Bump banged in. He said, "What do I smell? That's chili. Fuckin' chili. Right?"

Gruf came in right behind him. I collected their jackets and hung them on the new coat-tree while Bump invaded the kitchen and leaned over the chili pot with a big spoon.

Once we'd all grabbed drinks out of the refrigerator, John rudely chased us out of his way. We sprawled in various positions throughout the living room. There was a Charlie and Emilio movie on the tube. They were riding in a garbage truck.

Bump drank a slug of his Coke and said, "I found out who was working at Petey's the night of the murder. It was Petey himself. But I can't ask him about it 'cause he's out of town. Maybe until Tuesday or Wednesday."

We pigged out big-time on John's chili. Then Danny got a phone call, so he disappeared down the hallway to talk in his bedroom. We cleared the table and Bump washed it while Gruf and I started the dishes. Gruf washed, I dried.

After a few minutes we could hear Danny yelling. It became pretty obvious he was fighting with one of his girlfriends. We heard him yell, "Yeah? Well, don't hold your fuckin' breath."

In the sudden silence, Bump yelled, "Trouble in paradise there, Ignatius?"

There was no reply. After a few minutes, the skunky fragrance of burning marijuana wafted out to the kitchen. It probably sounds odd that Danny was back in his bedroom burning a bowl while John, a cop, was right there in the kitchen. The thing is, John's okay with it. He told us when he moved in that he used to burn a bowl himself now and then before he decided to be a cop. He can't do that anymore, and he has to stay away from the secondary, because the department has random drug testing. But as long as Danny's back in his bedroom with the door closed, it isn't a problem with John.

Gruf likes to burn a bowl now and then, too. He glanced wistfully toward the hallway.

I said, "Go on. I can finish up."

Gruf hurried back to Danny's bedroom. They came back out to the kitchen as I was putting away the last of the silverware.

I said, "Who needs a fresh one?"

Everybody did. I pulled a bottle of High Life out of the refrigerator for Gruf, Buds for John and Danny, and Cokes for me and Bump. Bump doesn't drink alcohol, either. It takes up the whole bottom shelf of our refrigerator, keeping everybody's brand in stock.

Bump dealt. We always play the same game. Flinch. Bump taught it to us the first time we ever played cards together. The way it works, you play with two decks. You deal out all the cards. Then you start out discarding sevens, lining them up in a row across the table. Then you can discard on the sevens, following suit. You can go in both directions from the sevens. Up and down. If you can't discard, you have to pass. Last one holding cards loses. Plain and simple.

The beauty of the game is its simplicity. You can play it and talk at the same time. But there's still enough to it that you can employ some strategy and dick over the other players. Hold back a key card, a seven if possible, and you block everybody holding the cards in that suit. Danny's a champ at this. And Bump. Anytime I have a long suit of cards I can't play, it's either Danny or Bump sitting there looking all innocent while holding back the flow.

I arranged my hand. No sevens, of course. I have the worst luck in the world at cards. Probably because my initials don't spell anything. Only I was trying to claim they do spell something. Twees. Which reminded me.

I said, "By the way, I haven't heard any of you call me Twees yet, and I'm getting plenty sore about it."

Bump said, "Not this again."

I laughed. "Would it kill you guys to call me Twees? I want a fuckin' nickname. Or we could go back to Muzzy, if you'd rather."

There were audible groans. Gruf threw down the seven of hearts. Hah! I held the eight.

Danny had hearts going the other way, and threw the six. He said, "Dude. It doesn't come natural, calling you anything but Terry. What's the big deal?"

I said, "Yeah, what is the big deal? It's not that much to ask. Just make an effort, is all I'm saying."

Gruf said, "Okay, *Twees*, think you could discard sometime this month?"

I said, "That's what I'm talking about." I tossed my eight.

Gruf said, "I've been thinking about that name Grodell. I know I've heard it before, but I can't think where."

I nodded. It rang a bell with me, too, and I'd only been in Spencer six months.

Bump said, "Wait a minute. Once in a blue moon we get a pizza delivery to Grodell's Plumbing. Out on Old Mill."

I said, "Sure. Grodell's Plumbing. Some guys in a Grodell's Plumbing truck eat breakfast at Brewster's. They sit in back at the lunch counter."

Gruf said, "We oughtta call Grodell's Plumbing tonight. See if Amy's one of those Grodells."

John said, "I doubt you'll get anywhere. Alan said if the family knows where she is, they're hiding her."

Bump turned around, pulled open the drawer under the breakfast bar, and lifted out the phone book.

John said, "You'll have to have a scam ready."

Bump looked around the table. "Ideas?" He tossed the five of hearts.

Gruf said, "Do we know anything about her?"

Everybody shook their heads.

I said, "The landlady said she was an old-maid-type chick. Plain Jane. Oh yeah, and she's got a big ol' beater car with a bad muffler."

Bump was running his forefinger down a page of the book. He said, "Maybe something to do with the car."

I said, "Yeah, like what?"

Gruf said, "Parts? Somebody wanting to buy it for parts?"

I said, "We don't know the make."

Bump found the number and stared at it. "Grodell. Oh, my God. *Pookie* Grodell."

Gruf said, "Pookie Grodell? Holy shit. I know him. Do you think it's the same Grodells?"

Bump said, "Jeez. That Pookie's a crazy son of a bitch. I don't know if he has a sister."

Gruf said, "There's about a million Grodells, isn't there?"

Bump said, "Yeah, come to think of it, you're right. Humongous fuckin' family. Come to think of it, I know a couple of the other brothers, too. Jeez. Pookie Grodell."

I said, "You wanna let the rest of us in on it?"

Bump said, "Pookie Grodell's this crazy, wild-ass dude."

Gruf said, "Yeah, and he's a cokehead."

Bump said, "Is that right? Huh. Anyway, last I heard, he was in jail again. Nonpayment of child support is what I heard. That tells us a lot about Amy Grodell, if he's her brother."

I said, "Well, come on. Let's see if we can get her on the phone. What's the story gonna be?"

Bump said, "I got it." He pulled his cell phone out of his vest pocket and dialed. When the call was answered, he said, "Yeah, is this the right number for Pookie Grodell? Oh, he's not there? Well, I was really calling for Amy. Oh, she's not there, either? You got a number where I could reach her?"

He began to get an earful. We could hear the rah-rah of a man's loud voice all the way around the table. Bump's eyes widened and he grinned.

He said, "Wo. Hold on there, Chief. I don't know anything about that. I'm just calling because somebody told me she has a beater car she might wanna sell."

His eyes ran across our faces as he listened. It seemed like the guy wasn't yelling anymore.

"Uh-huh. Yeah. Uh, excuse me? Excuse me? Hey, dude, I got another call. Can I just leave my number in case you hear from her? Yeah, it's Ignatius Tweeser Auto Parts, and the number is . . ."

We made choking, gagging, trying-not-to-laugh

noises while he rattled off the number for his cell phone. When he finally disconnected, there was a general exhalation of noise.

Gruf said, "Now you're gonna hafta answer your cell phone Ignatius Tweeser Auto Parts until she calls you."

Bump said, "I got a dollar says she calls me back within an hour."

Danny said, "What makes you think that?"

Bump said, "Because her old man got all friendly the minute I said I wanted to buy her car. Wanted to tell me her whole life story."

John said, "Tell us everything he said."

Bump said, "When I asked if he had a number for her, he went off. 'I ain't her fuckin' answering service. I get one more a these calls for her, I'm a-rippin' this fuckin' phone outa the fuckin' wall.' "

Danny laughed. "He's gonna punish the caller by ripping his own phone out of his own wall. That's harsh."

I said, "Ol' Amy's getting a lot of calls?"

Bump said, "But as soon as I said I wanted to buy her car, he's all, 'Well, pardon my French. You don't know what it's been like around here. Blah, blah, blah. But she might wanna sell if the price is right. She could use the money better'n she could use the car at this point.' That's where I cut him off. I figured if I sounded like I wasn't interested in her sad story I'd sound more like a genu-wine auto-parts dealer."

Gruf took a draw on his cigarette. "Yeah, that was good thinking."

I reached over to the window and opened it. We were all lighting up, except John, who doesn't smoke. The air was getting a little thick.

Gruf said, "It's your discard there, Mr. Tweeser."

Bump threw the nine of hearts. We went around the table a time or two and it came around to me. I had a shitload of diamonds and the seven wasn't even down yet. See what I'm saying? I threw the ten of hearts halfheartedly, knowing any turn now I was gonna hafta start passing like a Tijuana tourist.

Gruf pondered for a minute, tossed the jack of hearts, and flicked his smoke above the ashtray.

Bump said, "So, what do I say when Amy calls?"

Gruf said, "Say you think you can use her car for parts. Say you wanna look it over."

John said, "You set up a meeting with her tomorrow and then let me handle it. Us, I mean. Tell her the parking lot in front of Brewster's at noon, because you'll be there for lunch. We'll have some people there in plainclothes to grab her."

Bump stiffened. "Come on, John. It's our scam."

Danny jumped in. "No, John's right. That's where you gotta let the cops take it." He grudgingly gave up his seven of diamonds.

At the sight of that diamond, I let out a huge sigh of relief. Danny heard that and grinned. I could tell by the look on his face that he had more diamonds. Now that he knew I needed them, he'd hold them back to block me. Damn.

Danny looked over at Bump, who still hadn't conceded the point. He said, "Dude, the idea is to find out what she knows. The cops can do that better than we can, in this situation."

Finally, Bump said, "Okay. I guess you're right." He pulled his pen and his little notebook out of his inside vest pocket and thumbed through to a blank page. "What all questions do we want the answers to?"

I said, "Why did she suddenly get paranoid after they moved into that house on Washington? What was that about? Fuck, she could be a suspect. She coulda followed him that night."

Bump wrote quickly.

John said, "Hmm."

Gruf said, "Why did she move out so suddenly

that morning? She did that before the cops even had Tornow identified. How'd she even know he was dead?"

John said, "Yeah. That's a good one."

I said, "How'd her and Tornow get together in the first place? Where'd they meet?"

Bump nodded and added it to the list. "Anything else?"

Everybody concentrated. John asked Bump to read the list of questions back to us. Nobody could think of anything else. Bump tore off the sheet of paper and handed it to John, who folded it into his shirt pocket.

Danny said, "So, we get her. Find out what her deal is. What's next?"

I said, "We gotta figure out how it happened that Reese and ol' Marylou ended up at that trailer."

Bump said, "Reese worked third shift at Petey's. That's right on the corner of Green Meadows and Third. Right by Marylou's town house complex."

I said, "Yeah, but he wasn't working Friday night. Pete was. Tornow was getting dead in Chandler's at four thirty Saturday morning."

Bump said, "I gotta tell ya, I don't think we're ever gonna figure out how they got together unless Marylou's memory comes back."

I shook my head. "That's not gonna happen. She's never gonna remember that night. But there's gotta be some other way."

Bump said, "Maybe Pete'll be able to help us with that when he gets back."

"What I don't understand," Gruf said, "is what happened to the cars."

Bump said, "Huh?"

Gruf said, "Okay. At that trailer that night, you had Reese Tornow, Marylou, and the killer. If Tornow and Marylou went there together, then there should have been a second car that the killer drove. When the killer drove away after the murder, that still should have left one car. Reese's. Right?"

John said, "Maybe the three of them drove there together?"

Danny said, "Or there were four people there, and two people left after the murder, one in each car."

I said, "I heard two cars start up, one and then the other, right when I ran out to the street."

Danny said, "Somebody else dropped Marylou and Reese off there."

Gruf said, "Then where's Reese's car? He sure as hell didn't drive it away. If he and Marylou hooked up at Petey's and somebody else drove them to the trailer, then Reese's car should still be sitting at Petey's."

I said, "And why that trailer? The killer was somebody who knew it was deserted?"

John said, "No. How could the killer have taken them there? If that happened, then the killer would have had to kill Marylou, too."

I said, "Yeah. How did it happen that he left Marylou alive?"

Gruf said, "She was out cold when he killed Reese? So the killer figured she wasn't a threat?"

That was another one no one could answer. Play resumed. The discard was back around to Danny. He threw a club, looked at me, and grinned.

I was down to nothin' but diamonds. I muttered, "Shithead," laid my cards facedown on the table, and got up to go to the refrigerator. I was probably gonna be passing until Danny was forced to give up one of his diamonds.

I said, "Who's ready?" Everybody was. My turn came up as I handed Gruf his High Life. I passed. The play went around to Danny. He threw a spade. I pulled out Buds for him and John, Cokes for me and Bump, and passed again.

Bump's cell phone rang as I was sitting down.

He answered it with a breezy "Ignatius Tweeser Auto Parts. Buy, Sell, Trade."

His smug smile told us the caller was Amy Grodell. He briskly set up the meeting like John had requested and hung up.

Chapter 8

I got up early Monday morning, took a leak, and walked out to the kitchen where Danny was making coffee.

He said, "Whatever you do, don't look out the window."

Like a fool, I looked out the window. I saw nothing but white. Danny said, "It's a fuckin' blizzard. Gonna blow all day. Gruf called. Don't the Ridolfis ever sleep? Anyway, he says everything's closed. Brewster's is closed, and Carlo's isn't gonna open, and the new owners are coming tomorrow instead of today, and everything in town is buttoned up and shut down."

So I turned right around and went back to bed. Next thing I knew, it was noon. I belched and stretched, feeling muscles unknotting from my neck to my feet, cut a loud lonely one, and stayed there for another ten minutes, lying on my back with the covers pulled up to my eyes.

Danny's face appeared, peeking around my door-frame. He said, like he was talking to somebody behind him, "I can't tell if he's dead or alive. His eyes are open, but I can't see his nostrils moving."

I yelled, "How the *fuck* can it be snowing like this already?"

He said, "That's what you get for living in a hostile climate," and disappeared.

I jumped under the hot shower, forgetting again that there was no longer a bunch of hair there between my nearly bald head and the hot water. I yelped, and then relaxed and let the hot water do its work. Afterward I pulled on jeans, socks, and a T-shirt, wandered out to the living room, and stretched out on the sofa in front of the TV. Danny was sprawled in his La-Z-Boy, remote in hand.

Channel Five had cut away from regular programming and was covering the blizzard. Danny surfed. The other three local channels had done the same thing. The snow had hit Cleveland's west side almost as hard as us east-siders, which was unusual. TV reporters were all over the greater Cleveland area. We watched Channel Five's live report from Spencer's town square. A live report from Spencer is pretty much a requirement during a blizzard, since Spencer is more or less the snow capital of northeastern Ohio. Danny surfed again and found a reporter who was standing beside a road in, I think they said, Cleveland Heights. Then he struggled out of his La-Z-Boy to go get more coffee.

The reporter was standing in front of a stop sign at the bottom of a hill. Cars were coming over the top of the hill, hitting their brakes, and sliding helplessly all the way down the hill into the cars that slid to the bottom ahead of them. Every time the reporter tried to wrap up, another car came over the top of the hill and slid down into the mess at the bottom.

At least nobody was getting hurt. The cars weren't moving fast enough to cause injuries. The reporter was trying to look grim and to not laugh. I watched in perverse fascination.

I said, "Jeez. Look at that."

Danny came in to stand in front of his La-Z-Boy. We watched a big ol' Chevy Suburban with about a foot of snow on its roof crest the hill and go sliding down into the pile.

I said, "Boom. I can't believe nobody's closed off the fuckin' hill yet. You'd think the TV crew would run up to the top and flag off the traffic, at least until the cops get there."

Danny snorted. "Why would they wanna do that? They'd miss all this great footage. They'll be rerunning this for days."

A little foreign car appeared at the top of the hill. It was too snow covered to tell what make. Danny made the sound of a falling bomb as it began its slide down the hill and made a little puff sound with his lips as it slid right into the side of the Suburban.

I said, "Did you call old man Miller today and give him your notice?"

He gingerly lowered himself onto his recliner and picked up the remote. "Yes, I did." He drank a slug of coffee and settled back.

I said, "How did it feel?"

"Warm and gooey."

"Is he gonna want you to give him a full two weeks?"

"He didn't say, but I think I'm gonna tell him he's only getting one."

Suddenly, there was stomping on the porch, and John banged his way in the front door. He stomped snow off his boots onto the rug.

He said, "Holy *moly*. I never saw snowflakes that big in my *life*."

I said, "I thought you were still sleeping. How's your Geo getting you around if the roads are so bad?"

"They picked me up in an SUV this morning. I'm driving one of the SUVs right now."

I walked over to the window and looked out at the big black Bronco sitting in the mouth of our driveway. John kicked off his snowy boots and padded out to the kitchen.

He said, "I was working a fender bender out this way so I decided to stop home for lunch. I do that sometimes. I get sick of fast food."

I said, "How are the roads?"

"Terrible. Unbelievable."

Danny said, "Didn't anybody tell you Spencer is smack dab in the middle of the snowbelt?"

John turned away from an open cabinet holding a can of tuna. "Huh?"

I said, "That's right. The Lake Erie Snow Machine. Only place gets it worse than us most years is Buffalo."

John said, "Well, thank God for Buffalo, then."

Danny said, "There's something you don't hear every day."

Danny and I proceeded to tell him a few snowbelt horror stories while he stirred mayonnaise and pickle relish into the tuna. He seemed to be taking everything we said with a grain of salt, like he wasn't really buying it. Like he thought we might be lying to him.

I said, "Shit. I forgot about Amy Grodell. She was supposed to meet Ignatius Tweeser—the auto-parts dealer—at noon today in Brewster's parking lot."

John shook his head. "I called Bump this morning and told him to call her and reschedule for the same time tomorrow."

"Oh. That's good."

John said, "Yeah. So, what're you guys doing today?"

Danny said, "Sure as hell not going outside in *that*. Guess I'll loaf and do some chores around here. Catch some tube time."

I said, "I'm gonna call Bump. See about stopping over to see the Bitch."

Danny turned around and leered at me. "Is our conscience bothering us?"

John closed the refrigerator door and turned around.

I said, "No, smart-ass. I just think I oughtta put in an appearance over there. Simple human decency, that's all."

John said, "Simple human Bump's gorgeous sister, more like?"

I stared at him in disbelief. The remark meant everybody knew about my thing for Bump's sister. That was bad enough. But worse, the remark came from John. Of all people.

His expression went from a wide grin to a look of shock. Real shock, not fake shock.

He said, "Oh, my God. I can't believe I said that. Sorry, Terry."

I burst out laughing. In a few short months we'd transformed John from a corny Indiana farm boy to a, well, a guy who would stand there on a snowy Monday morning and rip on me.

Danny was howling. He pounded John on the back. "Good one."

John said, "So Marylou's gonna stay at Bump's sister's until this thing gets settled?"

I nodded.

He said, "Good. Okay. Because someone called the department trying to find out who she is and whether she's been arrested."

"What?"

"Take it easy. Her name's not being released, or anything about her. I just wanted you to know someone's interested in her. Maybe you could pass it along, when you're over there."

I nodded. "Was the caller a man or a woman?"

"I don't know. I'll ask."

I watched him stir his tuna concoction. "Here's something I've been wondering about. I heard three shots. But only one hit Tornow, right?"

"I don't know."

"Because I saw one head wound, but that was the only wound I saw. So I was wondering—where'd the other two shots go? Could the killer have been shooting at Marylou?"

"I don't know. You might have something there. I'll ask."

I picked up the phone and dialed Bump's house, figuring to ask him if he thought today was a good

day to pay my respects and, if so, to get Mike's number. While it rang, I walked back to my bedroom and
stretched out on the bedspread.

He answered on the third ring. "Hang on. I can't
hear anything. Wait a minute." There was a lot of
background noise. I could hear people laughing,
music, clatter, and what sounded like an undercurrent
of television chatter. Then I heard a door slam and it
was quiet.

He said, "Okay, what?"

I said, "It's Terry. Er, I mean Twees. What's going
on over there? It sounds like Carlo's on a bad night."

He laughed. "Everybody's over since it's a snow
day. The twins are teaching the girls how to bake pies.
Bud and my brother are here, too. What's up?"

I had to think for a minute. The twins? Then I
figured out that he was talking about two-thirds of the
Elliot brothers, of Elliot Brothers Landscaping, the
outfit that landscaped Bump's backyard after I finished building him his new deck.

The Elliots and Gruf Ridolfi grew up in the same
neighborhood. They've been friends all their lives.
Gruf and Emmett, the oldest Elliot, are good friends.
Emmett is the twins' older brother. He's a muscular,
tough-looking bruiser of a dude who you'd want on
your side in a fight.

The twins are built pretty good themselves. But
they're gay. *Way* gay. They were planning to work in
the bar when we got the New Part open. They wanted
to be servers.

Also, I'd gotten the impression that they'd formed
a cozy little friendship with Mike Bellini during the
time they worked on Bump's backyard. Bump had
mentioned them often enough over recent months that
he had me curious. Mike and the twins went to the
art museum. Mike and the twins went shopping. Mike
and the twins bought *Nutcracker* tickets.

Now Marylou was evidently part of the crew and

they were all baking pies, and I didn't know what to say. I didn't want to invite myself over into their Monday afternoon. Really, this pie-baking thing had gotten me off the hook, because I didn't really want to go see the Bitch anyway.

I said, "Uh, nothing. I was just gonna ask if this was a good time to stop over and pay that visit to Marylou for a minute, that's all. I can do it another time."

He said, "Bullshit. Come on over. Everybody's here."

Reluctantly, I said, "Okay. I'll stop over for a few minutes."

He said, "Hey, if Petey's is open, pick me up a pack of smokes on the way."

I shoveled out our driveway and moved the Bronco out to the berm. Then I headed for Bump's. The roads were horrible and the snow was still falling heavily, but I had no worries in my four-wheel-drive Tacoma. That truck goes through snow like it wasn't there. I only had to watch out for the other drivers.

I stopped at Pete's on the way and danced through the deep parking lot slush. As I stood in line with my six of Coke, I listened to the guy in front of me talking to the clerk.

The clerk, a middle-aged lady, had her graying hair held back off her long face by a wood barrette. She pulled her yellow cardigan tighter across her bony chest. "Yeah, I guess she'll be laid up awhile."

The customer said, "She never misses work. She musta hurt herself pretty bad."

The clerk nodded. "She musta hit every step on the way down." She handed him his change.

"Who's filling in for her, then?"

She shook her head. "Not me. I got more hours than I want now. For now, I guess LeRoy will have to cover, because Pete's out of town."

"He is? I just saw him in here, lemme see . . ."

"He worked third shift Friday night and left straight from work Saturday morning. But when he gets back, I guess he'll have to hire someone. Or do it himself."

He turned to go, then turned back. "Well, if you talk to her, tell her we miss her."

"Yeah, I will, Eddy. You be careful on those roads out there, now."

I stepped up to the counter and set down my Cokes. "And two cartons of Marlboros, please. Somebody get hurt?"

She reached for the smokes, set them on the counter, and looked up at me. "You know Nancy? Usually works mornings?"

Nancy. I remembered that Nancy was Bump's friend. The girl who had given him all that information about Reese Tornow the morning after the murder. The one with the headlights. I shrugged and nodded. I still couldn't picture her face, but I did remember those high beams.

The clerk said, "She called off sick. Said she fell down the steps Saturday night, or something. Wrenched her back, sprained a knee, messed up a rib." She started ringing me up.

I said, "Ouch. Poor kid."

She said, "Fifty seventy-two. That's for sure. Hasn't lost her sense of humor, though. She said the good thing is, at least she'll be able to catch up on her soaps."

I handed her a fifty and a one. "Hard way to do it."

She nodded and laughed as she counted out my change. "You be careful out there, now."

"Always."

I parked in Bump's driveway behind a white late-model Lincoln and Bud Hanratty's red Caddy. I grabbed one carton of Marlboros and the Cokes and walked to the house through the snow. It was already nearly a foot deep and coming heavier all the time.

Bump pulled the door open and stepped aside.

I said, "Whose big-ass Lincoln is that?"

Bump laughed. "One of the twins'."

He took the Cokes from me.

I stomped off my high-tops on his little blue throw rug, pulled off my black knit cap, and stuffed it in my jacket pocket. "Nice car."

Bump nodded. "They like to travel in style, I guess." He headed off toward the kitchen. I looked around. Bud and a guy I didn't know, but who looked like a diluted version of Bump and I assumed was Bump's brother, Ray, were sitting on the sofa. They each held a bottle of Corona. They were watching a replay of a football game on the tube.

Bud yelled *"Oooh!"* at a dropped pass and turned to me. "Hey, Terry, grab yourself a beer." He was wearing an old gray sweatshirt and gray sweatpants. His thinning, graying hair was tousled, like he just got up.

I walked over and shook Bud's hand. Then I turned to the other guy. "You must be Ray?"

He nodded.

I said, "I'm Terry Saltz. Call me Twees." I held out my hand. He shook it halfheartedly. He looked like maybe he didn't feel good or he was a little buzzed or something.

Bud said, "Twees?"

I said, "New nickname."

He said, "New haircut, too, huh?" He grinned at me.

From the dining room, Bump yelled, "Terry, get out here. Look at my backyard in the snow."

He was standing by the sliding doors. I tossed the carton of cigarettes onto the kitchen table, he handed me a can of Coke, and he slid open the door.

We stepped out onto the deck. His backyard looked awesome, the way the snow was draped over the fence, the terraces, and the bushes. Edges of brilliant green showed through the snow here and there. Fat flakes drifting in the air completed the picture.

He said, "Hang on. Lemme hit the lights." He reached

around the doorway and flipped the switch. The deck lights came on and glowed through the snow.

He grinned and said, "That's fuckin' laid *out*."

I felt his hand on my back, pressing, and we took a few more steps out onto the deck.

He leaned his mouth close to my ear and said in a low voice, "Somebody called the hospital, trying to find out who Marylou is, what she was there for, and where she is now."

I said, "Someone called the police, too, asking the same kinds of questions."

Bump said, "That's not good."

"No shit. How'd they even know to call the hospital?"

"I know. That's what's bothering me."

"Did they find out anything?"

He shook his head. "Fortunately, the woman on the switchboard is a friend of mine." His grin told me what kind of friend. "She told the caller she had no record of anyone being admitted that night. Then she called me."

"How'd she know to call *you?*"

"Because when I went down there that day to check on Marylou, she's the one who told me where to find her."

From the kitchen, a petulant male voice interrupted us. "Close that door. We're freezing our tushes off in here."

Bump and I stepped back inside, and I closed the door behind us. The twins, Marylou, and Mike were standing in a little knot near the sink, looking back over their shoulders at us. Marylou broke out of the pack and came toward me, smiling.

She said, "Hi, Terry." Her eyes were tearing up. She had flour on her nose.

I opened my arms to her. She came against me and I held her. I looked up from her hair and saw that everybody was discreetly fading out of the kitchen. Pretty soon conversation started up in the living room.

She had her arms up around my shoulders and my neck, and I could feel that she had started to cry silently. I held her and gently rubbed her back.

After a few minutes she settled down. She turned her head a little and said into my shoulder, "It's been so hard."

I said, "I know, but you're safe now. It'll get easier." I noticed her hair wasn't all teased up and sprayed stiff. It was just pulled back into a loose, soft ponytail. It smelled good. Clean.

She whispered, "I'm sorry for what a bitch I've always been to you."

I was astonished. Marylou, apologizing? I didn't say anything.

She said, "I think I've finally grown up a little bit."

This was an even more amazing thing for her to say. I was speechless.

She sniffled and pulled away. She walked over to the sink, tore a paper towel off the roll, and blew her nose into it. She turned back to me, pushing a smile. I noticed she wasn't wearing any makeup. Would wonders never cease?

She came back to me and spread the lapels of my pea jacket. I shrugged out of it. She took it away from me and fit it over the back of one of the kitchen chairs.

She said, "Your friends have been great. Mike, Ray, Bump. Bud."

I nodded. "We'll get the murderer. Just hang tight. We'll get him and everything'll be back to normal."

She nodded. "I know."

We looked at each other for a minute. She shoved her hands into her jeans pockets. "You got all your hair cut off."

I rubbed the top of my head self-consciously. "Whad'ya think of it?"

She smiled. "It makes you look different. One ex-

treme to the other, huh? But I think I like it. It makes
you look like that one guy."

Well, she hadn't changed completely. She still expected me to be a mind reader.

I said, "What guy?"

"He was a quarterback. *You* know. Always wore
sunglasses."

"What team?"

"Um, Chicago? Yeah. He played for the Bears. For
that one guy. Mike Ditka."

"Oh. McMahon? Jim McMahon?"

"Yeah. You look sorta like him now."

I said, "Huh." But I liked that. I always liked Jim
McMahon.

I ran my eyes over the cluttered counters and
said, "What's going on here? You guys are baking
pies?"

As if on signal, one of the twins popped back into
the kitchen. "Things are good here? Everybody's
happy happy?"

Marylou nodded. "Happy happy. Let's get back to
work."

He had flour all over the front of his acid-washed
denim shirt. There was even some in his long, straight,
sand-colored hair. He turned back toward the living
room. "Come on, Luther. That dough's chilled enough
now. Let's get the pies put together."

Luther appeared, a mirror image of his twin, whose
name, if I remembered correctly, was Reginald. Mike
was right behind him. Mike and I made eye contact.
She had her blue-black hair pinned up carelessly on
her head. Escaped curls hung across her pale forehead
and around her temples. She wore a white T-shirt and
blue jeans like Marylou. There was flour on one
cheek. She was barefoot, and there was pink polish
on her little toenails.

She looked so good I wanted to die.

She smiled at me. I smiled back. I decided there

and then that someday, that woman was gonna marry me. I'm serious. I began, then and there, to puzzle out the best way to make that happen.

While they clustered at the counter, Bump came out carrying a can of Coke. He spun a chair around and straddled it. I sat across from him, popped the top on my Coke, and lit up. He picked up the carton of smokes, opened one end, and tapped out a pack. He looked up at me and nodded thanks. I nodded back.

We smoked and watched the busy pie makers. A few minutes later, Bud walked out and announced that the game sucked rocks and he no longer wanted any part of it. He pushed his way through the bakers to grab another Corona from the refrigerator and pulled up a chair at the table.

I said, "Oh. Bump. Have you heard about your little friend at Petey's?"

He said, "What? Who?"

I said, "Nancy. I guess she's outa commission for a while."

Marylou, her back to us, said, " 'What the fuck. *You're* not Nancy.' " She turned around to face us. "What's that from? 'What the fuck. *You're* not Nancy.' "

Bud said, "You mean, like a movie or something?"

Bump said, "Like Bette Davis. 'What? A dump.' "

I gave him a blank look.

He said, "You know, she walks into the room, she's holding her cigarette out, she flicks the ash, she goes, 'What? A dump.' "

Bud ran his fingers through his thinning brown hair. He said, "I think that was Elizabeth Taylor."

Bump shook his head. "No, dude. Bette Davis."

Ray came walking out. He dropped his empty Corona bottle in the trash and pushed his way through to a fresh one in the refrigerator, just like Bud had done.

He faced us and pushed off the cap with his thumbs. "Bette Davis said 'Fasten your seat belts, boys, it's

gonna be a bumpy night.' " He cocked his hip when
he said it. It made me laugh.

One of the twins turned around from the corner,
waving a rolling pin. "I don't think she said 'boys.'
But the best one was, 'I'd like to kiss ya, but I just
washed my hair.' Now, that was a great line."

The other twin repeated it and they laughed.

Bump said, "That's a fuckin' stupid line. It doesn't
make any sense."

The twins glared at him. One said, "That's why it's
such a great line. That she would say that. It's great
because it doesn't make any sense." He whirled back
around to the work on the counter. Bump hooted.

The first time I met the Elliots was while they and
their older brother, Emmett, were landscaping Bump's
backyard. Gruf and I stopped by to see how the work
was coming. Afterward I asked Gruf about the twins.
It was the first time I'd ever met a gay guy, that I
knew of, anyway, and I was all like, What the fuck?

Gruf told me about a time when he was eight or
nine and made a crack about the twins at his dinner
table. Some kid in school had called them faggots, and
Gruf repeated it in front of his family. There was dead
silence around the table and then Smitty said, "That's
a word that can cause a lot of hurt. I'd rather not hear
you use it again."

Gruf said, "But they are faggots, aren't they? They
got dollies for Christmas."

His two older brothers were hurting themselves trying not to laugh.

Smitty said, "What the twins are is, they're a pair
of very old, very gentle souls. Don't ever let anyone
pick on them."

Gruf said, "Nobody does anyway. Emmett's the
toughest kid in the fourth grade. But did you say
they're old? They're only four."

Smitty said, "They're four in age. But a person can
be born with a soul that's any age. Their souls are
ancient. Now, shut up and eat."

Gruf said that was how he'd always thought about the twins, ever since that night at his dinner table. That they were a pair of gentle old souls. He said that all their lives they'd done pretty much what they wanted to do, in the manner they wanted to do it, and you could take them or leave them. They didn't particularly care either way.

I thought about that for a while. The world I grew up in wasn't very tolerant, and you tend to adopt the prejudices of the people around you. But here was the score sheet on the twins. They were lifelong friends of Gruf's. Bump dug the hell out of them. Bump likes people who go their own way and the rest of Western civilization can kiss their crusty asses. Mike apparently liked them, since she was hanging out with them. Any one of those factors would have been enough for me.

For myself, I'd seen enough of the twins to know that they were hard workers and they were very good at their jobs. They were meticulous and exacting, and they went about their landscaping like it was art. And I respect hard work above almost everything else. So I figured, What the fuck. Live and let live. That was my attitude as I watched them in Bump's kitchen that snowy afternoon.

One of the twins opened the oven door and positioned cookie sheets on the shelves inside.

I said, "What kind of pies are we building over there, anyway?"

One twin said, "Caramel apple."

The other one said, "And cherry sour cream."

I said, "You guys gonna have any extras? Little care package for the trailer boys?"

One of the twins said, "There'll be plenty for everyone, precious. Don't you worry about that."

I thought, Precious? I looked at Bump in time to catch his smirk. He wasn't laughing at the twins. He was laughing at me. He was certainly getting a kick out of watching me have a learning experience.

Marylou turned around from the counter, and I saw

that she had arranged sliced cheese and some kind of fancy crackers on a plate. She carried the plate over and set it in the middle of the table. Bud looked up at her and smiled.

Smiling back, she pointed at his Corona and said, "Ready for a fresh one, Bud?"

I thought, Marylou being considerate? Marylou thinking about someone else's needs?

He shook his head. "Not yet, darlin'. I'm good."

He watched her walk back to the others.

I thought, Darlin'?

I thought, Hmm.

I sat there smoking, watching Mike, sipping Coke, watching Mike, chatting. I hung out just long enough that I left for home carrying a beautiful cherry sour cream pie.

Chapter 9

Tuesday morning, Spencer looked like nuclear winter. Snow was still coming down at a good clip and there was already more than two feet on the ground. Schools were closed, of course, but Gruf called to report that some businesses had reopened. Brewster's was open for breakfast, and Smitty was gonna open the bar. Carlo's would also be open.

The roads were crowded with plows, salt trucks, and four-wheel-drives. I picked up Bump at his house because his two-wheel-drive truck isn't good in snow, and we drove over to Brewster's.

A funny thing happens in Spencer when there's a major snowstorm. People who have four-wheel-drive vehicles, and even some with front-wheel-drive vehicles, suddenly feel the overwhelming need to drive to the corner store for the morning paper or down to the crossroads to top off the gas tank. They venture out for two reasons. First, to prove they can get out of their driveways. Second, to see who else made it.

Within this group of hardy souls, there's a small hard-core subgroup. These individuals are the ones who go out driving in blizzard conditions without coats, hats, or gloves. It's like they're saying, I'm so cocky about both my driving ability and my vehicle that I don't have to even consider the possibility that I'll get stuck somewhere and be exposed to the elements.

These hard-core individuals are a rare breed, with

many imitators and wanna-bes. I've actually seen, on more than one occasion, a guy take off his coat and leave it in his truck so that he can walk into his destination looking hard-core when he really isn't. As far as I'm concerned, a person who would do this is beneath contempt and is never to be trusted or treated with respect.

I'm not hard-core. In bad winter weather, I wear my coat and my black knit cap (although I didn't used to wear it when I had hair). In my backseat are my gloves, a blanket, a tow chain, a shovel, and a bag of either cat litter or sand. These things in the backseat are not for me. I've got the four-wheel-drive. I carry these things in case I come upon someone else who's stranded.

Anyway.

So Brewster's was jammed with snow warriors that morning. It was busier than I'd ever seen it. But good ol' Mary had pushed our tables together and held our places for us. People were standing around the cash register waiting to be seated, and they were looking at the empty chairs around our tables with unpleasant expressions on their faces.

Bump and I squeezed through the milling crowd and headed for our tables. Behind me, I heard someone ask a waitress why we were being seated. I heard her answer that we had Reserved Seating.

Danny and John were already there, of course. We'd all left the trailer at the same time, but I'd had to swing over by Bump's house. Nelma and Alan were there, too. Gruf and Smitty came walking in about five minutes after me and Bump.

Gruf took a seat to my left.

I said, "Did you know that we have Reserved Seating here in Brewster's?"

He was blowing warm air into his cupped hands. His Jeep doesn't have any of those fancy sissy features like a heater.

He said, "I know it now."

I said, "One of the waitresses told somebody that— that we have Reserved Seating. It got me thinking about your problem."

He said, "What problem is that?"

I said, "Over at the bar. With the regulars?"

He stopped in midblow and looked at me. You could see the wheels going around. "Reserved Seating."

I nodded.

He said, "For the regulars."

I nodded.

He grinned.

After breakfast Bump caught a ride home with Alan. Gruf and I headed for the bar. We quickly installed the trim boards we had painted and stained on Sunday. The next step was to get all the electrical lines run out across the ceiling of the dining room to the spots where they'd be needed. It was tedious, because they had to be sited perfectly, so there was a lot of measuring and double-checking.

Plus, all morning we were preoccupied with the time. Wondering what would happen at noon in Brewster's parking lot. Would Amy Grodell show up? Would the cops get her? What would she have to tell them?

From noon on, Gruf started giving readouts from his wristwatch: twelve ten, twelve fifteen, twelve twenty. John had promised to call us or run over and tell us the second the cops had Amy Grodell, and to give us a detailed report on what she was saying.

Finally at twelve thirty, about the time we were hatching the idea one of us should drive over there and see what was going on, Bump came walking back into the dining room.

He was on a delivery. He said that as of the time he had left the parking lot, Amy Grodell still hadn't showed.

I groaned. "Oh, man. She spotted the cops and ran?"

Gruf shrugged. "Or she's snowed in. Or stuck in a ditch somewhere. Who knows?"

Bump came back at one thirty. She still hadn't showed, so the cops had called it off.

I said, "Well, keep answering your cell phone like you're the auto-parts guy. Maybe she'll call to set up another meeting."

We went back to work on the electric lines for the wall fixtures. When we were almost done I asked Gruf to call and see if Evan Lustig could come over and inspect the work so we could start snugging in the wall insulation in the morning.

He made the call, and came back carrying fresh iced teas for each of us. "Lustig said he'll be over around three. Insulation tomorrow. Pretty nasty shit, huh?"

I'd done the insulation in the kitchen and the wait-ress station one day when Gruf and Smitty were out trying to decide on the flatware for the dining room, so this was going to be Gruf's first insulating experience.

I said, "Not if you dress for it. Wear a couple of long-sleeved shirts you won't mind throwing away and bring a pair of work gloves."

He raised his eyebrows.

I said, "It's full of glass fibers. You get it on your skin and you'll get an ugly, itchy rash. And we gotta wear paper breathing masks. I ordered a pack along with the other stuff for tomorrow's delivery."

We finished the lines and only had to wait ten or fifteen minutes for Lustig. He passed us on the wall lines. Then he went out to the bar to talk to Smitty. Gruf and I walked back to the kitchen and had a cigarette. By that time it was a quarter of four. I headed back to the trailer. It was still snowing, but not as heavily.

The new owners never showed up at Carlo's that night. They didn't call or anything. Nobody knew what was going on with them. Gruf even called Kenny Carlo at the Fairfield store. Kenny didn't know what their deal was, either.

John came to Carlo's for dinner. While I waited for my next delivery to be ready I went into the dining room and sat with him. He gave me a big grin. "Guess what. We found Reese Tornow's VW."

I said, "No shit. Where?"

He said, "All the way down by LaDue Reservoir."

I said, "That's forty miles south of here."

He nodded. "And it was a lucky break we even found out about it. The license plates were stolen off another car six, seven months ago, and somebody'd tried to scratch out the VIN number. The cops down there did manage to bring up the VIN, but it wasn't registered to Reese Tornow, anyway. There would have been no way to connect it to anything up here."

I said, "Then how *did* you connect it?"

He said, "Alan Bushnell was talking to a friend of his down in the—I guess it'd be Akron PD, or maybe Highway Patrol, or someplace—about the case. He mentioned he couldn't find the gray VW. It happened that the friend knew about the gray VW they'd towed in from LaDue. So Alan got a flatbed truck and went down and got it."

I said, "How'd he know it was the same VW?"

John said, "He didn't. Not at first. Not for sure. But there was a stain on the front passenger seat. Once they had it back here, they ran tests. Semen and a little bit of blood and stuff. The samples matched up with Marylou's."

I said, "Shit. Well, that puts her in the car with Reese Tornow at some point."

He said, "Yup. The crime lab's going over it now. Oh. Something else. Those other two bullets? One was in the bathroom doorframe. The other was in a wall just past the bathroom. They both lined up like someone was firing toward the bathroom door."

"Think he was firing at Marylou?"

"Coulda been. We're gonna start sending a patrol car past Bump's sister's house at intervals. Just to keep an eye on it."

I nodded, relieved. Gruf called out, "Driver," just at that minute, so I left without telling John that someone had called the hospital to ask about Marylou. I thought of it as I headed out with my deliveries. I almost turned around to go back, but then I thought, Well, they're patrolling past the house now, anyway, so she's covered.

Business fell off around ten, so we were able to get an early start on the closing jobs. We got the place closed up fairly rapidly. I started for home around eleven-thirty. I turned onto Haskins, which is the main drive of Chandler's Trailer Park, and signaled to make the left turn to cut over to Sumner Court. But I stopped when I saw that a little Chevy had spun out and was stuck sideways in a snowbank that ran along the narrow side street.

Two guys were working with a shovel and a bag of salt, swearing, trying to dig it out and get it moving. I stopped in the intersection and walked over to help. With two of us pushing and the other one steering, we got it unstuck pretty quick. After that, instead of backing my truck up to turn onto the side street, I continued on down Haskins Court, intending to go down to the next cross street and cut over to Sumner Court on it.

Haskins Court was the street the murder trailer was on. I slowed down as I approached the dark trailer, but of course there was nothing to see. I passed it and rolled on, picking up speed, idly looking at the next couple of trailers in the row, wondering if the cops had questioned everybody all up and down the street.

Something caught my eye. I went by a few more trailers, thinking about what I'd seen. Then I braked to a stop, wondering if it meant anything. It was kind of a funny coincidence. Kind of made me wonder.

I looked back up the street, mulling it over. There

were still lights on in the trailer. What the fuck. It wouldn't hurt to ask a few questions. I pushed the gearshift into reverse and backed up to park in front of the driveway.

I stared at the truck that was parked in the driveway as I walked toward the front porch. Now I could see that it didn't have the extended cab like mine did. But still, from the back, these people's black Toyota Tacoma truck looked a lot like mine. I climbed the steps and knocked at the door.

A guy in a yellow T-shirt and green plaid boxers answered the door. A blast of hot air hit me in the face. I glanced at the boxers and wondered if his wife bought them for him.

He said, "Yeah?"

I said, "Hey, sorry to bother you so late."

He said, "What's up?"

I said, "It's about your truck."

He said, "My *truck?*" in a panicky voice. He looked out past me at his truck in the driveway, alarmed to think maybe something had happened to it.

I laughed. I love my truck, too.

I said, "I have almost the same truck. Black Toyota Tacoma. Parked right there. See?"

He stuck his head out the door to look where I pointed. I'd left my truck running and the headlights on.

He said, "Oh, yeah. Huh."

I stammered around, trying to figure out how to get into my questions. The problem was, I wasn't quite sure what my questions were.

I said, "Uh, the reason I stopped was, uh, you know that trouble up the street last week?"

He said, "The murder?"

I said, "Yeah. Well, see, the woman who was in that trailer at the time was my ex-wife."

He said, "Jeez." I had his attention now. He said, "Hey, don't stand out there in the cold. Come on in."

The temperature inside must've been eighty. After

the sharp, cold air outside, I felt like I was walking into an oven. I opened my pea jacket and said, "Oh, sorry. My name's Terry Saltz. Twees, for short. I live over on the next block."

"Sumner?"

"Yeah."

He said, "Mark Barr." We shook hands. He said, "The wife's in bed. Ya wanna beer?"

"No, no. Don't wanna put you to any trouble. The thing about that night is, we can't figure out what my ex-wife was doing in that trailer."

"What does she say?"

"That's just it. She doesn't know how she got there. She'd been drugged."

"Jeez." He stepped over to the little end table by the couch and picked up his beer.

I said, "I was coming home from work tonight and I saw your truck, and it made me wonder. Because your truck looks exactly like mine."

"I don't follow."

I said, "Well, I was thinking that if she was looking for *me* that night, and if she knew I lived in Chandler's, but she didn't know which trailer, and she was driving through and saw your truck . . ."

"She might've thought it was *your* truck?"

I nodded. "Exactly."

"Huh."

"So I wanted to ask you, did anything weird happen that night? Anything at all? Anything that might have had to do with your truck?"

He shook his head. "Nothing I remember. Hang on a second, lemme ask the wife."

I started to say, No, don't bother her, but he had already yelled, "Barbie! C'mere a minute."

Half a minute later, a pudgy little thing in a white terry cloth robe and a big ol' frown came padding out to the kitchen and squinted at me in a sour and disapproving manner. The man of the house explained briefly what we wanted to know, and she scratched her tummy through the robe, thinking.

"That was the night I had my candle party."

I said, "Candle party?"

Mark said, "Barbie invited a bunch of her girl-friends over so some woman could try to sell 'em all a bunch of candles."

I nodded.

Barbie said, "I sent you up to Smitty's to get you out of the way. Remember? Your truck wasn't even here."

Mark said, "Oh, yeah. That's right." He looked at me sheepishly.

I said, "Well, that's that, then. What time did you leave Smitty's?"

He looked at her. "You said to stay there until mid-night, right?"

She nodded. "Yeah. You came walking in, like, ten after, didn't you?"

He said, "Yeah, that's right. Ten after twelve."

I said, "Well, that takes care of that, then. You didn't see anything or notice anything up the street, did you?"

He shook his head. "Nothing. Sorry."

I said, "Oh, well. It was worth a try. Thanks for talking to me."

He said, "Sure thing," and reached for the door-knob to let me out.

I said to Barbie, "Was it a good party? Did you sell a lot of candles?"

Mark started to laugh. "They were still here work-ing on their orders when I came in. 'Member, hon? Ellen and what's 'er name and that other—hey, wait a minute. Wait a fuckin' minute."

He was snapping his fingers, trying to remember. "I came home and there were still three cars here. One of 'em was in the driveway. So I backed up the street. Oh, my God. I can't believe I forgot this. I knew that trailer was vacant, so I parked my truck up there until the last of the girls left."

He looked at me. "My truck was parked in that driveway from about ten after twelve until about one or so, when the last of them left. Then I went and moved it back down here."

Holy shit. I said, "Think hard, now. When you went back up to get your truck, were there any other cars there that weren't there before?"

He was starting to shake his head no.

I said, "Like an old gray VW Beetle?"

He blinked. "Yeah. Yeah, there was. Parked right under the streetlight. Gray Vee Dub. Yeah, there was. I remember it because it was so beat to shit. I wondered what kind of guy lets his car get like that."

I said, "Did you see anybody? See anything?"

He shook his head. "No, nothing. Sorry."

I said, "Any lights on in the empty trailer?"

He shook his head. "No. I'm sure about that. I'd have noticed that. I knew nobody lived there."

I said, "Hey, thanks. You helped a lot." We shook hands.

He said, "Whose car was it? The Vee Dub?"

I said, "The dead guy's."

He said, "Wow."

Barbie pulled her robe tighter.

Chapter 10

I was disappointed to see that Danny and John were already in bed. I wanted to talk about the case. They'd left a lamp on in the living room for me. I turned it off and got myself ready to hit the sack, but I thought I'd just toss and turn all night. I punched up my pillow, stretched out, and pulled up my bankies. That's the last thing I remember until my alarm went off Wednesday morning.

I hit the snooze and rolled over, but something was tickling around in my subconscious. My brain kicked into first gear and my eyes popped open. It was raining. Rain was drumming on the metal roof of the trailer and dripping down my window.

Boy, the weather in northeastern Ohio. You just never know.

I rolled over onto my back and tucked my hands behind my head. I began to hear the truly disturbing and ear-torturing sound of Danny singing in the shower. It would be bad enough if he stuck to other people's material, but the thing is that Danny generally has a habit of making up his own songs for his early-morning songfests.

This morning he appeared to be rapping, in a painfully unrhythmic white-guy style, on the subject of the weather. Something along the lines of: "Roofa! Roofa! I'm a bad mutha roofa got the rainy day off, got the day day, fucky day day, fucky day day off. . . ."

The stomping sound on the front porch meant

John was coming in from his morning run. Danny
and I have tried to persuade him to skip his morning
runs when the weather's bad, so he doesn't fall and
break his neck and freeze to death in a ditch somewhere, but he isn't having it. His only concession
has been to say that when it's icy, he'll settle for a
brisk walk.

I'd installed a second hot-water heater for my bathroom. I had to give up my linen closet to do it, but
I'd rather have hot water for my shower in the morning than a nice place to store a bunch of towels and
sheets that I don't own anyway. I took my shower
while Danny and John traded places in their bathroom, and by the time I walked out to the kitchen,
John and Danny were sitting at the table putting on
their shoes.

I lit up a cigarette, savoring the moment. "Guess
what."

John looked up. Danny said, "Huh," and went on
tying the laces on his high-tops.

"I found out why Marylou and Reese happened to
be in that trailer that night."

Danny looked up now. "No shit."

John said, "Why?"

"A guy who lives a few doors down from the murder trailer has a truck just like mine. It was parked in
the driveway of the murder trailer for a while that
night. Between around ten after twelve and one."

I could see them thinking that over.

I said, "See what happened?"

They were working on it, but I was too impatient
to wait while they got all the way through it.

I said, "Marylou wakes up in her town house after
being drugged and raped. She's stoned, scared, upset,
confused. She thinks if she can find me she'll be safe.
Somehow she hooks up with Reese Tornow, gets him
to drive her over here. She knows I live in Chandler's,
but she doesn't know which trailer. They turn in on

Haskins, start down the street. She's looking for my truck. The time is somewhere between ten after twelve and one a.m. And there it is, only it's not my truck—it's the other guy's truck."

They'd been nodding. John said, "Okay, that makes sense."

Danny said, "As far as it goes—"

I said, "The guy came back to move his truck down to his own driveway around one. He remembers seeing the gray VW parked out on the street. Marylou and Reese musta been inside, asleep or passed out or somehow out of it, because the lights were off and the guy didn't see or hear anything. A few hours later, the murderer showed up, did the deed, and disappeared, and so did the Vee Dub."

Danny lit a cigarette and puffed. "Well, well, well," he said sagely. He looked like Yoda. "Another piece of the puzzle falls into place."

John was nodding. "That's pretty good. And I've got something, too. Alan's been through the stuff Amy Grodell left behind at the house on Washington. You were right. It was Reese's stuff."

I said, "And?"

"There was a high school yearbook. It pointed Alan in the right direction."

Danny said, "What was the guy's deal? Was he a big fire-fightin' Navy SEAL?"

"He was a high school football hero from a suburb of Columbus who screwed up his knee big-time in the middle of his senior year. Went straight into drugs and fantasyland. Couldn't handle not being everybody's golden boy anymore. When his parents got sick of him laying around the house, stealing money out of their wallets, they gave him the boot."

Danny said, "Then he came up here?"

"He floated around Columbus for a few years first. All the suburban departments down there knew him, but they never actually caught him at anything."

The phone rang. John was closest, so he answered it. After a few minutes, he hung up and said, "That was Bump. Amy Grodell just called him and rescheduled their meeting for noon today."

I said, "Why didn't she show up yesterday?"

"Her car wouldn't start. Her dad told her he'll stick around today and make sure she can get it running. Man. I hope she shows up today. Alan's pretty sure either she did the murder or she knows who did."

In Brewster's, I was dying to tell Gruf and Bump my news about the other Toyota, but I couldn't while Alan was there or he'd know we were poking around after he'd told us not to. Nelma cut out early because she had a meeting, and John left a short time later. Alan had Mary top off his coffee. Then he sipped it and watched us a few minutes longer. But he must have finally faced the fact that we could sit there for hours if we wanted to. He shot me a stern warning look and left pretty soon after that.

The four of us moved into a booth. While I started telling Gruf and Bump about the other truck, Danny decided to order some more pancakes. My number four hadn't filled me up, so I ordered two more eggs, over easy, and another piece of Texas toast. We sat there awhile discussing the case.

Once we'd about exhausted the subject, Gruf bounced his eyebrows at me and grinned. "Are we working today, or what?"

I mopped my toast around in some egg juice and said, "Fuckin' A."

Gruf said, "Danny, you've got a rain day. Come work with us."

"Yeah," I said. "Get in a few bonus hours on the payroll."

Danny nodded. "Yeah, okay. I could do that."

Bump finished off his coffee and said, "I wonder if Petey's back yet. I'm gonna stop over there."

Gruf said, "Let's all go. I need a pack of smokes, anyway."

Pete was back, but he was busy when we walked into his store. We stood off to the side in front of the big beef jerky display while he rang up customers one after another. A breeze was beginning to turn the morning air icy so that the rain was freezing as it fell. Working men in Carhartts blew into cupped hands as they shuffled in line and waited to buy their stuff and head out to their jobs. Most were just buying Styrofoam cups of coffee and cigarettes, but once in a while somebody bought a pack of gum or instant lottery tickets. A few grabbed subs from the open cooler next to the register.

It seemed like Pete knew why we were there. He looked over after a few minutes and told us to help ourselves to coffee. Bump did. I was coffeed out from Brewster's and I guess Gruf was, too.

Pete waited till the last customer walked out the door. Then he said, "So, Reese Tornow got himself murdered, huh? And the cops think Pookie Grodell did it?"

We looked at each other in surprise. Gruf said, "They do?"

Pete motioned us around the counter so we could stand and talk in his back room. He lit a cigarette and sucked on it.

Bump said, "What makes you think the cops are looking at Pookie?"

Gruf said, "Yeah. How could he have done it? He's in jail."

Pete said, "No, he's not. He got out two weeks ago. But if you ask me, it's bullshit. Pookie didn't do it."

Gruf said, "No?"

Pete chuckled. "Alan Bushnell told me you guys might be in here asking questions. He told me not to talk to you."

We looked at each other.

Pete said, "Alan can go fuck himself. Anyway, where was I? Pookie, yeah. He talks big, but he's all hat and no cattle. Everybody knows that."

Gruf nodded.

Bump said, "You worked the night Reese got shot. Anything unusual happen?"

But Pete, peeking around the wall toward the register, said, "Shit. Hang on a minute," and went out to ring up another customer.

He glanced up at the wall clock as he walked back to us. "The new day girl was supposed to be here ten minutes ago. When she gets here, we'll be able to—hey, here she is. Nice a you to show up, Jeannie."

Jeannie, her curly blond hair badly windblown, came bustling back toward us, shedding her coat as she walked, blushing furiously. "I'm sorry, Pete. My dad's car was blocking my car and I had to wait for him."

Pete said, "Don't worry about it. Just get out there and make some new coffee. We're running low. And cover for me on the register until I finish my meeting here."

He turned back to us. "Jeez. I miss Nancy. Say what you will about her. She's got her faults. But that girl is punctual. You could set your watch by her. Where were we?"

I said, "So, you know Pookie pretty well, huh?"

Pete said, "Well enough. He used to work for me when he was a teenager. Trying to get away from the family. Didn't want to be a plumber. That kind of thing. Good worker, when he showed up. Screwed-up kid, but they're all screwed up at that age, huh?" He laughed. "He ended up quitting on me. Gave up and went to work for Daddy. But he still stops in regular. Say hi. When he's not in jail." He laughed.

Gruf said, "Has he been in here recently? The cops can't find him, you know."

Pete shook his head. "I haven't seen him for

months. But if I did, I wouldn't tell the cops. He didn't do it."

Bump said, "Who do you think did?"

Pete shook his head. "Hell, I don't know. But there were some incidents while Reese was working here. He had some stuff going on. People who really didn't like him."

Gruf said, "Like who?"

Pete pushed some papers around on the counter that seemed to serve as his desk and set his coffee cup down in the cleared space. He planted a boot on the edge of the counter and stretched his back in that position. From the front, we could hear the cash drawer pop open and some guys laughing at something Jeannie had said.

"Hell, I don't know. Alls I know is what the girls told me. Reese worked midnight until eight or so. His shift overlapped Nancy Sutton's by an hour or two if it was a busy morning, which it usually is."

I said, "How long did Reese work here?"

Everybody said, "Almost a month."

I nodded stupidly, remembering I'd heard that.

Pete said, "Okay, so sometimes the girls from the other shifts would stop in at night. Say hi. On their way home from the bar, or when they suddenly realize they're out of cigarettes. That kind of thing. Well, he was a good-looking guy. Single, good-looking. So they were stopping in to see him, too, no doubt. I'm pretty sure he slipped at least one of 'em his noodle." He winked at us.

I said, "But he was living with Pookie's sister."

Everybody said that wasn't until a week and a half before he got shot.

I said, "Oh, yeah," like a moron and decided to keep my mouth shut for a while.

Pete said, "Okay, so one night, one of 'em was in here and heard him get a phone call. He was arguing with somebody, and he was mad. Then she heard him say, 'Well, you come ahead on down, then. I'm not going anywhere.' He slammed down the phone and said, 'Pussy.' "

Bump said, "Who was it?"

Pete said, "I don't know. She didn't ask. She was nervous about it and took off. Didn't want to get caught in the middle of a fight. Then another night, one of the girls stopped in for milk for the morning. He asked her if she saw anybody hanging around the parking lot, sitting in a car or anything. She said she didn't. Why was he asking? He said somebody'd threatened him. She said he should call the police. He said he could handle it. He showed her a switchblade he carried in his pocket. There was other stuff. Odd phone calls. Stuff like that. All the girls knew about it."

Gruf said, "Sounds like ol' Reese had a busy life."

Bump said, "So, what about the night of the murder?"

Pete said, "Oh yeah. His regular night off was Wednesdays because he was in a pool league. I needed him weekends. Sometimes he'd work overtime. Sometimes I'd give him another weeknight off. That night I was covering third shift. Around midnight, along in there, Reese comes walking in for a six of Bud Ice and a pack of cigarettes. It was slow, so we stood there talking. I'd noticed he wasn't putting enough Swiss on the ham and cheese subs, so I brought that up. Third shift makes the subs, so they're nice and fresh for the customers in the morning."

We nodded intelligently.

Pete said, "We stood there talking, he turns around to go, and there's somebody outside, standing by his car. He goes hurrying outside. I followed him to the door, but I didn't go out. It was a girl, a blond girl, barefoot, really fucked up. I mean, really fucked up. Wearing one of those big long T-shirts, you know how they wear those shapeless things. I couldn't tell if he knew her or not. Who knows with that guy? Anyway, I already knew about the phone calls and this and that. I didn't wanna get mixed up in his goings-on, whatever they were."

Bump said, "Understandable."

Pete said, "Yeah. So I watched them talking for a minute, but I had better things to do. I got back to work. A few minutes later I looked back outside. The car was gone, and both of them were gone. That was it."

Pete took his boot off the counter and stretched backward, his hands on his hips. "Well, I gotta get at my paperwork. Anything else you boys want to know?"

We looked at each other. I said, "He wasn't a Navy SEAL."

Pete snorted. "Course he wasn't. He claimed to be a lot of things. For a guy to have done everything he claimed to have done, he'd have to be a hundred and seven."

I said, "You never checked his references?"

Pete laughed again. "It's a six-dollar-an-hour job. Who the fuck cares?"

By the time we got back out to our vehicles there was a sheet of ice on the windshields, and it didn't come off without a fight.

At Smitty's, Gruf, Danny, and I stood in the big open area that would soon be a fancy dining room and looked around. It sure didn't look like much now. It was just a big carcass of a room. We'd shown Danny the new kitchen and the waitress station, and now we took a few minutes to explain what all we were gonna do with this room. He looked impressed.

We were still talking when Smitty yelled that the truck from the lumberyard was pulling down the driveway. We hurried out back. We unloaded the rolls of insulation as the driver winched the stack of drywall sheets onto the pallets. He'd forgotten the plaster, tape, and breathing masks. He apologized and said he'd be right back with them.

We carried everything inside. The lumberyard guy brought the rest of our order. Then Gruf and I put on gloves, extra shirts, and breathing masks, and started snugging insulation. Meanwhile, Danny set up a work surface, ran an extension cord out from the kitchen for my circular saw, shot his plumb lines, and followed behind us, hanging drywall. He was smiling.

When the insulation was all hung, Gruf and I went to work drywalling. It was amazing what a difference having Danny made. We had three walls pretty much done by the time Smitty came in to tell us lunch was ready.

"Holy shit," Smitty said, looking around, grinning. "You guys are really going to town in here."

Gruf wiped drywall dust out of his eyebrows. "Hey, Dad. Have you been passing out the membership cards?"

Smitty nodded.

Gruf said, "Well? How's it going over?"

Smitty said, "You'd think it was Christmas out there."

As we trooped back to the kitchen to wash up, I said, "What's that all about?"

Gruf said, "Remember our little problem with the regulars? Your suggestion about the Reserved Seating?"

"Yeah?"

"Well, the solution went into effect today."

The solution was, at either end of the oval bar there was now a little floor stand sign that read RESERVED SEATING/MEMBERS ONLY. Gruf had also printed up membership cards, which Smitty had gotten laminated. Smitty was passing them out to the regulars as they came in.

The regulars were all neatly lined up along the back side of the bar, living large, grinning. There was an

unusually noisy amount of happy conversation. Gruf
slid onto his stool facing them and made eye contact
with Tiny. Tiny gave him a thumbs-up.

Gruf sighed contentedly. "Yup yup yup."

Danny regarded the plate in front of him. "So, this
is the famous French dip, huh?" He two-fisted the
sandwich up to his mouth and gnawed off a big bite.
"Yeah. Oh yeah. That's good."

I glanced at the wall clock. "It's twelve thirty. I
wonder if Amy Grodell showed up this time."

Chewing, Gruf said, "Gimme a minute and I'll go
call Bump."

But we didn't have to call him. He stuck his head
in the front door a few minutes later. "Gotta hurry.
Got a car full of deliveries. But the cops got Amy
Grodell. John says he'll call over here soon as he can.
Let you know what's going on."

Gruf and I were finishing drywalling the fourth wall
and Danny was rapidly taping and plastering by the
time we heard from John. He didn't call. He walked
in, big as life in his spiffy black cop suit. Rainwater
streamed off his cop hat. We stopped what we were
doing and lit smokes.

Gruf said, "Is she talking?"

John laughed. "They almost can't shut her up. She
says her brother did it. She says her family's been
keeping her almost like a prisoner out at their place
so she can't narc on him. She's pretty upset with the
blood relatives."

I said, "Pookie? That's the brother she says did it?"

Danny said, "How did Pookie know Reese Tornow?"

John said, "She says he didn't. But the other broth-
ers knew him, and they didn't like him. So as soon as
Pookie got out of jail, they put him on Tornow's tail.
Which is how Pookie found the trailer and killed him.
According to his sister."

I shook my head. "You'd have to have more of a

hard-on for a guy than that to kill him. Wouldn't you? That doesn't really add up."

Gruf agreed. "I never knew Pookie that well, but that doesn't sound right to me, either."

Danny said, "Did Pookie tell her? Himself? That he did it?"

John said, "She says he did. Bragged about it."

Gruf said, "What's Pookie say?"

John grimaced. "I guess he'll tell us when we find him. Well, I gotta get back. Just wanted to let you know what's going on."

He turned to go. Danny stopped him. "Hey, John?"

John said, "Yeah?"

Danny said, "That Vee Dub. That they hauled back from LaDue?"

John said, "Yeah?"

Danny said, "Was it dumped there, or did it break down there?"

John frowned. "Uh, I don't know."

Danny said, "Can you find out?"

John said, "Yeah. I'll check on it."

We finished the last of the taping and plastering. Then we installed one of the two big new bay windows that were going into the front wall. Our workday at the bar had to end by four so we could run home for our showers and be back at Carlo's by five. We busted ass to get that window in and weather tight before we left.

Gruf was sitting in our usual booth at Carlo's by the time I blew in at four thirty, but Bump was nowhere to be seen. I poured some coffee and sat down. "Where's Bump?"

Gruf frowned. "In back. The new owners are here. The Formans. Dawn Forman told him to slice some bread."

I raised my eyebrows, but Gruf didn't elaborate.

He said, "Bump says he's been asking around town, and he can't find anyone who even knew Reese Tor-

now, much less had a beef with him. He talked to
one guy who thinks he might have seen him down
in Logan's."

I said, "What's Logan's?"

"A bar down in Bagby. I asked some of the regulars
at the bar, too, this afternoon. I got the same thing
he got. Nobody even knows anybody who had a beef
with Reese Tornow."

I said, "Weird. The way news gets around in this
town. I mean, a guy gets dead, you'd think everybody'd be talking about who was mad at him and
who wasn't."

"Well, in this case, if anybody knows anything,
they're not talking. I wonder why Tornow's car was
all the way down at LaDue Reservoir." I shrugged.
Gruf drained his coffee. "Well. Richard Forman's in
the office. I guess I'd better go see what he's doing."

After a few minutes I walked down the hall and
glanced into the back room. Bump was standing at
the work counter slicing bread. A woman I'd never
seen before was standing next to him, talking. She was
skinny and had short black hair and wore glasses. I
figured she must be Dawn Forman.

I turned around and headed back out to the booth.
As I passed the office I caught a glimpse of the guy's
back. Richard Forman. He was standing in front of
the office shelves, moving cans of tomato sauce
around. Gruf was with him. They were talking.

I sat alone in the booth until it was time to clock
in at five. I went right out on delivery and was pretty
much in the car until after ten, so I didn't see much
of the new owners.

From what little I did see, it seemed like Dawn
Forman stayed mostly in the office. Richard Forman
stood a little over six feet, had short blond hair, and
wore glasses. It seemed like he mostly stood in the
doorway between the front and the back rooms. He
was right in the way, but from where he stood, he

could see what was going on in front where the girls were answering the phones, ringing up customers, and making pizzas, and the back, where the back boys were doing food prep and washing dishes.

When I came in from trips and stood at the front counter waiting for my next order, I noticed Gruf sometimes looked okay, but other times he didn't look too happy.

Once, when I came in around ten, Hammer was standing at the front counter. He said there weren't any more deliveries at the moment and that Gruf was in the shitter. He also said that the Formans had gone home for the night. He looked pretty glad about it.

Later, while we were all busting ass to get the place closed, Gruf said he hadn't made up his mind about the Formans yet.

By the time I walked into the trailer that night, John had already gone to bed, but Danny was still up, remote in hand, surfing the channels. He gave me a smug look as I hung my coat on the coat-tree. His bare, gnarled toes, propped high in the air because he had the La-Z-Boy rocked all the way back, twinkled happily.

He said, "I was right."

"About what?" I sock-footed it to the refrigerator and pulled out a can of Coke.

"The Vee Dub. Remember?"

I didn't have a clue. "No. What about it?"

"Remember I asked John whether it was dumped at LaDue or broke down there?"

I remembered, because I hadn't understood why it mattered. I still didn't. I said, "Oh. And?"

"And I was right. It broke down. Cracked radiator. *Pfft.*"

I slumped onto the couch. "Okay. So?"

He said, "So, it puts a whole different spin on who was driving it and why. Huh?"

I just looked at him.

He said, "Well, if it was driven down there and dumped, whoever drove it was just trying to lose it. But since it broke down, maybe whoever was driving it was going somewhere in particular. Huh?"

I stared at him. I was too tired to consider all the angles. I said, "Interesting."

His shaggy strawberry-blond eyebrows arched. "*Isn't* it?"

Chapter 11

Thursday morning was sunny and almost warm. The pavement was wet, not icy, and the only snow left was in piles made by the plows. I stepped out onto our driveway as John came running down the street from his morning tour of the trailer park.

"Beautiful day, huh?" he huffed. "Warm enough to work up a decent sweat."

I nodded.

We walked toward the porch and I stood in the sunshine while John did his stretching. He straightened and said, "We issued an arrest warrant for Pookie Grodell late yesterday afternoon. Suspicion of murder."

I was surprised. "Nobody who knows him thinks he coulda done it."

"Nobody at the department likes it, either. But what're ya gonna do? His own sister says he confessed to her." He clasped his fingers and stretched his arms straight behind his head.

"Man, I sure would like a chance to talk to Amy Grodell. Where is she now? How can we—"

"Forget it. They've kept her in custody. Material witness. They're afraid someone in the family might get to her. Talk her out of her story. Or worse."

In the kitchen, John got a glass of water and headed for his shower. Danny walked out, buttoning his flannel shirt.

As they passed in the hallway, John told Danny, "Boy, is it ever nice out."

Danny said, "Well, then, *leave* it out." Danny got a glass of water. We could still hear John laughing as he turned on his shower.

I said, "Hey, Danny, remember when you were talking about Reese Tornow's Vee Dub? Whether it broke down at LaDue or whether it was just dumped there?"

"Yeah."

"Well, I didn't really get the significance."

He turned around from the sink. "Maybe it means there was a witness there that night. Another witness, besides Marylou. Someone who ran for his life after it happened." He finished off his water and set his glass in the sink.

"How would a witness have gotten Tornow's keys?"

"Left in the ignition?"

I said, "Okay, how did this witness get there in the first place? Where's the witness's car?"

Danny said, "Huh. Maybe it was somebody that lives here in the park."

We thought about that for a minute.

"By the way, Terry. John overheard something that had to do with the Bitch."

I looked at him. "Twees. Yeah?"

"He had to go over to Bump's sister's with Brian Bell to double-check some stuff with Marylou."

I said, "Yeah."

"Well, anyway, while they were there, Marylou got a call, and when she hung up, she was all happy."

"Uh-huh?"

"It was that lawyer guy, that Alfred Hanratty?"

"Bud. Yeah?"

"He invited her to go out to dinner. It would have been last night, I guess."

My mouth dropped open. Marylou and *Bud?* Bud and *Marylou?* Then I remembered that day I'd gone over to Bump's when the twins and everybody were there. I'd *thought* I picked up certain vibes between Marylou and Bud.

I said, "How'd she act about it?"

"She was excited. Giggly."

I said, "Well, well, well."

Gruf and I busted ass at the bar. We installed the second of the two big bay windows in the street-facing wall. Then we spent the rest of the day on the tedious business of trimming both of them out. I raced home at four, showered, and headed back over to Carlo's. I got there just a few minutes before five.

I had two triple deliveries, and then, when I came in with my empty stay-warm bags, Gruf told me to go around and log out my car. That he was cashing me out.

I didn't understand that at all. It was only six-thirty. Deliveries were stacked on the five-shelf wire rack beside him and there weren't any other drivers standing around that I could see.

I drove the little green Carlo's Hyundai around back, locked it up, logged it in, and hung the key on the board in the back room. Gruf motioned for me to follow him up to the front register.

I said, "What's going on?"

He said, "I don't know, but Bump's on his way over and he says he needs you to go with him. Count up your money and let's get you cashed out."

I said, "Hang on. Are the Formans here?"

"Yeah, but don't worry about it. They won't have a clue one of the drivers is missing."

"And who's gonna close with Princess?"

"I already asked Jeff to stay."

"Is that okay with Princess?"

Princess and I always worked the same five nights a week at Carlo's, and we always closed the place together. Being a closing driver at Carlo's was an important job. You had to do all the food prep for the next day, wash all the dishes and equipment, and put it all away. You had to be thorough and you had

to be able to work very fast. Princess and I closed
Carlo's up like we could read each other's minds. We
could go all the way through closing in closely coordi-
nated ass-busting activity without ever needing to say
a word to each other. There oughtta be some kind of
prize for how good we were.

Princess's real name is Halle Mally. She's funny,
smart, works like a demon, and never complains
about anything. At that time, she had a full-time
day job and came to Carlo's after that, changing
from her office-worker clothes into her black Carlo's shirt and black sweatpants in the ladies' room,
five days a week. She wore black sweatpants instead of the black jeans the rest of us wore. I
assumed it was because she was kind of heavy, although lately I'd noticed that she seemed to be losing some weight.

I really like Princess. So I didn't want to stick her
closing with another driver unless she said it was okay.
While I wrestled with this, she walked in the front
door carrying a stack of empty stay-warm bags. Gruf
and I quickly explained what was up and I asked if
she minded if I took off.

She ran her fingers through her gray and brown hair
and smiled. "No. Course not."

"You're okay closing with Jeff?"

"Sure. No problem."

I shrugged and looked back at Gruf. "Okay. Lemme
count my money."

Gruf dispatched Princess and she hurried out with
another tall stack of deliveries.

A few minutes later, Bump's truck wheeled into a
space in the back lot. I hurried out the back door.
The air had gotten colder, and the wind was picking
up a little.

Bump was swinging out of his truck. "You mind
driving? All of a sudden this thing's missing a little
bit."

We climbed in my truck and I started her up. "Where're we going?"

"Get on 8. Heading east. I know where Pookie Grodell is hiding."

Once you leave the Spencer town limits, you get into farm country pretty quick. If you're going north or west, you come back into civilization, and a lot of it, before too long. But if you're going south or east, it begins to seem like the farmland goes on forever. I asked Bump a couple of times how much farther, and each time he just pointed at the dark highway ahead of us and said, "Forward."

Finally I remembered to ask him how he'd found out where Pookie was hiding. He stubbed out his smoke. "I stopped in the Thriftway after work. Wanted some onion bagels. I'm walking down the aisle heading for the bakery department and I hear two guys in the next aisle arguing about who's gonna pay for the beer. One of 'em says, 'I paid last time.' And the other one says, 'You only paid for a six of Shaefer. Pookie wants a twelve of MGD. He'll kill us dead if we come back without it.' "

I said, "Wo."

A pickup coming toward us had his brights on. I flashed at him.

"So I got to the end of my aisle and walked past their aisle like I was looking for something. There's Willie and Dirt Grodell, big as life."

"Dirt?"

"Don't ask me. I don't know. So they work out that they'll split the price. Then Dirt says, 'As long as we're in town, let's stop over at Smitty's for a shot of something.' Willie starts to object, and Dirt says if they had to drive all the way into town, the least Willie can do is give him a minute to sit at the bar and do a shot of something. Willie gives in.

"So I turn around without my bagels and hump out to my truck. A few minutes later they come out and climb into the worst rat-looking Chevy Nova I ever saw. I already knew they were going to Smitty's next, so I took my time heading over that way. I parked in the BP station across the street."

"Okay."

"I was starting to think I missed them." He was feeling around on the floor in the darkness like he was looking for something. "You got anything to drink in here?"

I shook my head.

"There's a little mom-and-pop in another half mile. We'll get a six of Cokes. Anyway, I was starting to think they changed their minds about stopping at Smitty's or something. They musta sat down for more than one. But eventually they came riding up out of the back parking lot. And I followed them out here. 'Cross 41, about a mile and a half down there's a little white church on the left. It's the next driveway on the right. Little dirt track."

I said, "Past 41? That's all the way out in BFE."

He chuckled.

Bump told me to kill my headlights just before we turned onto the driveway and to stop there, just far enough in to be off the highway. Yeah. Easy for him to say. He drives an old beater truck. He's tellin' me to drive the truck I *love* onto a narrow dirt driveway with big ol' country trees right up to the edge on either side, and big-ass country ditches on either side of the culvert? In absolute country pitch-black darkness?

I held my breath and did it. When we came to a stop, Bump said, "We'll just sit here until our eyes adjust."

It was so dark that I had my doubts our eyes could ever adjust that much, but after a while we could begin to make out the driveway. Amazing what starlight and quarter moonlight can do. The driveway was nothing but a rutted two-wheel dirt track with tall weeds down the middle. I could see faint lights way back through the thick woods.

I said, "You got a plan?"

He finished off his Coke and smashed the can. "Yeah. We go up to the door and pound on it."

"Subtle."

I tiptoed my truck up the long straight track. Way before we finally stopped at the edge of the woods we could hear loud music blaring. Pink Floyd. "Welcome to the Machine." I pulled on the hand brake so I could get the brake lights off.

We sat there a minute looking at a tiny little cottage. There had once been a small lean-to attached to the side of it, but it had evidently been built with an inadequate foundation. The outside wall had sunk into the ground, causing the roof of the structure to pull a good ten feet away from the house wall. Now it was a lean-away-from. Lights gleamed through the dirty windows on either side of the front door. Part of an old tractor carcass seemed to be growing up out of the front yard weeds.

There were two vehicles parked alongside the leaning lean-to. I couldn't tell in the dark, but the nearest one looked like a beat-up Nova.

I looked at Bump.

He said, "Go ahead and shut her off. We're hardly gonna need a fast getaway with these wussies." He picked up the rest of the six-pack and opened his door.

I tucked my keys into my back pocket as we walked around the tractor bones and up to the door. Bump pounded on it with his free left hand. Someone turned the music off abruptly. The echoes of it left my ears ringing.

Bump pounded again. "Pookie. Open up. It's Bump Bellini."

Somebody whispered, "*Shit.* Pookie, he says he's Bump Bellini."

Somebody else whispered, "I got ears."

The whispering was so loud it seemed like they were standing right in front of us. Nice heavy door. *Not.*

Now somebody whispered, "What're we gonna do?"

Bump whispered, "Open the fuckin' door."

After a lengthy, suspenseful silence, the door opened. A little freak stood there looking up at Bump with a gun bouncing in his trembling right hand.

Bump and I stared at it for a split second. Then Bump turned to me. "You believe this?"

Almost before the words were out of his mouth, his left hand made a sweeping motion. In the next split second the gun was backward in Bump's hand and the freak was yelping.

"*Ow.* Whad'ya have to do *that* for?" He raised his hand to his mouth and began to suck on his trigger finger.

Bump said, "Move," and stepped up on the doorsill.

The freak quickly jumped out of the way and we walked inside. The air was so heavy with cigarette smoke and man smell it made my eyes water.

Bump fanned his face with his gun hand "Jeez. You got a fan or something in here?"

Somebody said, "Just leave the door open a while."

A thin little balding guy with scared eyes and no chest stepped forward.

Bump said, "Hey, Pookie."

He wore baggy jeans and a faded black Harley-Davidson T-shirt that hung on his skinny frame. I remembered that he was supposed to be a cokehead and that he was supposed to be around our age, since he'd been in school with Gruf. But the way his cheeks and eyes were caved in and bruised, he looked like he was a hundred years older. Why do people think cocaine's glamorous?

Pookie's eyes kept darting to the open doorway. "You bring the cops, Bump?"

Bump snorted.

Pookie scratched his scalp through the thin brown hair on the top of his head. *If I had that little hair, I wouldn't be scratching at it.* "Whad'ya want then? What're ya doing here?"

Bump looked around the room in disgust. Against the left wall was a jumble of rolled-up sleeping bags and clothes. In the far corner was an old space heater, its coils glowing red. Along the back wall there was a counter with a sink in the middle and cabinets above and below.

A big, round, badly scarred table and the mismatched wooden chairs haphazardly placed around it took up most of the room. On the table were a deck of cards, a lot of empty beer bottles, two full ashtrays, and a little pool of something that had spilled. Three big, well-fed carpenter ants stood around it, having a party.

There was also a small dusty-looking mirror on the table. And a rolled-up sandwich bag with white stuff in it. And a razor blade and a sawed-off straw sitting on the mirror.

Pookie Grodell and his brothers looked almost like triplets. Pookie was a little taller than the other two. One of the brothers looked softer, almost pudgy, and the other one had quite a bit more brown hair. But if you knew one of them and then walked into a crowded room and somebody said two of his brothers were there, you could pick them out, no problem.

Bump walked to a chair, spun it around, and straddled it. He set his Cokes on the table. Then he gestured for everybody to take a seat. As everybody was getting settled, he tapped out the three bullets that were in the gun and dropped them into his vest pocket. Then he set the gun on the table and pushed it over to the brother he'd taken it from. The one with the hair.

He was still sucking on his trigger finger and giving Bump hurt eyes. He didn't reach for the gun.

Pookie chose the chair in front of the mirror. "I'm in a world of shit, Bump."

Bump said, "You aren't exactly a stranger in that world, Pookie."

"I didn't do it, Bump. I swear I didn't. But what am I gonna do? That bitch Amy is telling anybody who'll listen that I did."

He picked up the razor blade.

Bump said, "Uh-uh."

Pookie looked up, confused.

Bump said, "Put all that shit away. Where I can't see it. It offends me."

Offends him. I love that guy.

Pookie looked like he was about to argue. Then he changed his mind. He rummaged around through the crap on the counter and found a small grocery bag. Then he carefully, almost tenderly, loaded his stash and equipment into it and pushed it into an upper cabinet.

I said, "While you're up, maybe you could wash off this table and get rid of these ants."

Pookie turned around and gave me a stare. "Who're you?"

Bump said, "A friend. That a problem?"

Pookie turned to one of the brothers. The pudgy one. "Willie. Wash off the table. I gotta go take a whiz."

Bump looked around the room. "Where do you do that in this dump?"

Pookie shrugged. "Outside."

Bump said, "Terry, you mind watching these two while me and Pookie take a walk?"

I shrugged.

No sooner had Bump and Pookie gone out than Pookie's brothers started to move. I put my hands flat on the table. "You. Sit back down. You. Wash the table. And I bet Bump would really appreciate it if you'd empty these ashtrays and get rid of all these empty beer bottles, too."

The three of us did a lot of silent staring and sizing up while the table got cleared off and washed.

The one with the hair, who I now knew was Dirt, wore a dingy wife-beater T-shirt that went a long way toward showcasing his pasty, skinny, muscle-free upper arms. The pudgy one, Willie, wore a threadbare gray T-shirt that said SPENCER HIGH SCHOOL ATHLETIC DEPARTMENT in red letters across the front. The only other guys I'd ever seen wearing shirts like that were members of the Spencer football team. This guy was pudgy and he was only about half the required size to get anywhere near the Spencer football field. But maybe they'd had smaller guys back in Willie's day.

Pookie came stomping back in with Bump right behind him.

Once everyone was settled around the table, Bump pulled his Cokes out of the bag. He pulled off one for me and one for him. I popped my top and took a healthy swig. Looking down the barrel of a gun, however much it's shaking, works up a thirst.

Willie whined, "Are we allowed to drink beer?"

Bump said, "If it's at a moderate rate."

Chapter 12

The Grodell brothers are terrible liars. I don't mean that they do it all the time. I don't know if they do it all the time or not. I mean that they aren't good at it. I sat through about as much earnest eye contact and assertive head nodding as I could stand.

They were lying, and the nervous way in which they were lying told me that they knew a lot of the stuff we wanted to know. I started putting a few things together.

Finally, when Pookie told us for the third time, "I swear, Bump, what did we care who our sister was shacked up with?" I slammed my hand hard on the table. Everything on it jumped. So did the Grodell brothers.

I said, "That's enough of your bullshit, Pookie. All three of you. Here's how it's gonna go, starting now. We ask a question and you answer it. Plain and simple. Got it?"

They blinked at me. Willie said, "That's what we're *trying* to do."

Bump said, "No, you're not. You're lying through your teeth. But it stops right now."

The eye contact stopped. Three pairs of bloodshot blue eyes drooped down to their beer bottles.

I said, "Now, Willie and Dirt. You two knew Reese Tornow before your sister ever moved in with him, right? And I'm thinking you already had a big beef with him. Pookie was still in jail. It was you two that

were calling him all night when he was working at
Pete's. Wasn't it?"

Dirt said, "Oh, did he work at Pete's?"

Bump said quietly, "Dirt, you boys are getting on
my last nerve. That's not a good idea."

That sat everybody up straight. Finally Pookie let
go a deep exhale. "Fuck it. Just tell 'em."

Dirt said, "But—"

Pookie said, "They don't think I did it. If they did,
they'da brought the cops with 'em. Right, Bump? You
know I didn't do it, don't you?"

"I don't think you shot him, no. But you boys were
involved in this thing up to your grimy necks."

I said, "So, how did you get involved with Tornow?"

Willie and Dirt looked at each other. Willie said,
"Downtown Cleveland. In the Flats. It was back in
the summer, when the weather was nice and you could
sit out by the river most of the night, watch the boats,
the lights on the water, so many people down there,
hot girls, music coming out of all the bars—"

Pookie said, "Get to the point, Willie."

Dirt said, "Me and Willie met some guys from the
near west side down there. They lived over near Ohio
City. Nice guys. Three of 'em. We were going down
to the Flats about every Friday night and we'd always
see them. After a while we'd say hi. Then it got so
we'd sit together. Usually at the end of the pier in
front of Shooters."

Willie said, "Reese Tornow was one of 'em. He was
so tight with the other two, we thought they'd been
friends since school or they were from the same neighborhood. Something like that."

Dirt said, "Got so we'd take turns buying each other
rounds. Except Tornow never took his turn. I never
really noticed at the time. Did you, Willie?"

Willie shook his head and raised his bottle.

Dirt said, "And after a while the subject of blow
came up. Naturally."

Bump snorted. Air. "Naturally."

Willie said, "First, we oughtta tell how Tornow always wanted to hear all about Spencer."

Dirt said, "Yeah, I forgot. He was always asking questions about Spencer. About what it was like. About our family. About our dad's plumbing business. Any time we'd talk about home, he'd be there listening, like it was the most interesting thing he ever heard. Huh, Willie?"

"Like Spencer was the most wonderful place in the world."

"He only talked a little bit about himself. He said he used to be a Navy SEAL, and he was waiting for a big check he had coming from the government for his hazard pay. He said when it came, it'd be like winning the lottery or something."

Willie said, "Yeah. That was when we all started going out to the parking lots together to do the blow. That was when we started noticing that Tornow didn't ever bring. He just used everybody else's."

Dirt said, "Yeah, and that was when it came out that the west side guys hadn't known Tornow for very long. They'd hooked up with him in the Flats, just like we'd hooked up with them."

I drank a slug of Coke. Willie watched me. He said, "You want some beer?"

I shook my head.

"You, Bump?"

Bump shook his head.

Willie looked baffled. "How come you guys don't want any beer?"

Bump said, "We prefer soft drinks."

The Grodell brothers exchanged puzzled looks.

I said, "So, Tornow was freeloading off everybody. Go on."

Dirt said, "One of the last times we went down, it was just before Labor Day, we finally took Amy with us."

Willie said, "We didn't wanna take her. She's a pain in the ass. But she'd been raggin' on us all summer. 'I wanna go to the Flats.' "

"So we took her. And we hooked up with the west side boys like always, and she gets the major hots for Tornow."

"Meanwhile, we've pretty much got the guy scoped. He's a freeloader. Full of shit. If he was a Navy SEAL, I'm Chuck Norris."

Dirt said, "But what the fuck. It was the end of summer, another Friday night or two and we'd never see any of those guys again."

Willie said, "But, see, they knew our names, they knew we came from Spencer, they knew our dad had a plumbing business."

"Yeah, so it gets to be what, Willie? End of September?"

"Late September, early October."

"I get a call from one of the west side boys. What was his name, Willie? Something Irish."

"Callahan."

"Callahan, right." Dirt took a long pull. "So I got the call, just because Willie was out on a job and I was the one in the office. Anyway, it's Callahan. He got the number for the plumbing business from directory assistance. He's mad. I mean, really mad. Tornow had been crashing with him and the other guy, promising to pay them back and then some when he gets his government check."

Willie said, "Only they'd started to figure him out. Like we did. So Callahan starts pressing him. 'You gotta get a job. Start carrying some of the load.' "

Dirt said, "Start paying them back. Then all of a sudden, Tornow disappears."

"He took money both of them had put away in their drawers, he took Callahan's stash, and he took Callahan's car."

Bump said, "A gray Vee Dub?"

They both nodded.

I said, "I don't understand that. If it was Callahan's car, when the cops traced the registration they would have gone to Callahan and all this would've come out."

They were both shaking their heads. Dirt said, "Callahan bought it under the table from one a those chop-shop outfits. If the cops found numbers on it, it would have traced back to somebody in another city who got their car stole."

Willie said, "Yeah. So Callahan wants to know, has Tornow turned up out in Spencer? Has Dirt seen him?"

Dirt nodded "I said, 'No. Haven't heard from him.' Callahan says, 'Well, I have a feeling you will.' You know, because he was so interested in us and in Spencer."

"Callahan tells Dirt, 'Listen, I'll give you my number, and if you see that bastard, you give me a call. I want his ass.' "

"So I wrote down his number and stuck it in my wallet."

We were all quiet for a few minutes. I motioned to Bump for another Coke. Pookie went to the refrigerator and brought back fresh ones for his brothers. I lit a smoke.

"Okay. Then what?"

Willie and Dirt looked at each other. Willie said, "Then, around that time, our other brother, Murph, he starts teasing Amy. You ever met Murph, Bump?"

Bump shook his head.

"Murph's in a wheelchair now. Car wreck. So he's around the house and the office most of the time. He starts teasing Amy. She's getting phone calls and all of a sudden she's going out at night. I don't know if you know Amy . . ."

Bump shook his head.

Pookie said, "She's not what you'd call a looker."

His brothers snickered.

Willie said, "She's not exactly a raving beauty."

I said, "We get the picture. Go on."

Dirt said, "She's going out at night. Now, me and Willie, we hadn't noticed. We don't pay that much attention to Amy's social life, mainly because we never thought she'd get a social life."

The brothers snickered again.

Bump said, "You've made your point. Go on."

Willie said, "Amy works in the office, and she got paid for it all these years. She never had anything to spend her money on. She goes around the office all grungy, and she never goes anywhere, never does anything. She saved her money, and she had a lot put away."

Bump said, "Oh, jeez."

Dirt said, "Exactly. Amy's all of a sudden a busy girl, only nobody ever comes to the house to pick her up or anything. The guy who's calling her never leaves messages. Just hangs up if somebody else answers the phone."

Willie said, "At least we started to figure out that the hang-ups were a guy calling for Amy."

Dirt said, "So Willie and me start thinking. Where's she going at night? Who's she meeting?"

Willie said, "Really, we were thinking it was Tornow. Only we're thinking, No. It can't be. One night, we decided to follow her."

"She drove down to Bagby. Little bar down there. Parks right next to a gray Vee Dub. We knew the car. We'd leaned on it enough times when we were standing around in the parking lots in the Flats."

I said, "The bar was Logan's?"

They nodded.

Bump said, "Did you go in?"

They shook their heads. Willie said, "We didn't know what to do. Here you've got a guy who's a free-loader—"

Dirt said, "Worse than that. He's a fuckin' thief. And we're pretty sure he's after Amy's money now."

"Okay, yeah. Puttin' the moves on our sister, who's clueless as far as the real world goes."

"I don't think she ever even had a real date before."

"And then on the other hand, she's walkin' on air, practically. Happy."

Dirt said, "Yeah. So we didn't do anything that night. But along in there we saw the same Vee Dub sitting outside Petey's a couple nights in a row, so that's how we figured out he worked third shift there."

Willie said, "So we called him, trying to talk him out of seeing Amy."

"The jerk-off sat there and denied it."

"So we said, 'Either stop seeing her or we'll call Callahan.' "

"Then he gets all tough-guy. He was all like, Bring it on."

"So that's how things stood."

"Until they decided to live together."

Dirt said, "Man. There was no warning. She waited until our parents weren't home that day. Then all of a sudden she's carrying boxes out to her car. I'm like, 'What the fuck do you think you're doing?' "

Pookie said, "Our parents were down at the jail, picking me up."

Willie said, "Yeah. She goes, 'I'm moving into my own apartment. Pookie's coming home and he'll want his room back.' "

"See, my room is the best. It's big, and it's warm in the winter, and I've got a TV and a sound system all set up."

Willie said, "Your room's awesome. That carpeting. You put a lot of money into that room before it all started going up your nose."

Pookie said, "Shut the fuck up."

I thought about the Grodell parents. I wondered how they felt, all these messed-up adult offspring still living at home. Me and all my brothers and sisters, we got out of the house just as fast as we could. Course, it wasn't much of a house. And also, unlike the Grodells' situation, our mother was the first one gone. And also, our father was gone more than he was there.

Willie said, "Yeah, and Amy's room is tiny, and it's on the wind side of the house, so it's really cold in the winter. So I was like, 'What're you doing?' She goes, 'I didn't wanna tell anybody I was moving because they'd say I couldn't.' "

I said, "They, meaning your parents?"

Dirt said, "Yeah. So we're all asking her, 'Are you gonna have a roommate?' Because we had a feeling."

Willie said, "We just knew."

"So she carries the last box out and she hands me a piece of paper. 'Here's my new phone number.' "

"Soon as she drives away, we go inside and dial the number. Reese Tornow answers the phone."

Bump said, "Did you talk to him?"

Willie said, "No. We just hung up."

Bump stubbed out his cigarette, stood up, and stretched with his hands on his lower back. The brothers started to get up, too. Bump said, "Siddown. We're not done."

I leaned my elbows on the table and looked around. Nobody was wearing a watch. I wondered what the hell time it was.

Bump sat back down. "Okay, so Pookie comes home from jail. Then I guess you boys had a little meeting."

Willie said, "We'd been telling him some of this stuff when we visited him in jail."

Pookie said, "Yeah. So a while after I got home, we walked out to the back shed. There's a little shed down behind the garage back home. You know. We do a line, talk things over. They told me the rest of it, and I said we had to sit down with Amy. Tell her how things were."

I said, "Did you do that?"

Pookie said, "She tried to put us off, but I convinced her to at least talk to us. We went over to her new place. I think it was the next night."

He looked at his brothers. They nodded. "Yeah, a Thursday night. Tornow was at work. So we told her how it was, and she was all, 'You don't know him. He really loves me.'"

Willie said, "She's so dumb."

Pookie said, "Finally I just told her, 'Look. This guy's bad news. You either leave him and come home, or I'm calling Callahan and telling him where to find him. Period.'"

Willie said, "She went off. She was cryin' and everything. She was like, 'Maybe he was bad before, but he's changed. Don't do anything.'"

Bump said, "So then you figured, if she won't leave him, okay. We'll turn up the heat on him. Get him to blow town."

Pookie said, "Exactly. I called him at Pete's myself."

Willie said, "And we started following him."

This got our attention. Bump and I looked at each other.

Bump said, "Following him. Did you follow him the night of the murder?"

Pookie nodded. "We weren't going to. I thought he'd be working that night. Anyway, by that time I was starting to not see the point of following him. All he did was go to work, go home. But that night I was out at my buddy's because some of the guys got up a poker game. I left kind of early because I'd been lucky and I didn't want to lose it all back. I drove through town and I saw the Vee Dub parked in front of Petey's."

He stopped. He took a long drink of his beer.

I said, "You saw his Vee Dub."

"He was in the parking lot with this tall, sweet-looking blonde. She was cranked. Seemed like she was all upset about something. They'd bought a six of beer. He had it tucked under his arm. He got her in his car and they drove off."

Bump said, "So you followed them."

"Course I did. They went to Chandler's Trailer Park. He half carried her up to a trailer. They went inside."

I said, "What did you do?"

He shrugged. "I had the goods on him. I went home and called Amy."

Willie said, "Pookie goes, 'He's over in Chandler's right now, shacked up with a beautiful blonde. You don't believe me, go look for yourself.' "

I thought, Hmm.

Dirt said, "So Amy comes home bright and early the next morning with all her boxes."

Willie said, "She didn't wanna talk to us. Finally she said she'd talk to me and Dirt, but not Pookie. She said she'd never speak to Pookie again. She said she hated him now."

Dirt said, "We went in her room and closed the door. She couldn't stop crying. She said she waited all night for Tornow and he didn't come home, so then she knew what Pookie said was true. Reese had spent the night with the blonde. That was why she packed up and moved back home."

Pookie said, "Then, later on that day, come to find out Reese was shot dead."

Willie said, "And Amy just goes nuts. She's lying there on her bed going, 'Pookie did it. Pookie did it.' "

Dirt said, "Our parents freaked. Especially our dad. He was like, 'They'll find out where this guy lived and that'll bring Amy into it. When they talk to her, she'll point the finger at Pookie, and they'll believe her because he just got out of jail.' "

Pookie said, "So he told me to move out here until they found out who really did it. And he said he'd keep the cops away from Amy as long as he could. Maybe they'd turn up another suspect. Then the cops pulled a trick on Amy. About somebody buying her car."

Bump and I glanced at each other. He popped the top on another Coke. My can was half-full and warm.

Bump said, "Now I gotta ask a question and I want a straight answer. Do you boys think Amy did it?"

Pookie said, "Amy? Shoot Tornow? Fuck no. She's scared of guns. Won't even stay in the same room with one."

Willie and Dirt nodded vigorously.

Me and Bump sucked on our smokes, thinking over everything they'd told us. I looked at him. He shrugged, like, I can't think of anything else. Can you?

I finally thought of one other thing. "Last question. Did any of you guys ever call Callahan back? Tell him Tornow was in Spencer?"

They all shook their heads.

Chapter 13

Bump got on his cell phone as we headed back toward town. It was almost midnight when I turned into Chandler's. Gruf's Jeep was parked in front of the trailer and all the lights were on inside. Gruf and Danny were sprawled in front of the TV watching *Letterman,* Danny with his Bud and Gruf with his High Life. Gruf was still wearing his Carlo's shirt. John was puttering in the kitchen.

Gruf said, "What's up? Where were you guys?"

As I tossed our jackets on the coat-tree, Bump walked to the refrigerator and pulled us each out a Coke. He said, "Gather round, boys. We've got a little tale to tell." He pulled out a chair at the kitchen table, spun it, and straddled it.

Danny left the TV on. He and Gruf came out carrying their beers and their cigarettes, and we all parked ass around the table. Bump told them our news, with me filling in from time to time.

When we were done, John said, "Well, that seems to eliminate our prime suspect—if they were telling the truth."

I said, "It was the truth."

"And I guess it eliminates Amy Grodell," John continued. "I had my suspicions about her, too."

I said, "And it eliminates anyone from Tornow's previous life. I mean, if Callahan couldn't find him, then nobody from before Callahan could find him, either. Right?"

John thought about that. "Not unless he contacted someone himself."

Danny said, "You don't know Callahan didn't find him. You only know the Grodells didn't tell Callahan where he was."

I said, "Good point."

Bump said, "Maybe."

John said, "Anyway, you gotta tell Pookie to turn himself in. He needs to tell us his story." Us meaning the cops.

Bump said, "Me and Terry talked about that. We think it's better if Pookie goes on being the prime suspect for a while. Maybe with the cops looking for Pookie, the real shooter might get careless."

John frowned and thought that one over. After a pause he said, "Did I tell you guys that we're patrolling Carlson's Mill now?" He meant Mike and Ray Bellini's house, where Marylou was hiding.

Bump said, "Oh, good. I mean, with those dogs, I'm sure they're all safe enough over there. Still, when you think of those calls to the police department and the hospital asking about Marylou—"

John looked up sharply. "Someone called the hospital? Asking what?"

Bump said, "What's Marylou's name, was she admitted, where is she now?"

"If they don't know her name, how do we know they were asking about Marylou?"

Bump said, "They described her. A blond woman in her twenties admitted in the early-morning hours of—"

John said, "That's not good."

I said, "Now that I think about it, how did they know to call the hospital?"

John shrugged. "Could've been a lucky guess."

I said, "John, did you ever check whether it was a man or a woman that called the station asking about Marylou?"

"Yeah. The dispatcher doesn't remember."

I said. "Those calls fit together with the two bullets that were fired toward the bathroom. The guy must've fired two shots at Marylou, but he had to run without knowing if he hit her or not."

Danny said, "Wait a minute. You mean, you think the person who shot Tornow called the hospital to find out whether or not he also shot Marylou?"

I nodded. Bump's stomach growled. Loudly.

John said, "Did you guys eat?"

We shook our heads. John got up and started pulling Tupperware from the refrigerator.

I said, "Don't do that. You just got your kitchen clean."

John said, "You gotta eat. And I have all this meat loaf left."

Pretty soon, stuff was bubbling in pans. Pretty soon after that, Bump and I were stuffing ourselves on meat loaf and mashed potatoes. With gravy. We were just about done when there was a loud rumble of thunder in the near distance.

I looked at Danny. "What's the weather forecast for tomorrow?"

He smiled. "Rain. All day."

I picked up Bump's and my plates and went over to the sink. The pans were already soaking. I got to work washing everything.

John had been lost in thought. Now he said, "You guys put me in a bad position, going out to talk to Pookie like that. There's a warrant out for him. If I don't do something about this right now, we're all aiding and abetting, not to mention harboring a fugitive. Nasty stuff. It'd be the end of my career in law enforcement. We could all go to jail."

He'd said the magic words for me. I turned around. "Let's call Alan. Get him over here. Tell him everything."

Danny said, "Shit. He'd go nuts if he knew about this. He'd have you two's balls."

Gruf said, "Maybe not. Is he working tonight, John?"

John had to think about it. "Yeah. I'll call him. Right? Everybody agree?"

It wasn't long before Alan arrived. He came in, his holster and nightstick and handcuffs all thumping, rattling, and creaking from his belt, and pulled out a chair. John hadn't told him anything on the phone, but he already looked pissed off. John put a cup of coffee in front of him and topped off the rest of us.

Alan blew across the surface of his steaming cup and took a delicate sip. "Okay. Start talking."

We looked at each other around the table. Bump cleared his throat and began to tell the story.

You could see Alan was furious. As he listened, he got more and more furious. A vein began to stand out on his temple and his eyes narrowed to little slits. Once, he took his glasses off and polished the right lens good with a hanky he pulled from his back pocket. He glared at all of us around the table, but mostly he glared at me. Because he'd specifically told me in no uncertain terms to stay out of it. I tried to avoid eye contact.

I let Bump do all the talking. As mad as Alan was, at least he was listening quietly, not interrupting. I was pretty sure if I opened my mouth, he'd go off. So I didn't.

As Bump got near the end of the story, the rain started. It was gentle little pings on the trailer roof at first. Then it built into big pings. There was thunder and lightning in the near distance, too.

Bump finished and there was a heavy silence. Except for the TV. And the thunder. And the rain. Okay, it wasn't silent. Just heavy.

Bump said, "So we drove back and told these guys, and John said it was time to call you."

Alan shook his head. "You're wrong about that. The time to call me was right after you heard the conversation in the Thriftway."

I swallowed hard. "Alan, the Grodells wouldn't have told you what they told us. They'da denied even knowing Tornow, like they did at first with us. They'da lied and kept on lying. You've got Pookie charged with murder. The whole family woulda gone to jail to protect him."

Bump nodded. "Except Amy."

I shrugged.

Alan thought that over for a while. "Maybe. Okay, you might be right about that."

Bump lit a cigarette. I cracked the window because Danny and Gruf were smoking, too, by that time.

Bump said, "We think you should just leave Pookie out there. Keep the arrest warrant active, but let him stay in his hiding place."

Alan laughed at him. "We can't do that. Why would we wanna do that?"

Bump looked at me. "Tell him."

I thought, Oh yeah. Let me be the one to tell him our latest Hardy Boys strategy. The gravy backed up on me and I belched.

Alan smirked at me and gave me a look like, Well, out with it. I've waited all my life to hear this.

I said, "We were just thinking that if the warrant stays active and Pookie stays missing, the real murderer might relax. Get a little careless."

Alan shook his head in disbelief. "You been watching a lot of TV there, Terry?"

John spoke for the first time. "Just consider it for a minute, Alan. The idea might have some merit."

Alan stared at John. Then he pushed back from the table, carried his coffee cup over to the stove, and refilled it.

Friday morning, as I stood on our dark little trailer porch and watched John pound down the street and into our driveway, I had one of those sudden thoughts that seem to come out of nowhere. John pulled the white towel from around his neck and briskly rubbed his sweating head. Then he went into his post-run stretching routine. I walked down the steps and stood beside him, thinking.

Black, bulging clouds hung low in the dark sky, but they were moving briskly on the stiff breeze.

John straightened up and gulped a couple of deep breaths. "*Man*. That felt *great*."

I said, "Listen up, Johnny. I just thought of something." His eyes snapped over. I had his attention. "You know that chick that works mornings at Petey's? The one who told Bump Reese Tornow's name before you guys had him ID'd?"

"What about her?"

"I heard another clerk in Petey's talking about her. That she's gonna be off work a few days because she fell down her steps."

He nodded. "Okay. So?"

"Dude. She lives in a trailer. Right up the street from the murder trailer. How could she hurt herself bad enough falling down three or four steps that she can't work?"

He shrugged. "I don't know. I guess if she hit just right or landed funny. Are you sure that clerk said she fell down her trailer steps? Maybe she fell down some other steps."

"Come to think of it, there's something else funny about her. She told Bump she knew it was Reese Tornow because she recognized his body when they carried him out of the trailer. She said her and her boyfriend watched them carry him out. But he would have been covered up, wouldn't he? The cops wouldn't carry a dead body away without covering it, would they?"

"No. I don't think so."

"I didn't think so. Isn't that kind of odd?"

"It's very odd. I'll find out for sure whether he was covered up or not."

* * *

The sun came out during breakfast. Which the TV weatherman had said rain all day. And Bud Hanratty came crab walking into Brewster's. He looked pretty dapper for a fat balding guy. He wore a sincere navy blue suit, white dress shirt, and a navy blue tie. Lawyer costume. Trust me.

I've never owned a suit, or even a sports coat, in my life. Closest I ever came, I bought a black sweater-vest once. What was I thinking? I never wore the hideous thing.

I never went to any of those high school dances where you have to rent a tux and buy the girl flowers and go to a fancy restaurant the same night, and maybe even go in with a few other couples and rent a limo. On the nights those kinds of dances were held, I hung out with a bunch of kids who sat around saying how stupid it all was. Which, really, the reason we didn't go was none of us had the how-you-say discretionary income to get in that game. You know?

Bud dragged a chair over to the near end of our breakfast tables. Mary was right there with the coffeepot. She asked him if he needed a menu. He winked at me and ordered the Number Four. Most of the rest of us had only just ordered, so he wasn't too far behind.

Once Mary hurried back to the waitress station, Bud caught my eye and cleared his throat. "Hey, Terry. Can I get a quick word with you?"

I said, "Sure, Bud."

He picked up his coffee cup, looked around, and pointed to a nearby empty booth. I grabbed my cup and my smokes and we resettled.

I'd never seen Bud Hanratty nervous before. Matter of fact, I'd about decided Bud didn't have a nerve in his body. But he was nervous that morning.

He squirmed and uhed a few seconds. Then he said, "I should have talked to you sooner. I meant to. But, I, uh . . ."

"Bud. What's wrong?"

"Uh. Well, shit. Terry, I went out to dinner with Marylou the other night."

I said, "I know. So?"

His head jerked. "You know? How'd you find out?"

I shrugged. "I don't know. Somebody mentioned. Is that what this is about?"

He played with his big, shiny gold wristwatch, twisting it side to side on his thick hairy wrist. "I know I should have talked to you first, and I meant to. But, uh, well, fuck. All of a sudden I'd already called her."

"Bud. You didn't have to talk to me. I got nothing to do with it."

"Legally, she's still your wife. And I consider you a friend. I feel like I went behind your back."

I shook my head no.

He said, "I guess I half expected her to laugh at me or make up some excuse. But fuck me dead if she didn't accept. And we had a good time. I, uh—jeez, Terry, I think she likes me."

I said, "Good. Listen, she and I have no future together, if that's what you're thinking. Except maybe as friends." I stopped. "That sounds like I'm saying you're her second choice. That's not the way it is. She was trying to get me back there for a while, but that was just out of habit. If you wanna see her, go for it. Watch out for her, though. She can be a little snake if you give her half a chance."

He nodded. "She told me some of the stuff she pulled on you. She's pretty ashamed of that stuff now. You should know she's changed." He looked up at me. "Maybe if the two of you gave it another shot, it could work this time."

I shook my head. "I know what you're trying to do, and it's pretty damn decent of you. You're a good man, Bud. To tell you the truth, I think you're way too good for Marylou. But maybe she has changed."

He nodded earnestly.

I said, "I hope so, for your sake. And don't worry about me. I'm interested in someone else now, anyway."

"Well, that's good, then. I really care for her, Terry."

I lit a smoke. He sipped coffee.

He chuckled. "Marylou and Mike. *Man*. They're double-teaming me. They've about got me off the booze. Thank God I don't smoke, or they'd be after me about that, too." I laughed. "There's one more thing. Uh. This is hard."

"What?"

"Your divorce."

"You wanna finish it off?"

He found new interest in his wristwatch. If it aggravated him so much, why did he wear it? But then, he wore that white dress shirt with that strangling top button, and he wore that navy and white polka-dot necktie. Every time I have to look at a guy in a suit and tie, I thank God I'm a carpenter.

I said, "It'd be a big favor to everyone concerned if you'd finish the thing off. So go ahead and get it done. I got no problem with that."

He let go with a big sigh of relief. He reached out a hand and we shook.

I said, "She's probably broke now. Not working, hiding out at Mike's. I said I wouldn't pay for it, but—"

He looked horrified. "No. I don't want your money. *God*."

Whatever. I shrugged. His eyes slipped past me toward the back of the restaurant.

He said, "Here comes breakfast." He looked back to me. "So, we're okay?"

"All good."

We moved back to join the others. Alan and Nelma were sitting across from each other at the far end of the table from me and Bump, and they were busy fighting about their huge family's Thanksgiving plans again. This good-natured tug-of-war between Alan and Nelma and the family factions they represented had been going on since the middle of the summer. We listened to them argue all the way through breakfast.

After breakfast, Gruf and I went over to the bar and poked around awhile, looking over what we'd accomplished so far. Smitty had evidently assigned someone to the job of washing the new bay windows. Someone had peeled all the stickers off the panes and washed them good. Or maybe he'd done it himself, as excited as he was about them. The glass sparkled in the morning sunlight.

I told Gruf about my early-morning conversation with John and that John was going to check to make sure Tornow's body had been covered when they carried him out of the trailer.

Gruf said, "That would've happened way after you guys left, wouldn't it? Is she claiming she and her boyfriend stood around in the cold all that time in the middle of the night?"

I shrugged. "I guess. Unless they could see from their window."

"Does she live close enough—"

"I don't know. Something else, too. She's off work now. Hurt herself falling down her steps. But trailers don't have that many steps. How can you hurt yourself that bad—"

"Bump knows her, huh?"

"Yeah."

"We'll have to ask him about her."

"Yeah. Well, let's get to work and do something, even if it's wrong."

There was no use delaying it anymore. The next step was the ceiling work. No getting around it. We dragged out the ladders, got out our measuring tapes and pencils, and went to work.

It's slow going and tedious work to begin with, working on a ceiling, marking where all your electrical and sprinkler connections have to be sited. Plus, we were putting an exhaust system in the ceiling that would suck out cigarette smoke. Add to all that the fact that you're working overhead, leaning back away from the ladder and reaching up over your head all day, and you've got instamatic pain. Shoulders, neck, back. Butt. You carpenters, electricians, and painters, you all know what I'm talking about.

Running the lines for the wiring, exhaust, and sprinkler systems, and then, just when you've had so much fun you can hardly stand it, trying to hang the ceiling grid so it'll make the room look like it's not out of plumb and leaning one way or another. All the weird distortions in the structure from seventy, eighty years of the foundation settling. Getting this ceiling in was going to be a bear.

There used to be this guy who worked for one of Red Perkins's crews. He had a pair of stilts. Whenever his crew had to do ceiling work, he'd climb a ladder and get on his stilts and work walking around on them all day. Rough in the wiring, install the sprinklers, no problem. Install the grid, hang the light fixtures, drop the tiles in. It was amazing. That guy could install a ceiling three times faster than anyone else I ever saw. He saved himself all that wasted time of up the ladder, down the ladder, move the ladder.

He made it look so easy. I'd watch him work, walking around on those stilts, and I'd think, Jeez, why doesn't everybody do it that way? Then I got up on 'em once. I did okay, just walking around, but there was no way I could have worked on 'em. You'd have to put in a lot of practice time to get used to that.

So I still do it the slow way—up the ladder, down the ladder, move the ladder. After endless measuring and marking and checking with the level, Gruf and I climbed ladders and went to work roughing in the wiring for the overhead lighting. It was one of those days where you just set your mouth and get through it.

We'd been working for about an hour when John came in. The three of us sat at the bar, and Smitty hooked us up with coffee.

John said, "Nancy Sutton was at the station this morning when I got there."

That surprised me. "What was she doing at the station? I thought she was hurt too bad to leave her trailer."

"Yeah, that was odd. No one seemed to know why she was there. She just hung around awhile, until I started asking her questions. Then she seemed to get all paranoid and left."

"Did you ask her how she got hurt that bad falling down three or four steps?"

"Three steps. I asked her and she got all flustered, but she stuck to her story. Brian Bell was there. He's been around a lot longer than I have. He says her injuries are the result of a domestic. No doubt in his mind."

I said, "A domestic? Her boyfriend did something to her?"

Gruf said, "What makes him think that?"

"Because. No visible marks. Brian says that's how abusers work. Leave the bruises where they can't be seen."

I said, "What's her boyfriend's name?"

"She lives with this guy named Jack Moberly. As soon as she said that, Brian knew. Brian says Moberly's had his problems with the Spencer police a time or two. DUIs. Got a little problem with the hooch."

"When did she get hurt, anyway? I was never clear on that."

"Uh. Lemme see. She says it was the night after Reese Tornow was shot."

"How could the two be connected?"

He shrugged. "She says they're not connected at all. She claims she just took a bad fall down her steps."

"What about her recognizing Tornow? Did you ask how she recognized Tornow's body when it was covered up?"

"Yeah. And that shook her up. She claimed she was upset because of the murder. And she stuck to that story, too. She saw his face when they were carrying him out. But after she left we talked to the guys that carried him out. They say he was covered. She couldn't have seen his face."

"So she's definitely lying about that."

"Definitely."

"Still, she knew all about it when Bump saw her the next morning, hours before you guys knew who he was. How'd she know?"

"That's what I'd like to know. She must've seen him in the trailer, or she saw him and Marylou when they went into the trailer, or she saw his car parked in front of the trailer, and she put two and two together when they carried him out."

I looked at him. "That's right. She would have recognized the car. She'd seen it enough times at Petey's. But why's she lying?"

He shrugged, shook his head, and drained the last of his coffee. "I gotta run. Call me if anything comes up."

After he'd gone, I said, "Nancy Sutton's story stinks."

Gruf nodded. "Yeah, but so what? You don't think any of this has to do with the murder, do you?"

I shrugged. "People lie for a reason. I'd like to know what her reason is. I'm thinkin' maybe we need to talk to her ourselves."

Gruf nodded. "Okay. When do you wanna do it?"

"Right now. The boyfriend oughtta be at work by now. And Bump should be available. It's not even ten yet. He doesn't start at Carlo's until eleven."

"Good with me."

While Gruf called Bump and asked him to come over to the bar, I thumbed through the phone book. There was no Haskins Court listing under Sutton, but Jack Moberly was listed. I wrote his address in the little notebook I'd remembered to grab that morning and tucked it back into my shirt pocket.

Chapter 14

Gruf and I were sitting in Gruf's Jeep with the heater blasting and giving off exactly no heat whatsoever by the time Bump rolled down the driveway into Smitty's back parking lot.

He climbed into the backseat and sat there blowing into his bare hands. "What's up?"

I threw my elbow over the back of my seat to turn around. I told him about our conversation with John. "We're thinking maybe we'll take a quick ride over to Nancy Sutton's. See if we can clear up a few questions."

Bump was all good with it. "Let's go."

On the way over, we decided we'd tell her we stopped by because Bump was concerned about her. Ease into it that way. But we could have saved ourselves the effort. When Gruf pulled up in front of the trailer, we discovered we had a little problem. Bump knew Nancy's car was an old green Honda, and it wasn't there. The only vehicle in the driveway was a white Chevy pickup with a ladder and a stacked pair of sawhorses in the bed.

Gruf said, "She's not back yet? How can she be out running around all morning when she's supposed to be hurt so bad?"

We turned around to look at Bump, unanimously nominating him as the one to explain this chick's behavior.

He squinted at the trailer. "Well, it looks like somebody's here," he said. "And we're here. Let's go see what's going on. If she's gone, we'll talk to the boyfriend."

As soon as we climbed out of the Jeep, we could hear the music. I knew almost from the first note what song it was. The tune ended as we walked to the porch. It started up again right away.

Bump led the way up the steps, but he turned back to us before he knocked. "I know that song. What is it?"

I said, "Van Morrison. 'Into the Mystic.' "

And I'll tell you what, Chief. Just hearing that song again, I knew instinctively that someone inside that trailer was suffering. I knew why it was blasting out through the walls. There were a couple of painful weeks in my own not-too-distant past when I kept that very tune on more or less permanent repeat.

Bump turned back to the door and knocked loudly. He had to do it again. Then we heard the music break off, and the inside door flew open.

The guy who looked out at us was wasted. "What the fuck?" He took a staggering step backward when he saw the three of us. Then he chested belligerently back up to the door. *"What?"*

His curly black hair swirled wildly around his head. He wore a threadbare T-shirt and old, ripped jeans washed almost white, and his feet were bare. He was a slender guy, but you could see by his Popeye arms that he was a working man. And you could see by his bloodshot eyes and day's growth of beard that he was also a drinking man.

Bump said, "Sorry to bother you. You must be Jack, huh?"

Jack Moberly's dark eyes narrowed, and his mouth hardened into a deeper frown.

Bump said, "We were just stopping by to see how Nancy is. We—"

Jack looked really pissed. "What. She's doing you all in threes now?"

Bump glanced back at us with his eyebrows raised.

"No, dude. Jeez. Nothin' like that. We heard she was sick." As he talked he pushed the button to release the screen door and pulled it open.

Jack said angrily, "Well, she ain't sick and she ain't here." He tried to slam the inside door, but Bump got his big high-top in the way and caught it. He pushed to open the door and Jack pushed from inside to close it.

There was quite a Tough Man contest there for a few seconds. I fully expected to see the door come loose from the trailer altogether. But Jack suddenly stepped back and said, "Shit, don't break my door." He faded away into the trailer's gloom and we filed inside.

There was no sign a woman had ever lived in that trailer. No curtains, no frillies. There was an old, worn, faded blue sofa and an entertainment center with a humongous sound system, stacks of CDs, and a big TV, and that was it for the living room.

A guy who has that in his living room, unless he's got a woman living with him, he thinks he's good to go. But you add a woman into the mix, she's all of a sudden gotta put some plastic flowers on the kitchen table. She's got to brighten the place up with a bunch of breakable shit that you have to watch yourself around. She's got to hang something up on the wall. She's got to have lamps.

This trailer didn't have any lamps. There wasn't any of that woman stuff at all. When I saw the way that living room was, I got curious about just how things were between Jack Moberly and Nancy Sutton.

Moberly sank back onto the end of the sofa and picked up his half-empty bottle of Jack Daniel's off the floor. Jack and Jack went down the hill. I glanced into the kitchen. There was an empty bottle of JD and a string of Bud empties lined up along the counter.

Bump took a seat on the opposite end of the sofa and stretched out his long legs. I stepped into the kitchen, picked up a kitchen chair with each hand,

and sidewaysed them into the living room for Gruf and me.

Bump was saying, "That was a nice tune you were playing there. Van Morrison, huh?"

Jack drank a sullen slug and didn't respond.

Bump said, "You're Nancy's boyfriend, Jack, huh? I think I've seen you a few times at Petey's. In the mornings. You know, pick up a pack of smokes, say hi to Nancy."

Jack gave Bump a sideways look, then lost interest.

Bump said, "She always seems like a nice girl. Your Nancy. Cheerful."

Jack regarded his bottle. "Yeah. Nancy likes to spread the joy. That's probably where she is right now, matter of fact. Out spreading the joy." He took another swig.

The three of us exchanged looks.

It was a small one-bedroom trailer. Not even half the size of ours. Closer to a quarter the size. From where I was sitting, I could see into the bedroom. I could see the end of the bed, the bare mattress with the blankets half hanging off, and I could see power tools lined up along the wall.

I said, "Hey, you're a carpenter?"

Jack looked up, looked me over, and nodded.

"Me, too," I said with a lame smile.

Jack held up the bottle in a mock toast and took another long pull. As he lowered the bottle, Bump reached over in one swift motion and took it away from him.

"Hey!" Jack lunged for it. Bump held him off with one hand and passed the bottle to Gruf with the other.

Bump pressed Jack back into his end of the sofa. "You'll get it back, dude. But we need to ask you some questions before you pass out."

Jack settled back, folded his arms tightly across his chest, and sat there breathing heavily.

Bump said, "Now, where's Nancy?"

"How the fuck should I know? I haven't seen 'er since yesterday morning."

Gruf said, "Somebody said she hurt herself. Somebody said she was too hurt to work."

Jack fixed him with a glare, then looked down at his bare feet. "People say a lot of things. That don't mean they're true."

Gruf said, "Are you saying she's not hurt?"

Without looking up, Jack said tightly, "I'm saying fuck off."

I said, "Jack. Is Nancy hurt, or isn't she?"

His chin sank deeper into his chest. He sighed and closed his eyes.

I said, "Jack, Nancy told Bump here something we wondered about. She said you and her watched the cops bring Reese Tornow out of the trailer the other night. That guy who got shot down the street."

He looked up at me and I noticed he didn't have any trouble getting me in focus. His bloodshot eyes were alert and wary. He looked surprised. Then he smiled unpleasantly.

He said, "She said that, did she?" His voice was sarcastic and his expression was almost mocking, like he knew a joke we didn't know.

Bump said, "Yeah, she did. She said she saw his face and she recognized him."

His face changed. The hardness and mock went out of his eyes and mouth. He looked shocked. He turned to stare at Bump. "She told you that?" He let go with what almost sounded like a chuckle. "Fuckin' Nancy."

The three of us looked at each other in confusion.

I said, "She didn't just say it to Bump. She said it to the cops, too."

His dark eyes met mine and I saw the agony in him. There was so much raw emotion in his eyes I almost couldn't stand to look at him. It was probably only a split second before he looked back down at his empty hands, but it seemed a lot longer.

I didn't wanna be there anymore. I stood up and motioned for Gruf to get up, too. I carried the chairs back to the kitchen table. Bump didn't move. He sat there watching Jack.

I took the bottle from Gruf and handed it back to Jack. Then I jerked my head at Bump that we were leaving. I said, "Come on. We're done here."

Bump gave me a long arguing look, but he slowly picked himself up off the sofa. Gruf pulled the door open. As they stepped out onto the little porch, I turned back to Jack Moberly. He was watching me. I reached into my back pocket, pulled out my wallet, and fished out one of the business cards Gruf had printed up for us. It had my name and the trailer phone number on it. At the bottom I wrote my cell-phone number.

I held it out. He took it and looked at it.

I said, "I don't know what's going on with you, dude, but when you decide you need a friend, you call me at one of these numbers."

He looked up at me.

As I pulled his door closed behind me, I heard him say softly, "Thanks."

I looked back. He was lifting the bottle to his mouth.

I joined Bump and Gruf at the Jeep and we piled in. Bump was mad. He leaned forward and nudged my arm as Gruf pulled away from the trailer.

"Why'd you cut it off, dude? We didn't get anything out of him at all."

I was staring at the trailer. I shrugged.

Bump said, "Because, I mean, something funny's going on there. That guy knows something. Right, Gruf?"

Gruf nodded and glanced over at me.

Bump said, "Fuck."

I said, "I'm sorry. Something happened. I can't explain it right now."

Gruf shifted into second gear.

Bump said, "We're not gonna get anywhere if we start feeling sorry for every poor drunk we come across."

I said, "It wasn't that. It was something more important than that. I gave him a business card. Maybe he'll call when he's ready to talk."

I couldn't explain it to them. I didn't understand it myself. I don't know if I can explain it even now. It was something to do with his familiar eyes, something about his curly black hair, and the way his thin, unhappy face set itself in familiar expressions. The way he sat with his arms folded across his chest and his ring finger tapping a rapid drumbeat on his elbow. That's an unusual thing to do, tapping only the ring finger, but I'd seen someone else do it lots of times. Lots of times. My brother Berk.

He was a carpenter, and he was a dead ringer for me and my brothers, all five of them but especially Berk when he was in his midtwenties. And my old man. And he obviously had a serious problem with alcohol like me and my brothers and my old man all do. And I didn't want him to be a murderer. It was something to do with half a year earlier. I'd had that night in that bar, when I'd gotten stoned and drunk and hit guys and trashed the place, and that had been bad enough. But what if I'd killed somebody? If this guy, who looked enough like my brothers that he could be one of them, if he'd killed somebody, then maybe that meant I could've, too.

Back at Smitty's nobody said much. Bump took off right away because he had to be at work at Carlo's at eleven. Gruf and I went quietly back to work on the ceiling. At lunchtime he called Evan Lustig and asked him to come around in the late afternoon to inspect the work.

We were just finishing installing the exhaust system Smitty'd bought to take care of the cigarette smoke when Evan walked in. He took a quick look. By that time he'd seen enough of our work to know that I knew the Grand County building codes forward and backward and I don't ever ever ever cut corners.

Evan went out to the bar and we could hear him and Smitty laughing together for the next hour. Building inspector must be nice work if you can get it.

With the sprinkler and exhaust systems and the wiring okayed, we were clear to go ahead with the grid work for the ceiling tiles and get the thing finished. But by that time it was nearly four, so we cleaned up for the day and headed our separate ways.

Friday night Carlo's was very busy. When I got my break around nine thirty, Gruf and Richard Forman were in the office with the door closed. A few minutes later, Gruf came walking out to the dining room, not looking too happy. He refilled his coffee cup, took a seat across from me, and lit a cigarette.

Almost immediately, Dawn Forman came around the corner from the back room, started into the office, looked out at us, did a double take, and came toward us.

It was the first time I'd seen her up close. I didn't like the tight line of her mouth, the slightly raised right eyebrow. She reached up and poked her glasses higher on her nose with Pointer Man.

She said, "Just what are you two doing?"

Gruf had to turn a little to look at her, since he was sitting with his back to the hallway. "About what?"

She made a show of controlling something. An exhaled breath, a settling of her shoulders. "Why are you sitting here?"

I said, "We're on break."

She shook her head. "Not in the dining room, you're not. How do you think that looks, having employees sitting around in the dining room?"

Gruf said tightly, "Where do you want employees to take their meal breaks?"

She shrugged dismissively. "Not in the dining room." Then she whirled and walked down the hall and into the office, closing the door behind her.

I said, "Does she think the employees are gonna eat standing up in the back hall? Or does she plan to add on an employees' lounge?"

Gruf smirked. "I'm starting to get a bad feeling about those two."

We gathered up our stuff and relocated to the back hall. I ate standing up and went right back out on delivery. By the time I parked the car, logged it in, and locked it up, the Formans had gone home.

Closing was an unusually quiet and thoughtful process that night. While we were sweeping and mopping, Gruf told me he thought we ought to not work at the bar the next day. Just take Saturday off and get a little R and R. He looked tired and stressed. I could see he felt bad, having to admit he was worn out.

I said, "Yeah, we've been hitting it pretty hard. It would be a good idea to rest Saturday." He looked relieved.

Chapter 15

I slept in Saturday morning. By the time I woke up and walked out to the living room, scratching my ass, Danny had already been to breakfast and was sitting in front of the TV, banging on his PlayStation. It was just after eleven.

He said, "Gruf called. Shit." He gave the thing a final thump and turned it off. "He wants you to call him."

"Oh, man. I shouldn'ta slept in. He probably changed his mind and wants to work on the bar today."

Danny shook his head. "He just called maybe fifteen minutes ago. I think he slept in, too. So, *are* we working on the bar this afternoon? Boss?"

I looked at him. "Are you done at Miller's already? Has it been a week?"

He grinned. "I said bye-bye forever to Miller Roofing yesterday at five-oh-five."

"Excellent. Okay, lemme call Gruf."

Gruf sounded like he was still crashed in bed. He made a grunting noise like he was trying to sit up and I could hear rustling sheets. "Okay, yeah. I'll meet you over there."

I set the phone back on its base and headed for my shower. Then I stopped in my bedroom doorway.

"Hey, Danny."

He looked up.

"Don't call me Boss."

He smirked.

*   *   *

Gruf sat at the bar with a big cheeseburger and a pile of fries in front of him. And his High Life. He looked a hell of a lot perkier than he had the last time I saw him. Almost as soon as we sat down, Benny walked out of the kitchen with similar plates for me and Danny. Smitty drew Danny a Bud draft and Benny brought me my iced tea.

Smitty leaned on the bar and watched us chew. "So, Danny's with us for good now? Man, I hope the groceries'll hold out."

We laughed and nodded, but saying anything at that moment was out of the question for any of us unless we wanted to spray cheeseburger all over everything.

When our plates had been cleared away, our beverages refilled, and we had lit up smokes, Gruf elbowed me. "Did you notice the regulars over there? Their new fashion statement?"

I stole a glance across the bar toward the Reserved Seating section. Some of the regulars were sitting there hunched over their beers. I could see that two of them had something hanging around their necks. I took a closer look. They'd poked holes in their laminated membership cards and strung them on chains. They were wearing them like necklaces. I looked at Gruf.

He said, "First Tiny did it. Then most of the rest of them. They pull 'em out of their pockets and put 'em on over their heads when they walk in the door. At first they were mainly doing it as a joke, to rip on my dad, but now I think they're doing it because they like it."

After lunch, we poked around in the new dining room for a few minutes. Then we got busy on the ceiling grid. With Danny working, it went pretty fast. We got the grid up, dropped in the tiles, and started installing the lighting fixtures.

There was a honkin'-big brass chandelier for the center of the room. Smaller versions of it would be evenly spaced across the rest of the ceiling. A dimmer switch controlled them all, so that you could dim the lights while there were customers at the tables and then turn them up bright while the place was being cleaned and closed.

We started with the smaller light fixtures, because we were waiting for Smitty's insurance man to come and inspect the mounting for the big center light. Also, I wanted us to have the experience of hanging those smaller ones before we tackled the monster chandelier that was going in the middle of the ceiling.

We worked slowly and carefully. The things were so heavy and fragile that one careless move would've been a catastrophe. We were about half-done with the smaller fixtures when the insurance guy came. He gave the mounting for the big center chandelier a thorough inspection. He even climbed a ladder and shined his flashlight all around. Then he stuck around to watch us hang it.

Getting that thing hung was hairy. It was so heavy, it took all of us and all the extra muscle we could round up from the bar to get it up and hold it steady while I attached it to the support I'd built in from the center beam. I'm a strong guy, but my knees were noodly when I finally climbed down off the ladder and looked up at the finished product. We were all drenched with sweat. The insurance guy shook hands with Smitty and took off.

By quitting time all the lights were hung, turned on, and glittering brightly. The rest of the big room still looked like shit, but the finished ceiling looked amazing. Smitty's face was so filled with awe as he gazed at that big chandelier in the middle, you'd have thought he'd never seen electric light before.

While Danny collected the tools, Gruf and I rolled up the orange cords of the trouble lights and stacked them back on a kitchen counter, glad to be done with the damn things for the time being. Since there were three of us to keep track of now, Gruf had printed up a bunch of time sheets. He filled out our hours while Danny and I carried our tools and the radio back to the new kitchen. I walked out feeling satisfied we'd put in a good day's work.

It was a typical Saturday night at Carlo's. Busy as hell. And it was amazing. If you had told me there would ever be a night at Carlo's when all those happy people I'd come to know and love were cross and even rude and nasty to each other, I'd have said you were full of shit. But that night arrived, and it was that Saturday night.

Richard Forman suddenly decided to make Hammer the main focus of his attention. He planted himself in the middle of the tiny, cramped kitchen and stood there, right in the way, watching Hammer's every move and asking stupid, annoying questions during the busiest part of the night.

Hammer put up with it for a surprisingly long time for a redheaded teenager. But when he'd finally had enough, he stalked out to the front where Gruf was in the middle of taking a phone order and said loudly, "There's one too many people in my kitchen. Either get that cocksucker outa there, or I quit."

I was standing on the other side of the counter at the time, waiting for my next delivery to be ready. I really thought Hammer would be gone by the time I got back, but Gruf somehow managed to get Richard Forman out of the kitchen. Hammer was still working, but he was majorly pissed.

It was Debby who walked out. I found out about it when I got in from my delivery. What happened was, Debby was working with Cindy that night. Which was not good. By this time Debby had had her fill of Miss Cindy and didn't mind saying so. Her problem with

Cindy was that Cindy was an artist at not being around when there was work to be done. She did okay taking care of her tables, because that was directly related to the size of the tips she'd get, but the prep work and cleaning in the waitress station, the clearing and washing of tables between customers, all the other work that needed to be done throughout the evening, Cindy managed to avoid in a pretty consistent way.

Cindy shirked all her nontipable duties all night as usual, and Debby busted her butt to take up the slack. At a certain point, Debby carried out the orders for one of her tables, and it was going to be a few minutes before Hammer had her next order up, so she went to slice bread and discovered there were only a few loaves left back in the walk-in. She knew the next bread order wouldn't be coming in until Monday morning, so she went up front to let Gruf know there was a problem.

She had just finished telling him when Dawn Forman came bustling up to them.

Dawn said nastily, "Debby. Every time I look at you, you're standing around talking to someone. Maybe when you get a minute, you could actually do some work around here?"

Then Debby said, "Dawn. Maybe when *you* get a minute you could go fuck yourself."

She took off her apron, folded it neatly, handed it to Gruf, and walked straight across the back room, down the back hall, and out to her car.

One down.

After my last delivery I pulled the car around back, parked it, logged it in, and locked it up. Princess and Gruf had already started closing. They were over at the dishwasher. She was washing and he was putting away the cleans. There was no laughing, no clowning. Nobody was even talking.

Somebody had started making subs on the work counter in the back room. I read the list Barb Pannio had left, telling how many of each sub she wanted put together for her day crew, and got to work finishing the job. I hadn't been at it for very long and was just thinking I oughtta go out and drop some quarters in the jukebox because everybody in the place needed some music to lighten the mood, when Richard Forman came walking into the back room from the front hallway.

I was unpleasantly surprised to see him. I'd hoped our new owners had done their damage and gone home by that time. He came up beside me and watched me fold the baked ham onto the triangular slices of provolone. That's irritating, when someone stands there watching someone else work.

Without looking at him, I said, "Don't be shy, dude. Slice a bun open and start loading it up."

I expected him to say something nasty to put me in my place. But to my surprise, he selected a knife from the knife holder on the wall, sliced a bun open, and started folding ham onto it.

I said, "No. The cheese first. Take a stack and cut it corner to corner, so the pieces are shaped like this. See?" I pointed my knife at one of my triangular-shaped cheese slices.

I thought, What, was he absent from his New Owner Training Class on Sub Day or something?

We worked awhile, proceeding from the ham to the hard salami to the turkey breast, until we had Barb's quota wrapped in foil and ready to store on a tray in the walk-in. Then he vanished somewhere and I got busy sweeping and mopping.

I didn't see him again until Gruf was cashing me out. Gruf and me were standing at one of the front computers. Princess had just cashed out and left for the night. Hammer had closed his kitchen in record time and was long gone. I caught peripheral movement in the kitchen and turned to see Richard Forman heading our way.

Gruf was totaling up my deliveries and I was counting my money. You don't interrupt somebody in the middle of counting his money.

But Forman said, "I didn't catch your name."

I turned around to see who he was talking to and immediately forgot how much I'd counted so far. Now I'd have to start over. And I had a big ol' stack of money sitting there. And I was tired. And so was Gruf. And now Gruf would have to stand there and wait for me to count it all over again.

And Forman was talking to me.

"Twees," I said. "Twees Saltz."

Forman said, "Saltz? And you would be a driver?"

"I would be, yes."

He tapped the nail of his pointer finger on his upper front teeth. It actually produced a clicking sound. I'd never seen anyone do that before. I watched in fascination.

Then he pointed the same nail at me and said, "Well, Saltz, where's your hat?"

I didn't know what he was talking about at first. I wondered if he meant my black knit cap. I hadn't worn it that night because it wasn't that cold outside. I glanced at Gruf. He didn't seem to know, either.

I said, "My hat?"

Forman said, "Your Carlo's hat."

Then I remembered the big, dumb, high-peaked, black Carlo's baseball cap that Bump had handed me the first day I started working there. The one I had immediately carried back into the office and returned to the shelf beside the other Carlo's baseball caps that were sitting there. In the whole time I'd been working at Carlo's, I'd only ever seen two, maybe three people actually wearing those goofy caps.

I said, "I didn't want to wear it. I put it back in the office."

He turned around and walked away. A minute later he came back carrying one of the caps. He handed it to me. "Here you go. I need you to wear it. Without the hat, you're out of uniform."

I glanced at Gruf. He was scowling at the figures on the computer screen. Even from the side view I could see how stressed and pissed off he looked. But he'd already lost Debby that night. He didn't need me flying off the handle right then. So I took the hat and set it down on the counter beside my money. "Hey, thanks. Well, gotta count out my money now."

I started counting out the bills again. Gruf turned around to face Forman. "So, Richard, have you got some interviews scheduled yet? To find yourself some new employees?"

Forman laughed. "Not yet. There's time."

I thought, No, there's not.

Gruf said, "No, there's not."

Forman turned around and walked away.

Chapter 16

Sunday morning I woke up just after six and walked barefoot out to the kitchen of the quiet, sleeping trailer for a glass of water. I carried it to the front door, pulled the door open, and stepped out onto the cold little porch to drink it. It was a dreary morning that was just beginning to think about dawning. I ducked my head to see more of the sky, but all I saw was very, very dark gray. I put my glass in the sink and went back to bed.

The phone rang a couple of times around noon, or I don't know how late I might've slept. I got up and walked out to the living room. John was in the kitchen putting groceries away. Danny was in his recliner, clicking the remote.

Danny said, "Bump's sister and Marylou wanna have cards at their place tonight. Jackson's coming, and Bud, Bump's brother, Debby, and the twins. They're gonna have two tables, and we keep switching places, like when you play bridge."

I said, "Like when *I* play bridge?"

He shrugged. "Like when *some*body plays bridge. And they're gonna have food." He bounced his bare toes. "And dessert."

"What time?" John asked.

Danny said, "Around six."

John said, "Sounds good. I'm gonna take a nap." And he headed down the hall toward his bedroom.

I went back to my bedroom, pulled my blanket off

my bed, and carried it out to the living room. I slouched on the sofa with my bare feet propped on the coffee table and tossed my blanket out over them. After a few more clicks of the remote, Danny decided on a documentary about mummies and we settled into it.

We were the first ones to arrive at Mike's. Because of Danny. He all but carried John and me out to John's car at five-thirty. We stopped at Pete's on the way to pick up some beer, pop, Fritos, and French onion dip because John said we shouldn't show up empty-handed, and we still got to Mike's ten minutes early.

I couldn't figure out why Danny was so anxious to get there until I saw the look on his face when Debby walked in. Her eyes found him right away, too, and she gave him a nice smile.

I stared at him. Danny and Debby? I never saw that one coming. But really, when you think about it, sure, Danny and Debby.

But I'm getting ahead of myself. When we got there Marylou answered the door. She looked nice. She was still going with the natural look. Her hair was loose, soft, and clean, and she wore only a little bit of mascara. That was a good sign.

I stuffed my black knit cap into my coat pocket, and she took my coat along with the other guys'. While she put them on hangers and stuck them in the front closet, I looked around the living room. It was the first time I'd been inside Mike's house.

Everything was shades of pink and green. The walls were papered in a light bluish green. The big sofa and love seat were a dusty pink color, and the throw pillows on them were all different shades of green, from light to dark. The carpeting was very pale brown. The drapes were plaid and seemed to pick up all the shades of pink and green from around the room.

There was a lot of copper stuff. There were copper bowls hanging on the walls and large copper buckets on the floor. A wide, shallow copper bowl near the end of the love seat was piled with paperback books. A big copper bucket by the fireplace had logs sticking up out of it. Another copper bucket on the floor by the coffee table held a bunch of stuff that turned out to be squeaky toys for the dogs. All that gleaming copper mixed in with the soft pinks and greens made the room look like a place where a person would feel healthy and happy.

I carried our bags from Pete's out to the kitchen. Mike was pouring pretzels into a copper bowl. Her hair was loose, too, in a tumble of shiny black curls. She was wearing a neat white T-shirt and a pair of little straight-leg stonewashed jeans.

She looked at the bags I was carrying, put her hands on her hips, and gave me a smile. Then she reached out to take one of the bags from me.

"What's this?" She peeked inside. "Cool. Thanks for bringing this stuff."

I said, "Where's the doggies?"

We unloaded the bags on her kitchen counters. "They get to have a sleepover at Uncle Bump's tonight. They get too excited when there's company. They're so big, just wagging their tails tends to throw people through walls and stuff."

I said, "That's not good."

She said, "No. For the people or the walls." She folded up the bags and stashed them on a shelf in her broom closet. Then she turned to face me.

"So," she said, and she smiled. God, that smile.

There was a commotion in the living room just then, and we heard one of the twins laughing and the other one singing, "Mikey! We found it!"

Mike yelled, "We're out here. Hey, Twees, what can I get you to drink?"

I said, "Coke's good. I'll get it." I turned around,

pulled open the refrigerator door, and pulled a can loose.

She said, "Grab me one, too." I did, and I handed it to her.

By that time the twins had descended on us. They were both carrying large, bulky objects that turned out to be Tupperware containing a variety of appetizers and snacks from their kitchen. They also had two square cardboard boxes that turned out, when I read the lids, to contain two copies of a game called Flinch.

I picked up one of the Flinch games and studied the box with interest. One of the twins watched me. He said, "You wouldn't believe how many places we had to go to find those."

The other twin was lifting lids off Tupperware and letting Mike peek inside and sniff.

Then Bud, Ray, and Bump pounded on the front door. Ray and Bud were carrying chairs they'd brought over from Bump's house, and Bump was carrying his kitchen table. I hustled to take one end of the table and guide it through the front door.

While Mike directed the placing of the furniture, Marylou motioned to me and I followed her down the hall to a bedroom, where she began pulling folding chairs out of a closet.

I said, "Hey, Marylou." She turned around. "Can you sit a minute? I wanna talk to you."

She sat on the edge of the bed looking solemn and folded her hands in her lap. I sat next to her.

She said, "What?"

"It's about Bud."

She gave me a guarded look. "I went out to dinner with him."

"I know."

"What's wrong with that? He's a nice person."

I nodded. "He is a nice person. That's why I wanna talk to you about him."

"What?"

"Marylou, don't play around with Bud. Not if you don't mean it. He's gonna fall for you like a ton of bricks, if he hasn't already. Don't hurt him."

She was genuinely shocked. "Hurt him? I would never hurt Bud."

I said, "I hope not. Because Bud's a good guy."

She said, "I know he is."

I said, "Good. You can make him the happiest man in the world if you want to."

She nodded and was about to say something else when we heard new noises in the living room. Gruf and Jackson were laughing at something one of the twins had said. Marylou tucked two chairs under each of my arms, and I followed her out to the living room.

Once the chairs were set up around the tables, Mike and one of the twins got busy getting everybody's drink of choice. The other twin started passing out these card things that had a bunch of numbers on them and explained how you were supposed to look at your card before each hand to figure out which table you were supposed to sit at. Bump and I happened to catch each other's eyes, and we shrugged, like, Okay, whatever.

Then Debby arrived, Danny's heart went *boom chucka lucka,* and now we're caught up.

We ended up with about seven people sitting at each table. Something like that, if I counted right. With the extensions in the tables, it didn't feel too crowded. Mike stood up TV trays around the tables to hold ashtrays and people's beverages and plates and bowls of snacks.

Flinch, played with cards that had been printed up for the purpose and by the rules, was different than the game we'd been playing. But it was a lot of fun once we figured out the rules. Everybody was funny, especially the twins. There was a lot of laughing.

About midway through the evening I found myself sitting at a table with Mike, Marylou, Jackson, Luther,

Danny, and Gruf. I don't think I've talked about Jackson yet in this story. Her real name is Lauren King. She was still a senior in high school at the time, but she was already Gruf's assistant manager. That was because she'd been working at Carlo's since she was fifteen, and she knew how to do every job in the place, and she worked harder than any other two or three of us put together.

Jackson is beautiful and wise beyond her years, and Gruf's been in love with her probably since the first time he saw her, and as of that night at Mike's he hadn't done anything about it yet. Because she'd just turned eighteen. Judging by the way I caught them looking at each other every now and then, I was sure they were gonna get together any day.

While Gruf dealt out the first hand of cards, Jackson began to ask Mike questions about nursing as a career. Six months earlier a guy had tried to kill her, and the nurses she'd met during her brief stay in the hospital had made a big impression. She was asking Mike about the nursing programs at Lakeland Community College and at Kent State University. It sounded like she was seriously thinking about applying to one school or the other.

I glanced at Gruf. He was listening and smiling. A few times he asked a question. I watched Mike. She answered Jackson's questions enthusiastically and gave her a lot of encouragement.

Mike said, "Jackson, if you decide to go for it, Ray and I will give you all the help you can stand. I mean that." From the other table, Ray nodded.

As they went on talking about nursing, Gruf leaned toward me. "I'm worried about the Formans managing the place alone tonight."

"They're gonna hafta solo sooner or later."

He nodded. "But I'm afraid they'll piss everybody off."

"Who's working?"

"Of the ones that matter, Jeff, Princess, and Hammer. I'm not too worried about Jeff and Princess. The Formans can't ruffle Princess, and if they start to mess with Jeff, Princess'll smooth it out. But I'm real worried how they'll be with Hammer."

I nodded.

Eventually the question and answer session about nursing hit a slow spot. Mike brought up Reese Tornow's murder. She wanted to know if we'd gotten any farther figuring out why Nancy Sutton was lying.

Gruf and I stared at her.

She said, "Well, of course Bump fills us in as much as he can." At the other table, Bump heard his name mentioned and turned to listen.

Mike said, "Marylou *is* just slightly involved in the thing, isn't she?"

I said, "Oh. Well, sure. We haven't gotten any farther, no. John and another cop interviewed Nancy Sutton and she stuck to her story."

John looked over from the other table and nodded.

Mike caught her lower lip in her teeth. "I keep thinking about something Marylou said one day. It was the day we were all baking pies at Bump's. Remember, Marylou? You were there, Twees. Remember?"

I didn't have a clue, but I was grateful to her for calling me Twees. She'd done it twice now. I shot Bump a look. He rolled his eyes.

Mike said, "Remember when she touched off that funny conversation about famous movie lines? When Luther and Reginald were doing Bette Davis? Remember?"

"Vaguely."

Luther nodded uncertainly, trying to remember.

"I asked her about it yesterday. Remember, Marylou? She can't connect it to anything, but the line is stuck in her mind. 'What the fuck. *You're* not Nancy.' "

I said, "I do remember that now." I thought about it. "Wait a minute. You mean you think it was something that was said the night of the murder? The Nancy was Nancy Sutton?"

Gruf started nervously snapping his fingers, working on the idea. "In the trailer. Someone came up on Marylou in the trailer thinking she was Nancy Sutton and said that?"

He turned to Marylou.

She frowned and shrugged. "I don't know. I just can't remember."

Jackson put down her can of Coke and said, "What would be a possible scenario that would have made someone say that? Who would have said it?"

Danny said, "Nancy's boyfriend? Jack Moberly?"

By this time everybody at both tables had laid their cards down to listen.

Gruf loaded another chunk of nachos onto his plate. "Okay, how about this? Nancy Sutton and Reese Tornow worked together at Petey's, or at least their shifts overlapped when he was finishing up night shift and she came on for early-morning shift. Right?"

I had a mouthful of stuffed mushroom, so I just nodded.

Gruf said, "Okay, and Nancy's drunken boyfriend is supposedly abusive."

Luther said, "Did someone say her boyfriend is Jack Moberly? We know him. Remember, Reginald? He's on a team in the bar pool league."

Reginald nodded. "He plays for Logan's."

"That's right." Luther looked back to me. "But did you call him abusive? He's not abusive. He's a sweetie."

Bump said, "We heard he's a violent drunk. Likes to beat up his girlfriend."

They looked at each other, shaking their heads. Luther said, "We never saw that. He drinks too much, that's true, but he isn't one of those mean drunks."

Reginald said, "Beating up *that* girlfriend would be self-defense if it's the one we know. Right, Luther?"

Luther nodded vigorously.

Mike said, "Reginald, that's a terrible thing to say."

Luther fixed Mike with a challenging stare. "Oh, really? Do you know her?"

"Well, no."

Luther pursed his lips and nodded like he'd proved his point.

Reginald said, "The girl we're talking about works mornings at Pete's."

Bump said, "Yeah, that's her. Nancy Sutton."

Luther and Reginald exchanged nods.

Gruf said, "Anyway, so Jack Moberly maybe stops at Petey's for coffee in the mornings on his way to work. Maybe a few times he sees Reese and Nancy talking or laughing. Or a little too friendly or something while they're working. He doesn't like it."

Jackson said, "Maybe he thought they were messing around."

Bump said, "Maybe they *were* messing around."

I said, "And Tornow probably parked his VW right out in front of the store. Be able to keep an eye on it while he was working. Jack could have known the car."

Mike said, "Oh, my God. So maybe Jack came home drunk that night, saw the VW parked in front of what was supposed to be a vacant trailer, just a few doors away from his own trailer."

Gruf said, "He's drunk, he assumes Reese is in there with his girlfriend, Nancy."

Danny said, "Grabs his gun."

The words hung in the air. We all sat there, stunned. Me, especially. I didn't want Jack Moberly to be the murderer. But still, it was all starting to fit together.

Mike said, "We're only jumping to about a million conclusions here."

Luther said, "You certainly are. You've got Jack Moberly all wrong."

Gruf said, "Still."

Jackson said, "How does Nancy Sutton come into

it? A few hours later, once she was at work, she told Bump that Reese Tornow was the guy who got murdered. How did she know?"

Bump said, "She was upset that morning. I remember that. She said it was because of seeing Reese Tornow dead."

Gruf said, "Maybe she knew Jack did it. She made those things up to cover for him."

Mike said, "But if it was Jack who shot Tornow, and Nancy was covering for him, why would he beat her up the next night?"

Reginald said, "Beat her up?"

We all nodded at him.

Luther said, "Not the Jack *we* know. I'm telling you, he's not like that."

There was silence while we all thought about it.

Danny said, "Hey, Twin."

They both looked at him. I thought that, as usual, Danny had solved a knotty little problem in his usual direct and not-overly-sensitive way. Having trouble keeping track of which twin was which? No problem. Just call 'em both Twin and save all the aggravation. I had a closer look at their faces. They didn't look annoyed or offended. Hey, Twin. Huh.

Danny said, "That bar pool league you mentioned. That you and Moberly used to play in."

Luther said, "Still do."

Danny said, "Moberly still does, too?"

They looked at each other. Luther said, "He was there last time we played Logan's. Wasn't he?"

Reginald thought a second. "Yes. Remember? He played Maureen. She beat him, too."

Danny said, "And Reese Tornow was on a team, too? Did he play for Logan's?"

The twins looked at each other, shaking their heads. Luther said, "No. I've never seen his name on any of the rosters."

I said, "That's funny. Several people have said he was on a team."

Gruf said, "Maybe it was another one of his lies."

I said, "Jeez. Did that guy lie about everything?"

Danny said, "What night are the games?"

Luther said, "Every Wednesday night."

Danny said, "Logan's, you said. That's the bar in Bagby."

They both nodded.

Danny said, "I played in a bar league. Some nights we played in our home bar and some nights we played at the other team's bar."

They both nodded. Luther said, "We've got fourteen teams in the league, but some of the bars sponsor more than one team. I think there are only nine or ten bars with teams this year."

Danny said, "You wouldn't happen to have a schedule with you, wouldja? So we could look up where Logan's is playing this Wednesday?"

They grinned. "We don't have to look it up. They play us. At Logan's."

Danny said, "Huh. Interesting." He leaned forward, so he could look around Gruf and see Debby sitting at the other table. "Hey, Deets."

I said, "Deets?"

Danny said, "It's her nickname. Debby Duncan. Double Dees. Deets. Get it? Everybody calls her that."

I said, "Oh, like everybody calls me Twees?"

He said, "Whatever. Hey, Deets, wanna go watch some pool Wednesday night?"

She grinned at him. He nodded and leaned back in his chair.

Mike said, "Well, John, I think what the police have to do now is take Jack Moberly's fingerprints and run them against the prints they lifted from the trailer and from the Vee Dub. Oh, now Bump's got me saying Vee Dub. From the VW."

I looked at John. "Did you guys even get prints? Come to think of it, I haven't heard a thing about fingerprints."

Mike nodded. "They lifted a ton of them, both from the trailer and from the VW."

I looked at her with my eyebrows up.

She said, "Right, John? I asked you about that the day you came over here to check some things with Marylou."

He nodded.

I said, "Hey, John."

He turned around a little farther so he could see me.

"You never told us what forensic guys put together from the evidence in the trailer. Can't they get a pretty good idea what happened that night by picking up threads and stuff? Blood splash and stuff?"

It made him laugh. "Boy, Terry, from one friend to another, you need a little work on your crime-fighting lingo."

I waited for him to stop laughing. "Still, you understand what I'm asking. What do they know about what happened that night?"

He thought about it. "Well, they know Marylou spent some time in the bathroom. She barfed on and around the john."

Marylou groaned and turned red.

John said, "Sorry, Marylou. And you were crouched on the floor between the john and the wall. Maybe you could have been hiding there? Because two rounds were fired in the direction of the bathroom, which could indicate the killer shot at you and you ducked in there and hid behind the john."

She shivered and shrugged.

Mike said, "Will you get a set of Jack Moberly's prints and see if you can match them up with prints from the trailer and the VW?"

He nodded. "I'll suggest it in the morning."

Gruf said, "If you can, do it without mentioning any of our names."

John grinned. "No shit."

It occurred to me that our Indiana farm boy was

acquiring quite a potty mouth. Like the rest of us. I smirked as we got back to the card game.

The party broke up about midnight. As we put on our coats, I asked Bump if he wanted some help carrying his table and chairs back to his house. He said no, he was leaving them at Mike's because she'd need them again for Thanksgiving. Just that afternoon Mike, Marylou, Jackson, and the twins had decided to do a huge Thanksgiving dinner blowout.

Mike said if anyone didn't already have plans, she'd love it if they'd come. And she looked right at me when she said it. So I said I would. John explained he was going home to Indiana. Gruf said he had to eat with his family but he'd stop over later. Danny looked at Debby—ahem, *Deets*—and they both said they'd come.

I watched Mike, half listening to everybody saying what they'd do or not do, realizing that Thanksgiving was only four days away. Just four days until I'd see her again.

As John and I were leaving, Mike stepped up to me, put her hands on my shoulders, went up on her toes, gave me a little kiss on the cheek, and said she was glad I could make it for Thanksgiving. I felt that place where her lips had touched my cheek all the way home.

Danny rode home with Debby. Only she didn't bring him straight home. John and I puttered around and got ready for bed and he still hadn't come home. I never did hear him come in.

Chapter 17

After breakfast Monday morning, I drove over to the lumberyard to pick up wood for the dining-room trim while Danny and Gruf went over to the bar to get organized for a ball-buster day.

Coming down Third Avenue on my way back to Smitty's, I saw a guy standing unsteadily in front of Hollister's Motel. He looked familiar. I slowed down. Once I got close enough, there was no mistaking the guy. Fred Oatley is big and gross and Cro-Magnon-looking, and that morning he was really fucked up.

I'd met Fred Oatley a few months earlier, during the time we were trying to find the person who murdered one of our delivery drivers. All I really knew about him was that he dealt a little pot from time to time.

This has absolutely nothing to do with the story I'm telling here, but he stood there weaving, with his battered black high-tops sticking out into the street from the absolute edge of Hollister's driveway. Cars picking up speed from the stoplight were only missing him by inches. It seemed kind of untidy to just leave him there and let his brains get splashed all over Third Avenue, so I turned around in the KFC parking lot and headed back up the street to Hollister's driveway. He was oblivious as I edged my Tacoma past him. He didn't move a muscle or bat an eye.

I parked quickly and walked toward him. "Hey, Fred."

He turned slowly toward me and I could see that
he was going to take a step backwards, right out into
the path of the next car. I quickly closed the space
between us, grabbed him by the shoulders of the filthy
jeans jacket he was wearing, and pulled him farther
up the driveway. He put up about as much resistance
as a big bag of cement mix. A very big bag of cement mix.

"Easy, dude," I said, laughing and trying to keep
him erect. If you ever looked into his big, stupid face,
at his narrow hint of a forehead, his bushy, connecting
eyebrows, his ugly, slack-jawed mouth, his repulsively
huge lips, you'd have to suspect that his particular
species of human being hadn't actually *been* erect all
that long.

I got him a few lurching steps away from the edge
of the street and made sure he was steady before I
let go of him. He turned his head from side to side
like he was looking for somebody.

I was about to ask him what he was on, when he
spoke. He said, "You know Mitchell?"

He swung his face to me, and I could tell his eyes
were having just a little trouble focusing.

"Mitchell who?"

"You know. Mitchell."

"I don't think I know anybody named Mitchell.
Dude, you're fucked up."

He giggled.

I said, "How'd you get so fucked up this early in
the morning?"

He said, "Is it early already?" and tipped back to
look up at the sky. The movement made him lose his
balance. He took a staggering step backward toward
the traffic. I grabbed his shoulders again until he
stopped swaying. This time I kept hold of his arm,
walked him to my truck, and more or less pushed him
up into my passenger seat.

I already knew he lived in King's Row Apartments,

but we had a little confusion about which building. I finally got his key chain away from him and found that his apartment number, B-302, was etched on his key. As I walked him into Building B and up the steps to the third floor, he was upset because we'd left his car parked in Hollister's parking lot and because he was supposed to meet this Mitchell guy there.

I said, "Hasn't Mitchell ever been over to your apartment?"

He reared back, indignant, and I had to grab him again to keep him from going backward down the steps.

He said, "Sure he has. Lotsa times."

I said, "Then if he wants to see you bad enough, he'll come over here."

I got the door open and pushed him inside. He took a few steps into his front hall and slowly sagged onto the carpeting. He was snoring before his head settled on his arm. I stepped over him, set his keys on his kitchen counter next to an empty can of lima beans, and quietly closed his door behind me.

Back at Smitty's, Gruf and Danny were well under way sizing the upper two-thirds of the walls. They started to climb down off the ladders to come and help me carry in the wood, but I waved them back up.

"It's not that much. I can get it."

It only took a few trips. I set up a work surface out at the front of the game room and started cutting and routering boards for the cornices. Over the course of the morning, we got the walls sized, primed, and painted, and the cornice and baseboards and the chair rails cut, routered, and sanded. The color for the lower third of the walls was a very dark, rich shade of red. I finishing sanding the last chair rail about the time Danny and Gruf finished with the second coat of the red paint. We stepped back to admire our work.

I said, "That's gonna look awesome when we get the brass light fixtures put up."

Danny said, "It's gonna be laid *out*."

Gruf said, "I cannot wait to see this room finished. It seems like it'll never get done."

Danny said, "You guys've already done all the tedious shit. Now we're gonna rock and roll."

I said, "Matter of fact, I think you can tell your dad to go ahead and call for delivery of the wall fixtures. We'll be ready to put 'em up tomorrow."

Danny said, "How are we finishing the floor?"

I said, "Carpet."

"Better get that delivered sometime tomorrow, too, then."

I said, "You think? There's a lot of those light fixtures."

Gruf said, "Three of us working . . ."

Gruf had to work at Carlo's that night. By the time he had to leave, he and Danny had finished wallpapering the upper two-thirds of the walls with the heavy, textured, dark green covering Gruf and his dad had chosen. I'd painted the cornice boards white and mounted them. After Gruf left, Danny and I got the chair rails and the baseboards painted. We left them spread out over the tarp on the kitchen floor to dry.

When Danny and I walked into the trailer, John was at the oven, checking his baked chicken. He looked around as we came in the door.

He said, "Guess what? We took Jack Moberly's fingerprints this morning and matched them up to prints that were found all over the trailer and the Vee Dub." He straightened and tossed his oven mitt on the counter. "The report came in just as I was going off shift."

I skinnied out of my pea jacket and hung it on the coat-tree, feeling sick at heart. "Is that enough evidence to charge him?"

He shrugged. "Unless he's got a real good story how they got there."

Danny said, "You think they'll arrest him tonight?"

John shrugged. "They'll question him tonight. After that, it depends what he says."

We were all antsy during supper, not knowing what was happening. I wanted to take a walk around the block, just to see if there were cop cars parked in front of a certain trailer over on Haskins Court, but it started snowing and a cold wind was blowing.

I tried to talk John into calling the station to see what was going on, but he wasn't having it. "We'll find out at breakfast tomorrow. If Alan doesn't volunteer the information, I'll ask him."

After supper we watched Danny channel surf. Danny settled on a news magazine show about a murder mystery in Iowa or someplace. We stared at the tube for a while before Danny dragged himself into the kitchen for a fresh one. He popped the top and knocked back the first slug while standing in the kitchen doorway.

"Hey, John?"

John looked over at him.

"The night of the murder, right before the shots were fired, there was a fight in another trailer up the street. What did the cops find out about that?"

John shrugged. "Where'd you get that? I never heard anything about a fight."

"That night, while me and Terry waited for you out front, we were talking to a couple out on the street. Frankie and Janice Abbott. Remember, Boss?"

I nodded. "But don't call me Boss."

"They said they were already awake that night, because there was a fight across the street from them. So who was fighting?"

John said, "Beats me. I never heard anything about any fight. Abbott, you said?"

Danny nodded. He climbed back into his recliner.

"I'll check on it tomorrow. See if somebody talked to them."

I started to get drowsy early, like maybe nine or so. I told the guys, "Wake me up if you hear anything." Then I went to bed.

* * *

Alan never showed up at breakfast Tuesday morning. When we left Brewster's, Danny, Gruf, John, Bump, and me stood on the sidewalk out front and watched the snowplows work the parking lot. We'd gotten almost six inches of snow overnight, but the morning was pleasant. The air felt fresh and almost balmy.

John said, "I'll find out as much as I can about Moberly, and I'll let you know first chance I get."

Bump said, "Then somebody call me."

John took off, but the rest of us stood around awhile longer, watching to see if the snowplow guys were going to leave one of their piles where it was, or if one of them would push it on over to the side of the parking lot.

I turned to Bump. "Hey. How old is Bud Hanratty?"

"Bud? Hmm. I know he's not forty yet. Because when he turns forty, I'm gonna rag on him like a motherfucker."

I was surprised. Gruf was, too. He said, "Bud's not forty yet? He's gotta be older than that."

Bump shook his head. "He was twenty-six when he took custody of us. I was fourteen, Mike was thirteen, and Ray was twelve."

Danny said, "When Bud took custody of you? What does that mean?"

Bump said, "You haven't heard that story?"

Danny shook his head and looked at me. I'd heard a little of it, but I just shrugged.

Bump said, "Well, lemme see. My parents got divorced when I was in sixth grade. I started getting a little out of hand. Then the summer I was going into eighth grade, my old man died. I went to about the first week of eighth before I dropped out. Then I got in my motorcycle accident almost right away. You've heard about my motorcycle accident, right?"

Danny nodded. "Thirteen, drunk, stoned, riding a

stolen BSA 650. And that's why you don't drink or do drugs."

Bump gave him a wry smile. "Right. Put me in the hospital for a long-ass time. Then, while I was in the hospital, my sister and brother started getting way out of hand. My mom couldn't really deal with how bad I was hurt plus handle two younger kids at the same time. Ah, there he goes. He's moving it out of the way."

One of the plow guys had decided to push the pile over to the perimeter of the parking lot. We watched him.

Bump said, "After I got out of the hospital and started working part-time for Carlo's was when Kenny Carlo introduced me to Bud, and once *he* got involved with us, handling our inheritance case, he saw how—"

Danny said, "Inheritance case?"

"From my dad. Our stepmother and her lawyer were trying to screw us out of our inheritance."

Danny said, "Was your old man rich or something?"

"Fuck yeah. And our stepmother and her lawyer were trying to hide everything, claim there wasn't anything left. Kenny hooked me up with Bud, who was Kenny's lawyer at the time, and Bud shut them *down*. It was funny. No shit. Anyway, during that time, he saw how outa hand we all were, and to make a long story short, it ended up he took us all in. Me and my sister and brother. He straightened us all out, and he hooked me up with Nelma Wolfert and she helped me get my GED. So we all ended up okay."

I said, "That was okay with your mom? That Bud took you all in?"

"Ya gotta understand. I mean, I love my mom, okay? Me and my brother still have a good relationship with her. Not Mike, but we do. She's a good person in her own way, but she's no June Cleaver.

Yeah, it was okay. She knew she couldn't handle us. She figured maybe Bud could. Plain and simple."

Danny said, "What judge would give custody of three teenagers to a guy who was only twenty-six?"

Bump laughed. "Urquhart. You gotta remember, Kenny Carlo was involved. Kenny throws a lot of weight around, both here and in Fairfield. Kenny and Judge Urquhart play racquetball together or something. Plus, my mom was all for it."

I said, "Why'd Bud even wanna do it? That's a big load to take on for a twenty-six-year-old guy."

He shrugged. "That's Bud for ya." He laughed. "Fuckin' Bud. He told me that first night, 'Bump, there's nothing you can pull that'll fool me. I know every trick you could possibly think of and plenty more. So you might as well play it straight with me and get your act together. I want us to have a happy, fun little family. But each and every time I catch you trying to break one of my rules, I'm gonna kick your ass.' "

Danny and I laughed.

I said, "Did it work?"

Bump said, "Fuck yeah. I knew he meant it."

We split up, laughing. Danny, Gruf, and me headed for Smitty's. The rest of the morning I thought about Mike, imagining her as a little girl. Her parents get divorced. Then her dad remarries, and then he dies. Then her big brother nearly kills himself on a stolen bike. She starts running wild and fighting with her mother. She gets taken in by bighearted ol' Bud Hanratty, gets herself straightened out, starts to bring her grades up in school, starts to think about going to college, decides to become a nurse. And sometime along in there, she musta realized she was quite a bit more beautiful than most people.

We didn't hear anything about Jack Moberly until right around noon. Danny, Gruf, and me were sitting at the bar getting ready to eat lunch when John walked in the front door. A minute later, Bump walked in. He'd seen John's patrol car parked out front on the way back to Carlo's from a delivery.

John started over. "They took Jack Moberly in for questioning last night. He absolutely denied killing Reese Tornow. He was really steamed. He had a lot to say about, 'You cops are so stupid,' et cetera. Then he clammed up and demanded a lawyer."

I said, "Did they charge him?"

John shook his head. "He couldn't find representation until early this morning. When he finally did, his lawyer said, 'Charge my client or let him go.' They decided they didn't have enough to charge him with yet, so they let him go. But they told him not to leave town."

Bump said, "They let him go?" He looked pissed.

John shrugged. "What else were they gonna do?"

Bump said, "What about Nancy Sutton? Could she be in danger, if they're putting the heat on Jack? I hope somebody called her and warned her."

"I called her myself. I asked her if his release was going to cause her any problems, and she said, 'Why would it?' She didn't seem worried."

In the afternoon we were able to finish mounting the wall fixtures, and we laid the carpet padding. But Danny and I agreed there wasn't enough time to get the carpet completely installed and we didn't want to have to stop in the middle, so we knocked off a little early and went home.

The snow continued to fall and the wind picked up. Carlo's home delivery was busy that night. People were getting home late from work and ordering out because they were too tired to cook and they didn't want to have to go back out and face the weather again.

Delivering pizza is a lot more fun in the summertime. Princess slipped and fell in somebody's icy driveway and came back in limping badly. She'd landed on her shoulder and her hip. She stood at the front counter trying not to cry while she told us that she was fine.

Gruf told her to go sit in the dining room while he made her a pizza to take home for her supper, that she was done for the night. I watched her limp across the dining room to our usual employees' booth. Cindy got her a Coke to sip on while she waited.

Gruf was just lifting the next delivery bags onto the counter when Richard Forman walked up from the back room. He looked at me and frowned at my black knit cap.

"Hey, sport. I thought I told you to wear your Carlo's hat."

I didn't even have time to react because at that moment I heard Dawn Forman's raised voice out in the nearly empty dining room.

"I'm not a baby-sitter for you people. I shouldn't have to check the dining room every two seconds to make sure the employees aren't lounging out here."

I took some backward steps to look around the partition and see what was going on. There was Dawn Forman, yelling at Princess. See what I'm saying? The bitch was yelling at Princess.

The only customers at the moment were an older couple who sat in a booth by the windows. The woman had turned around to watch.

I looked back at Gruf. Behind him, Richard Forman was saying he was going to write me up, whatever that meant.

Gruf and I stared at each other. Then he broke into a slow grin. So did I. I unbuckled my fanny pack and handed it to him. He set it on the counter by the cash register and took off his apron.

He said, "Go get Princess. Tell her we're taking her out to dinner."

I nodded. I walked out across the dining room,

where Princess was struggling to get herself out of the booth. Dawn Forman had her hands on her skinny hips and was tapping her toe as she glared angrily at Princess.

I said, "Which shoulder hurts, Princess?"

She touched the one closest to the wall. I took her by her outer arm and supported her while she slowly rose from the booth.

When she was upright, I said, "Take off your fanny pack and hand it to the baby-sitter. We're outa here."

Princess looked at me while she unbuckled. She handed the fanny pack to Dawn, who still didn't understand what was going on. As Princess and I started down the back hall, Gruf and Jackson came out of the office with their coats on.

Gruf was saying to Jackson, "I believe Terry and I owe you a trip to Denny's, don't we, young lady? From a long time ago? Something about Moons Over My Hammy?"

I'd forgotten all about that. A few months earlier we'd promised Jackson a trip to Denny's if she'd cover for Gruf at Carlo's one night when we wanted to go off investigating.

Jackson laughed. "That's *right*. You do."

Princess said, "Moons Over My Hammy? Yum." She pulled her jacket off the coatrack and I helped her on with it. Then I quickly shrugged mine on as we headed toward the back hall. Hammer and Cindy were waiting for us by the back door.

Out in the parking lot Princess said, "I think we can all fit in my Blazer." She flipped me her keys. "You drive, Terry. I'm in pain." We all piled in and drove up to the Fairfield Denny's, laughing our asses off.

Afterward, I drove Princess home. She kept insisting she was okay to drive, but the Blazer was manual shift and it was the hip of her gas pedal/clutch foot and the shifting arm shoulder that were injured, and I wasn't willing to take the chance. Matter of fact, I wanted to drive her to the hospital and get her x-rayed. She talked me out of that, but not out of driving her home.

Gruf followed us in his Jeep. Then he drove me back to my truck in the Carlo's parking lot. We pulled into the Carlo's lot just after ten. The place was closed up tight and all the lights were off.

When I saw that, I said, "Oh, closing early, are we, Dick? I think I'm gonna hafta write you up for that."

Gruf thought that was hilarious.

Chapter 18

When Bump walked into Brewster's Wednesday morning, I could see he was mad all the way across the room. At first I thought he was mad because we'd all walked out on the Formans. But he walked straight over to Alan's end of the table and stood there glaring down at him.

"Where's Nancy Sutton?"

Alan leaned back and stared at him. "Am I supposed to know?"

Bump said, "That's my point."

Alan wrinkled his eyebrows. "Maybe you'd better sit down and tell me what you're talking about."

Bump pulled up a chair. "I stopped in at Petey's this morning for a pack of smokes. Pete was all worried. He called her trailer late yesterday afternoon, like he's been doing every couple of days, see how she's coming along. Jack Moberly answered the phone. Said she wasn't there."

Alan said, "So?"

John cleared his throat. "Uh, Alan? Supposedly she's on medical leave. Too badly injured to work."

None of this was making any sense to me. Was the girl hurt, or wasn't she?

John said, "I talked to her twice yesterday. I drove over to her trailer in the early afternoon. She was moving around like a cripple, but she said everything was fine, not to worry about her."

Alan looked back at Bump.

Bump said, "This morning, just before I came in, Pete called the trailer again. Moberly went off on him. He goes, 'She's gone and she's not coming back. Don't call here anymore.' "

Danny said, "She's not coming back? Jeez. What does that mean?"

Alan frowned, drained his coffee cup, and looked at John. "Drink up there, kid. Let's go look into this."

John drained the last of his coffee and pushed back from the table. He looked from me to Danny. "Oh, just so you guys know. I'm leaving right after work to drive home to Indiana for Thanksgiving. I'll be back Friday afternoon."

Bump sat there steaming after they'd left. When Mary asked him if he wanted to order breakfast he shook his head and just pointed to his coffee cup.

I wanted to tell him about how we'd all walked out on the Formans the previous night, but I wasn't sure whether the story would cheer him up or piss him off more. Finally, Gruf brought it up and told him what happened. Bump listened to the story without any reaction.

After a short but uncomfortable silence, Bump drained his coffee cup, stubbed out his smoke, left a five-dollar bill on the table, and walked out without a word. The next time I saw him, he looked a lot happier. He and Flute, the other day driver, came walking into the bar at around eleven thirty. They were wearing their Carlo's shirts under their open jackets. Neither one of them was wearing a fanny pack. I knew right away why they were there by the way they were laughing.

It hadn't taken long for the Formans to piss them off. Carlo's doesn't even open until eleven.

Danny, Gruf, and I were crawling around on our hands and knees, trying to get the heavy, floppy carpet stretched straight. We stood, worked the kinks out of our backs, and walked out into the game room to talk.

It'd been a while since I'd actually talked to Flute, although I'd seen him almost every day as he lurked around Carlo's shadowy corners, trying to whisper gossip to whoever he could get to listen. Remember I said there were only two or three people who worked at Carlo's who actually wore their stupid Carlo's hats? Flute was one of those guys. The bottom edge of his hat always made his gray hair stick out in a ratty little fringe around his head.

Flute's a droopy, pessimistic guy who goes through life always pissed off about something. But he looked like he was in a pretty good mood that day. He wanted to be the one to tell what happened. Bump took a step back and waved at him to go ahead.

Flute said, "So we g-g-get in there. F-f-finally—"

Bump interrupted. "Barb had the day off, so it was up to the Formans to open the store. They were fuckin' fifteen minutes late. We were all sitting in our cars with the heaters running, waiting for them to come and unlock the fuckin' doors."

Flute nodded. "S-s-so we get in th-th-there. Finally. And the D-d-dick tells us that we're all g-g-gonna hafta p-p-pull a double shift, because all you g-g-guys q-quit last n-n-night."

Gruf said, "Fuck that."

Bump said, "Exactly. We were all standing around in the back room—"

Flute said, "And thc D-d-dick says, 'You all hafta p-p-pull a d-d-ouble shift.' B-bump says, 'No, we d-d-don't.' Then the D-d-dick goes, 'Yes, you d-d-do. That's an order.' " He snorted. "An order m-my ass. So then B-b-bump s-says—"

Bump draped a heavy forearm over Flute's shoulder. It looked like Flute drooped a little more. "This was right after he told me he was writing me up for not wearing my Carlo's hat."

Flute said, "Yeah. Wr-wr-writing him up. So B-b-bump goes, 'You know what, D-d-dick? Fuck you, f-f-fuck your ugly h-hats, and f-f-fuck your ugly *wife*. Write th-th-*that* up.' "

He barely got it out. He laughed so hard he doubled over. When he straightened back up, tears were running down his cheeks.

I'd never seen Flute laugh before. I watched him, thinking a hearty laugh was probably doing him a world of good. Chronically depressed guy like that.

Bump said, "So we all walked out. Laura the day cook, me and Flute, even that new day waitress, who until then was kissing up to the Formans so bad it made me wanna puke. There's nobody left over there now but Dick and Dickless."

That cracked us all up.

When we finally started to settle down, Flute peeked around us to see into the dining room. His eyes got big. "Wow. It's g-g-gonna be f-fancy."

Gruf nodded.

Flute said, "Well, n-now we're outa w-w-work. How long t-t-till this p-p-place is up and r-r-running?"

Gruf said, "Enjoy your Thanksgiving, and come in Friday morning at eleven, ready to go."

Flute said, "*This* F-f-friday?" Gruf nodded. "That's g-g-great! S-s-see ya Friday, then."

We watched him walk out. His black corduroy pants were too long. They dragged the floor in back of his heels.

I looked at Gruf. "You're gonna start the training Friday?"

He shrugged.

I said, "How are you gonna do that?"

He grinned. "I have no idea."

I said, "Well, shit. It's almost lunchtime. Might as well break now."

We collected our cigarettes and took stools at the bar. The special of the day was shredded barbecued pork. Danny, Gruf, and me had been smelling it cooking all morning, since the exhaust fan in the old kitchen was even worse than the one in the kitchen at Carlo's. So the three of us all ordered it with a side of fries. Bump went with a cheeseburger.

Smitty and Benny got us hooked up with beverages, and we lit up while we waited for the food.

Bump said, "Oh. Nancy Sutton's okay. Alan tracked her down and talked to her."

I said, "Tracked her down? Where is she?"

Bump said, "I guess she moved back in with her mother."

Danny said, "Where does her mother live?"

Bump shrugged. "South of here someplace. Hartville or something."

Danny raised his eyebrows.

Gruf said, "Well, that's good she's okay."

Danny said, "Something's funny about those two. Nancy Sutton and Jack Moberly."

Bump leaned forward to see Danny past me. "Funny how?"

Danny shrugged. "I don't know. We're missing some pieces there or something."

I said, "That's just what I was thinking."

Bump said, "Are you and Debby still going down to Logan's tonight? To watch the twins' pool team shoot Moberly's team?"

Danny nodded. "But Moberly probably won't even go now."

I shrugged. "You never know."

Danny said, "Well, even if he doesn't show, we can ask some questions."

Smitty walked out of the kitchen and leaned on the bar in front of Gruf. He said, "So, now everybody has quit Carlo's?"

I don't know how he'd heard the news already, but not much gets by Gruf's old man.

We all nodded.

Smitty said, "Boy oh, boy. Are those new owners ever screwed."

Gruf shrugged. "We were more than fair with them. They were obnoxious jerks to all the employees. They made their own bed."

I said, "Meanwhile, Smitty, we'll get the carpet down right after lunch, and that's it for the dining room. You can call for delivery of the booths and tables."

He made fists and shook them, the way a ballplayer does when he goes yard. *"Yes."*

I turned to Gruf. "What else absolutely has to be done in order to get the dining room up and ready for business?"

Gruf said, "The new bathrooms."

I said, "I was afraid you were gonna say that. Putting in those bathrooms is gonna be very labor intensive. Almost as bad as the kitchen."

Gruf nodded. "I know. But you can't expect people to come in here and drop a hundred dollars for a meal and then take a whiz in those foul old bathrooms. Especially the men's room. That thing's hideous. No offense, Dad."

Smitty waved a hand at him. "No, you're right. It is."

Danny said, "A hundred dollars for a meal? What kind of menu are we gonna have, anyway?"

Gruf said, "An expensive one." He winked at him.

I said, "But still, we're gonna be priced a little under other, like, steak places in the area, aren't we?"

Smitty hooted. "Hell no. My male heir here shopped the area restaurants. Then he set all our prices twenty percent higher than the highest ones he found."

We all stared at Gruf. He grinned around at us. He said, "Because our motto at Smitty's Eats is gonna be *Twenty Percent Higher Prices, One Hundred Percent More Fun.* It'll work fine. Trust me."

We looked at each other with raised eyebrows.

I said, "Well, okay, so we get the new bathrooms

built. Anything else that absolutely has to be finished before we open?"

Gruf and Smitty looked at each other, thinking. Smitty said, "The front entrance."

Gruf nodded. "And we gotta get the new signs hung outside."

I said, "That shouldn't be too bad. That stuff'll take a day, maybe a day and a half."

Gruf said, "And that's about it. Everything else can be worked on after we're open for business."

Benny came out carrying two of our plates. Smitty hustled back to the kitchen for the other two.

When he returned, I said, "Well, Smitty, I guess you'd better call for delivery of everything on the bathroom lists, too. Tomorrow's Thanksgiving, and everybody's already made plans, but starting Friday, we'll just have to bust our butts and get it all done."

Bump took off after lunch and we went back to our struggle with the dining-room carpet. After another hour or so we finally managed to get it tugged into shape. I was duckwalking, driving in carpet tacks along the front wall, when I happened to look over and found myself staring at a shiny pair of four-inch black patent leather high heels.

There were feet in the high heels, and the feet were attached to slender, black-stockinged legs. My eyes traveled up the legs to the hem of the black-and-white herringbone straight skirt, up to the hem of the matching jacket, up the buttons of the little white blouse under the jacket, and I found myself staring at our little erstwhile work-shirking waitress, Cindy. She was smiling down at me. A big, huge, fashion-model smile.

I said, "Jeez. What are *you* so dressed up for? Somebody die?"

She said, "You silly."

Danny was on the far side of the room, pounding carpet tacks over there. He glanced at her. She patted her blond hair and batted her mascaraed eyelashes at him. "Hi, Danny."

He nodded at her and went back to work.

Cindy said, "Gruf says if I'm gonna be the hostess here, I'll have to dress up, so I'm getting used to wearing high heels." She gave a little kick. "I've been in these things three hours today and counting. By the time we open, I'll be ready for an eight-hour shift."

I shrugged. I told her she looked nice. What the fuck. I didn't like her much, because she was so phony and she wasn't much good as a waitress, but she did look nice.

Then I said, "Cindy, did you ever call Debby and apologize to her? Because you're gonna have to do that before—"

She wiggled her fingers at me. "It's already taken care of. We're best friends now."

I had my doubts about that best friends thing, but as long as she had apologized.

She said, "Where's Gruf?"

I stood up and looked around. "He was here a minute ago. Maybe he's in the can."

She giggled. She looked around at the big empty room. Then she looked up at the big chandelier. "Wow. How much did that thing cost?"

I shrugged. "I don't think I heard anyone say."

She narrowed her eyes and studied it shrewdly. "I bet it cost ten thousand, easy."

I swallowed. "Ten thousand dollars?"

She nodded. "Easy. This place is everything Gruf said it was gonna be and then some. It's really gonna be nice, isn't it?"

I nodded. Gruf came walking in through the poolroom. "Hey, Cindy. Who's funeral'd you go to?"

She hurried over to him. I was dropped like a bad habit. Fine with me. I was trying to get that damned carpet all nailed down so we could move on. I squatted and got back to work.

Cindy said to Gruf, "You silly. I'm just trying to get used to my new high heels. I drove by Carlo's. It's all closed up."

He said, "Yeah. Their day shift walked out on them this morning. As far as I know, they don't have any employees at all anymore."

She said, "It's their own stupid fault, the jerks. Well, I went shopping this morning and bought myself some hostess clothes. What do you think?"

I glanced over. She was turning, modeling her new clothes. Gruf had his lips pursed and was studying her. He said, "You look good. That's just the kind of thing I want you to wear. Dressy but not flashy, like I told you."

She sighed. "Oh, good. I'm glad you like it. How soon do you think we'll be open?"

He glanced over at me. "Maybe two weeks? If we're lucky?"

I shrugged and nodded.

Gruf said, "But I'm gonna have people come in starting Friday at eleven. There'll be some organizing and shit to do, and we'll try to start some training."

She said, "Okay. I'll be here."

He said, "Yeah. Take a nice Thanksgiving vacation and be here ready to work Friday morning."

I laughed to myself about that line. Cindy. Ready to work.

Once she left, Gruf went back to work. I duck-walked around the corner and started along the next wall. Gruf was coming toward me from the other end, and Danny was just about finished on the back wall.

I said, "Hey, the big chandelier. How much did that thing cost?"

Gruf placed a tack and pounded it home. "Nine something."

"Nine hundred something?"

He looked over at me. "Try nine thousand something."

Son of a bitch. I wondered how Cindy knew a thing like that. I said, "I'm glad I didn't know that when we were hanging the son of a bitch. I'da been scared shitless."

We finished the carpet pretty quick after that. Then we went back to the area where the new bathrooms and the new hallway were gonna be and started gutting the old storerooms.

We'd been working for nearly an hour when we heard thumping and banging in the back hallway. Gruf ducked out to see what was going on. He came back and told us that the dining-room tables, chairs, and booths were being carried in. He said that Smitty had called in just about all his employees to help get everything in place.

A little while later, Jackson came in. We all stopped working and went out to the bar to take a smoke break and talk to her. Gruf asked her to come in early Friday morning, ready to do whatever. Kind of be his gofer while he started organizing. She was excited and eager to get started.

A while after that, Smitty came back to tell us that some of the deliveries of the bathroom fixtures and materials were coming in. He said he had some of his guys move the back pool table forward, so the bathroom stuff could be stacked there. That way, when we tore out that back wall, the bathroom stuff would all be sitting right there waiting for us.

It was nice not having to quit before four in order to get home, clean up, change clothes, and get back to work at Carlo's. We finished gutting the two back rooms and we tore out the back wall. Danny stayed until six-thirty. Then he hurried out for his shit, shower, and shave before he went to pick up Debby. Gruf and I worked until a little past seven, not quitting until we had carried all the crap out to the Dumpsters.

Then we dragged our sweaty, filthy carcasses to the front of the building to look in at the dining room. Smitty and his guys had vacuumed the new carpet, moved in all the furniture, and put it in place. The room looked awesome. Tits and ass, as Bump likes to say.

The big, plush, dark green–upholstered booths were

all in place along the walls, with their oak tables perfectly centered on the glittering wall light fixtures. Out in the middle, the rectangular tables were all centered under the ceiling fixtures, with their thickly padded green-upholstered captain's chairs spaced around them, just as we'd planned.

And in the very center of the room, under that huge, incredible nine-thousand-dollar brass and crystal chandelier, was a big eight-person oak table. We stared at the spectacle with our mouths open.

Smitty and his guys were still working. When I left, they were cutting open boxes in the kitchen, unpacking the brass candleholders, bringing them out, and centering them on all the tables.

Chapter 19

I was halfway home before I realized I was going back to an empty trailer. John was probably near the Indiana line by now, and Danny and Debby were on their way down to Logan's. Sure enough, the trailer was dark when I got there. I unlocked the door and flipped on the living-room lights.

I hadn't even thought about how I was going to feed myself. I looked around, running through my options. I thought I remembered somebody—one of the twins, maybe—saying Logan's ran a kitchen at night.

Bagby was only a fifteen-minute drive. I decided to take a run down there, eat, and see if Danny and Debby were getting any interesting information. I took a quick shower, threw on a fresh pair of jeans and a clean flannel, and was probably pulling out of Chandler's Trailer Park about the time Jack Moberly was thinking about what to say in his suicide note.

Logan's is a long, thin bar wedged in between a hardware store and the post office on Bagby's one and only business block. You wouldn't think that a little one-block town like Bagby would be able to pack a bar on a Wednesday night, but it was packed. There was a row of crowded tables along the wall across from the bar. People had to squeeze sideways to get past each other to walk back to the bathrooms. The place was crowded with tired, rowdy workingmen and hard-looking women, and the jukebox was cranked.

I spotted the twins easily. There was a crowd around

the nearest pool table watching the game intently. One of the twins was shooting and the other was sitting at a table nearby, tapping his teeth with a pencil, evidently keeping score. I scanned the crowd carefully, but I didn't see Jack Moberly. I found out why later.

Danny and Debby were sitting with a couple of guys I didn't know. Danny spotted me trying to wedge my way over to their table. He waved his arm. I saw that he was grinning and yelling to me, but I couldn't hear him over the noise.

I dragged over an empty chair and everybody scooched to make me a place. Danny and Debby were sharing a platter of hot wings, so when the bartender came by I pointed to their platter and yelled, "And a Coke."

There was no use trying to talk over the noise of everybody yelling and the jukebox besides. I looked the crowd over for a while until a particular chick caught my eye. She'd caught a lot of people's eyes. She was cranked on something and seemed to be attempting to lap dance anybody sitting down.

In between songs, she planted herself in front of a guy at the bar and pulled up her shirt. He laughed and reached out to cop a feel. She squirmed away from him, laughing and pulling her shirt back down. Then she looked our way.

I was pretty sure she was cranked on coke. There's something about a chick on coke—an air of tension around her, or edginess or something. Like she's not quite all the way in the moment. Some little part of her is somewhere else, worried about something. Also, she's often the life of the party.

I elbowed Danny and saw he was watching her, too. I leaned close to his ear, because the next tune was blaring. "Is that who I think it is?"

He said, "Nancy Sutton?"

And just then we heard one of the guys crowding around her yell her name.

The two other guys at our table were also watching

her. Debby leaned over for one of them to say something to her, and then she shouted something into Danny's ear. Then he yelled to me, "Come on. We're moving upstairs where we can talk."

I hadn't noticed the stairs. They were tucked around the corner behind the jukebox. Everybody grabbed their stuff, I caught the bartender's eye and pointed toward the stairs, and we relocated.

Upstairs was much better. Quieter, cooler, and not as smoky. There was a small bar and three pool tables. There were a few small groups of people sitting around tables near the bar, so we settled around a table over near the wall.

As we were sitting, the bartender came upstairs bringing my wings and Coke, and Danny introduced me to the two guys. Joe was a friendly looking little balding guy. Tony was bigger and older and walked with a bad limp.

Danny said, "They're on Jack Moberly's pool team."

We shook hands. I said, "This is league night, isn't it? Don't you guys play tonight?"

Joe said, "Tony shot first. They'll come up and get me when it's my turn."

Tony said, "If you even get to shoot tonight. If Smitty's holds back Reginald Elliot, we'll have to put Lucas up against him. No offense, but you wouldn't stand a chance against Reginald Elliot."

Joe nodded glumly. "Oh, well. Whatever helps the team."

I said, "The twins' team plays for Smitty's Bar?"

Everybody, including Danny and Debby, said, "Yeah." Somehow I'd missed that piece of information.

I said, "I didn't see Jack Moberly. Isn't he supposed to be here?"

Tony said, "Hasn't shown up yet. He may come wandering in."

Debby said to Tony, "What you were trying to tell

me downstairs—start over so these guys can hear. I
missed half of what you were saying, anyway." She
turned to us. "He was trying to tell me about Nancy
Sutton."

Tony said, "Nancy *Slutton,* more like." He grimaced
and readjusted the bad leg under the table.

Danny said, "No duh. Is she always like that?" He
jerked his head in the direction of the stairs.

Tony said, "No. Sometimes she's worse." He cut off
his laugh with another flinch, reached down, and tried
to ease the bad leg into a better position. You could
see by the deep lines around his mouth that he'd been
living with pain for a good long time.

Debby said, "Tell 'em about that night. What you
were telling me."

Tony said, "Yeah, okay. So this one night—"

Debby said, "Two weeks ago, did you say?"

"Two, three. Way before Reese got shot, anyway."

I said, "Did you know Reese Tornow?"

He nodded. "Sure. He practically lived in this place.
All the regulars in here knew him."

Danny said, "Which team is he on? Yours?"

Tony looked confused. "He was always hanging
around on pool night, but he's not on any of the
teams."

Danny and I looked at each other.

Debby said, "Tony, go on with your story."

"Yeah. So, anyway, it was maybe the week before
he got shot. It was pool night, so it was a Wednesday.
Nancy and Jack were fighting, as usual. Only this one
was worse. Nancy was drunk and stoned, as usual, and
Jack had had enough. So Jack walked out on her as
soon as his match was over—which he lost, because
he was too distracted watching her trying to dry hump
Reese." He turned in his chair and caught the bartender's eye.

I said, "Holy shit."

Danny said, "Were Nancy and Reese getting it on?"

The bartender got close enough to hear, and Tony waved his empty Zima bottle at him. "And a shot of mescal."

He turned back to us. "I thought they were before, but then I wasn't sure, because another chick started coming around and Reese seemed to be involved with her. Some mousy little plain Jane. Who knows, with that guy? He was one of those guys who can't keep it in his pants. We started calling all his little sluts Reese's Pieces."

Debby said, "So Jack walked out that night and left Nancy here."

"Yeah. I'd already shot, but I was hanging around because my—uh, a guy I know was supposed to come by, uh, to see me about something. Anyway, he didn't show, so I settled up with everybody and got ready to leave, and Nancy asked me for a lift home."

Danny said, "Because she'd come in with Jack?"

"Well, yeah, that night. But I mean, she was always asking somebody for a ride home, a ride here, a ride there. Her car's been sitting in the BP station up in Spencer for a couple of months. Freeloading bitch. That car was one of the things they were always fighting about."

I said, "Nancy and Jack?"

He nodded. "It needs a new fan belt. She was trying to make Jack pay for it, but he was getting sick of always paying her way. I mean, she's got a job. She oughtta be able to scrape up enough to do something for herself once in a while, right? Anyways, Jack thought so."

The bartender came over with Tony's Zima and shot and Tony handed him a ten.

The bartender smiled at Debby. "Hey, Deets. Long time no see."

"Bradley, I didn't even see you over there. How ya doin'?"

"Not bad." He pointed at her half-empty bottle of MGD. "Ready to go again?"

She smiled and nodded, then turned back to Tony. "So she asked you for a ride home."

He nodded. "I woulda made up an excuse. I really don't like that woman. But I guess she caught me off guard or something. I said okay. I took the back way, up Bagby-Spencer Road, because it's so much faster, but I completely forgot we're into rutting season. I came around that long curve there by Gleason's, and a fuckin' deer ran right across in front of my car."

Danny said, "Did it getcha?"

"Fuck yeah. The corner of my bumper caught its back legs and flipped it into the ditch."

Rutting season, if you don't know, is in the fall when deer get horny. Horny deer running out in front of cars is the number one cause of car accidents in Grand County. Seriously.

Tony said, "I slammed on my brakes, but I didn't react fast enough. So I'm sitting there, spun sorta sideways, catching my breath, and the deer is on its back in the ditch and we can see his legs kicking in the headlights."

Danny said, "Shit."

"Yeah. I'm sitting there taking stock, you know, getting ready to put 'er in gear and go on my way, when I look over and see Nancy pulling a gun out of her purse."

I said, "What?"

"Yeah. Fuckin' little handgun. I was so surprised. She gets out of the car, walks around the front in the headlights, leans down into the ditch, and boom. No more kicking feet. Turns around, walks back to the car, puts the gun back in her purse, and looks at me, like, Well, what are we sitting here for?"

Danny said, "Jeez."

"Yeah. That's what I thought. I thought, If I live through this night, I swear to God I'm never gonna find myself alone with this head case again."

Debby said, "I don't know if shooting the deer

makes her a head case. I mean, really, she was just
putting the thing out of its misery."

Tony shook his head. "No. That wasn't an act of
kindness. The look on her face . . ."

Danny said, "Describe it."

Tony shrugged. "She was, I don't know. Maybe it
was that she didn't have any expression at all. Just
blank. I don't know. Whatever it was, it scared the
shit out of me. And I don't scare easy. I got over
being scared in 'Nam. Anyway, I drove her to their
trailer. Then she wants to know, do I wanna come in?
Have some fun? No, bitch, I wanna get as far away
from you as I can get, thanks all the same."

Danny said, "She invited you in? Wasn't Jack
home already?"

"Fuck yeah. The lights were on and I could see him
moving around in there. To tell the truth, I think her
deal is, she wants to stir up trouble. I think she wanted
to drag me inside that trailer and watch me and Jack
go at each other. I think every time she goes from
one guy to another in this bar, what she's hoping is
that she can get a fight started. She's a fuckin' head
case."

He drained his Zima and waved for another.

We chatted awhile longer. I got another Coke and
finished my wings. Danny and Debby shot a game of
pool, Tony kept knocking 'em back, Tony and Joe
talked about pool league, which sounded like a lot of
fun, and I started getting sleepy.

I said good night to everybody and left at nine, nine
thirty. It was getting cold outside. The air was crisp
and sharp and you could smell snow in the air. I
started seeing flakes in the headlights about halfway
to Spencer. I watched carefully for deer.

Driving out Route 8 toward Chandler's, I pulled
over for an approaching ambulance. When I came
over the last hill I could see the pulsing red glow of
the police cars that were parked along Haskins Court.

I turned into the trailer park and realized they were parked in front of Jack Moberly's trailer. I parked behind them and ran for the trailer. Brian Bell and two other cops were standing there talking.

"Brian," I puffed. "What the fuck happened?"

He turned around. There were big flakes of snow landing on his cop hat. "Jack Moberly just shot himself in the head."

"Shit. Is he dead?"

"Not yet. Doesn't look good for him, though."

"*Shit.*" I stood there helplessly for a minute. Then I thought of something. "Did he leave a note?"

He nodded. "I didn't read it. They've still got it in there."

The other two cops started to move toward the trailer. Brian said, "Catch ya later, Terry," and went after them.

I took one last look at that trailer and started back toward my truck.

It tore me up bad that he'd never called me. I didn't even turn on the lights when I got home. Just shrugged off my jacket and sat on the sofa in the darkness.

You could say I barely even knew the guy. But that's just it. I did know him. I knew those tools of his, lined up along his bedroom wall, gleaming in the gloom. I knew that bottle of Jack Daniel's sitting on the floor by his feet. He was the spitting image of my brother Berk and I couldn't accept, I didn't *believe,* that he was the one who shot Reese Tornow. Especially after watching Nancy Sutton in action.

I was still sitting there like that when I saw Danny's headlights stop on the street in front of the driveway. A minute later, he and Debby came stomping in.

Danny popped on the lights and looked at me curiously.

"Whew," he said, hanging his jacket on the coat-tree and reaching for Debby's jacket. "It's startin' to come down pretty good out there."

He pried off his high-tops, signaled for Debby to

make herself comfortable, and sock-footed it into the kitchen for a couple of beers. She joined me on the sofa.

I tried to rouse myself out of my black mood. "You guys missed all the excitement."

From the kitchen, Danny said, "We know. We just got an earful from Janice Abbott."

I couldn't remember who that was. "Janice Abbott? Where'd you run into her?"

He smirked. "Right in front of her trailer. Her and Frankie were standing out on the street, talking things over with their neighbors. They invited us in for a cup of coffee." He came back into the living room, handed one of the beers to Debby and climbed into his La-Z-Boy.

I still wasn't connecting who she was. "Where's their trailer?"

He said, "Over on Haskins Court. Right across the street from Jack Moberly's trailer." He looked at me. "Get it?"

I said, "Across the street."

Danny said, "Remember? That fight they told us about? That they overheard the night Reese Tornow was murdered?"

"Oh. Those people we talked to the night Reese Tornow got shot. Out on the street, while we were waiting for John."

Debby said, "Turns out the fight was between Nancy Sutton and Jack Moberly. The Abbotts say Nancy was screaming and yelling like a crazy woman."

"No shit?" I stared at them, trying to make sense of it. "What was she yelling? Could they make out any words?"

Danny said, "Just general abuse. You son of a bitch, you fucking bastard, I'll kill you for this."

I said, "What was *he* yelling?"

Danny said, "I asked 'em that. They couldn't remember hearing *him* yell at all. They just heard him throwing stuff."

"Could they see anything?"

Danny shook his head. "They looked over, but Moberly's trailer was dark as far as they could tell. They heard her yelling, and a lot of crashing sounds, stuff being broken and thrown. Then everything went quiet. The next thing they knew, they heard the shots. They were afraid the shooting was out on the street. They hit the floor and stayed down until they were sure it was all over."

I shook my head sadly. "Well, it is now. All over, I mean."

Danny said, "Is it?"

I said, "Brian Bell said it doesn't look good for Jack Moberly. But I don't think he killed Reese Tornow."

Danny said, "Neither do I."

Alan Bushnell put down his coffee cup at breakfast Thanksgiving morning and heaved a big sigh. Jack Moberly was still hanging in there, but nobody was giving him much of a chance.

We'd been talking about Moberly's suicide attempt and what it meant all through breakfast. Alan said they'd sent the gun Moberly used for testing, to see if it was the same one used on Reese Tornow. It was the right caliber.

Everybody but Danny and me thought the case was over. That Moberly had shot himself because he'd killed Tornow and the cops were closing in on him. Danny said he disagreed.

Bump said, "Come on. We know he was violent."

Danny said, "No, we don't. We don't know that at all. In fact, the Elliot twins say he wasn't. But even if he was a wife beater, it doesn't make sense that he tried to kill himself."

Bump said, "Nancy wasn't his wife. She was his girlfriend."

Danny waved his free hand. "You know what I mean."

Alan said, "Why doesn't it make sense?"

Danny said, "I knew a guy once who liked to hit his wife. He wanted her to jump whenever he snapped his fingers. If she'd run away, he'd have tracked her down and brought her back. He would've looked until he found her. But he would never have hurt himself. He was a pussy."

Bump stubbed out his cigarette. "Different strokes for different folks, I guess. By the way, Alan, does Nancy know about Jack?"

"She knows. She's over at the trailer right now, supervising the cleanup. She's got it figured that if he dies, it's her trailer, since they cohabited and she helped pay the bills."

I leaned over to Danny and muttered, "God. She's a cold-blooded thing, isn't she? Over there cleaning, and he's not even dead yet."

Bump said, "I'm gonna swing by the trailer. Ask her if she wants to come for Thanksgiving dinner."

I didn't care much for that idea. The nasty memory of her working the bar the previous night was still fresh in my mind. I didn't want Thanksgiving trashed up. But, I mean, Bump was more or less one of the hosts of the shindig. It wasn't really *my* place to say who could come and who couldn't. What the fuck. Maybe we'd be able to get some information from her.

Chapter 20

At Mike's house that afternoon, smoke was billowing from the chimney. I climbed out of my truck onto the snowy driveway and watched the round white puffs stretch out and streak away across the pewter-gray sky. I sniffed the ancient fragrance of burning logs and felt nostalgia for something I couldn't possibly have been remembering from my own life. Fat snowflakes landed on my cheeks and hands like quick cold kisses in the frosty air.

Although I didn't think it out in words right then and there, I'm pretty sure that was the second when I decided someday I'd build a house of my own and it would have a humongous fireplace.

It seemed like everybody was there ahead of me. Danny's truck was parked just ahead of mine. On up the driveway was Reginald's big white Lincoln. Bud's big red Caddy was parked on the street.

Just as I noticed that someone had shoveled a path across the grass from Bump's front door to Mike's driveway, Bump's front door opened. An oven-mitted twin came bustling out carrying a large bowl covered in aluminum foil. Jackson appeared in the doorway behind him. She peeked out at me, waved, and said, "Reginald, don't forget the cornstarch."

Reginald spotted me and called out, "Happy Thanksgiving, Terry." His words made fat white puffs in the air. "Run ahead and get the door for me, will you? This bowl is heavy."

I shook out of my daydream and hurried up to Mike's porch. I pulled the storm door open, pushed open the inner door, and was greeted with warm air, rich fragrance, and a wall of sound that seemed like hundreds of happy conversations. I stepped around to the back of the storm door to let Reginald squeeze in ahead of me.

Meanwhile, he was giving a breathless play-by-play of the meal preparations. "We're cooking in both kitchens. We've been at it since eight this morning. Marylou and Jackson are still in Bump's kitchen, mashing the potatoes. Bud's over there, too. These"—he raised the heavy bowl for emphasis—"are the *yams*. We've got a turkey just coming out of each oven. And Mike and Luther should be about ready to start their gravy."

He stepped through the doorway and raised his voice to be heard over all the chatter. "Here are the yams. Quick. Someone put a trivet on one of the tables for them."

Bump set his Coke can on the corner of the nearest table and hurried to the kitchen. He was back in a second with a square tile, which he placed in the middle of the table. Reginald relieved himself of his burden and looked around.

"Now, where'd I set my Chablis?"

Ray appeared behind him and tapped him on his shoulder. Reginald turned around, took the wineglass Ray held out, sighed, and sipped happily and importantly as he surveyed the scene around him.

"Is everyone here? I think everyone's here now. I'll run back to Bump's and see how they're coming. Just let me top off my wine—"

I said, "Don't forget the cornstarch."

"*Oh*. The cornstarch." He hurried out to the kitchen, and the sounds of general confusion and busyness coming from that vicinity seemed to crank up a decibel or two. In a few seconds he came rushing back out, his wine in one hand and a box of cornstarch in the other. I held the door for him and he streaked back across the yards.

The football game on TV provided background noise, but no one seemed to be watching it at the moment. Ray was busy tucking napkins under the flatware at the place settings on the near table. Danny and Debby were each working a table, pouring water into fancy glasses. They passed each other as he filled the glass at the foot of his table and she filled the glass at the head of hers. As they did, he reached back without looking and grabbed a handful of her ass. She jumped and giggled.

Bump had retrieved his Coke and was standing in the dining room talking to someone who was out of sight in the kitchen. Even though I'd had advanced warning he was going to invite her, I was still shocked to see Nancy Sutton standing beside him holding a glass of wine.

I watched her. She was average height for a girl, a few inches shorter than Marylou, who stands five-ten, and Mike, who's five-ten-plus. Her brown hair was shoulder length and curled under slightly, so that when she turned my way, I saw that it sort of framed her face. Her face was pale, heart shaped, and pretty, but her mouth looked hard.

She stepped out of sight into the kitchen and reappeared carrying a wine bottle. She refilled the glass she was holding, set the bottle on the table, and drank a healthy slug.

I don't like wine myself, and I'm no expert, but I thought you were supposed to sip wine, not toss it back. Anyway, she tossed hers back and returned to listening intently to the conversation, her shiny brown hair bouncing when she laughed. She tucked her free hand possessively under Bump's arm.

She wore low patent leather heels, a short, tight gray skirt that showed off her long slender legs, and a lavender, lacy, tight, scoop-necked, somewhat-see-through little T-shirt. Even though she was actually wearing a bra that day, it was a fuck-me outfit if I ever saw one. Fuck me, fuck me, fuck me. Right now. She turned toward Bump so that her body pressed against his.

Bump glanced toward the living room and noticed me standing there for the first time. "Terry, you made it."

I walked over to him. We shook hands for some reason.

He said, "You've never actually met Nancy, have you? Nancy Sutton, Terry Saltz."

I said, "Call me Twees. Happy Thanksgiving." I stuck out my hand. So, this was the famous Nancy Sutton, up close and personal. Now I clearly remembered her from my morning stops at Petey's.

She smiled at me, winked one green eye, and we shook hands.

From the kitchen, Luther cried, "Where'd we put the platter? It was here a minute ago."

Also from the kitchen, I heard the softer sound of a female voice. Then Luther said, "Oh. Thank you, precious."

Then I heard Mike's voice. "Bump, get in here and lift this thing out of the pan for us, wouldja?"

I said hi to Ray and the short little brunette with him, whose name, when he introduced us, turned out to be Heather. Then I went on around the corner to the kitchen in time to see Bump, his elbows out wide, center a huge golden-brown turkey onto a large white platter. He carefully withdrew the long roasting forks he'd used to lift the thing. A piece of meat came away with one of the forks. He blew on it and dragged it off the tines with his teeth.

He growled with pleasure. "*Umm.* Is it almost ready? How much longer?"

Mike laughed at him. "Put the bird on the table, then stay out of the way."

She was wearing a tailored gray dress that hugged

her little waist, then flared a little bit in the skirt before it ended just above her knees. She had on a white lacy apron that was tied in a big white bow in back. She wore gray heels that were just high enough to flex her cute little calf muscles.

I stared at that big white bow. A guy could catch the end of one of the tails and tug gently, slowly pulling the bow untied, and the apron would slowly begin to slide . . .

Bump picked up the heavy platter and Mike watched him start toward the table. Then she saw me. She gave me a happy, beautiful smile, then glanced around the kitchen. "Oops. He needs a bowl for the stuffing. Twees, grab that big white bowl and tell Bump to spoon out the stuffing, would you?"

I carried out my mission. When I turned to go back in the kitchen, Luther was positioning two trays of dinner rolls in the oven where the big roasting pan had been. Mike was watching me. We smiled at each other again, and she blew a glossy black curl off her cheek and rolled her eyes.

Then she turned back to the stove, where the roasting pan now sat across the front burners. Mike chopped giblets and scraped them into the gravy while Luther stirred the juices and outlined the finer points of gravy making. I went to the refrigerator, careful not to get in anyone's way, pulled out a can of Coke, and went to supervise the removal of the stuffing.

The cooks from Bump's house came in, all in a flurry. Bud carried the foil-wrapped turkey platter, and Reginald, Marylou, and Jackson were all heavily loaded with foil-wrapped, important-looking bowls and plates. It took forever for all the dishes and platters and bowls to get carried to the tables and for everyone to sit.

Finally, as we all settled around the tables, Luther lit the fat green candle centerpieces. Ray added two more logs to the fire, where they began to spit and sizzle, and took his seat. Mike remembered the cranberries at the last second and ran out to the kitchen to get them. Then she sat down and turned around to Bud, who sat at the head of the table I was at, just to my right.

She said, "Bud, would you please say grace? Just like old times?"

I groaned inwardly. Something to do with a prejudice I've always carried around with me, which I don't even know where it came from exactly—against Bible-thumping, hypocritical, do-gooding, lip-service, hard-hearted, mean-spirited Sunday Morning Religiosity with a capital R.

But when I saw a look go around between Bud, Mike, Bump, and Ray, I got a much clearer picture of what these people meant to each other. I reminded myself of who they were and what they were all about. Then I knew this wasn't going to be the kind of grace I was prejudiced against. This was going to be something different.

Bud looked at Marylou. Her head was already bent forward over her folded hands. I saw him swallow hard. He cleared his throat and everyone bowed their heads.

"Heavenly Father." His voice was thick. "Today's Thanksgiving, and we who sit here today have a lot to be thankful for. You've blessed each of us with some combination of talent, intelligence, sense of humor, beauty . . . well, except Bump. But I guess you have your own reasons for how he turned out."

Everybody laughed.

"You've blessed us all with work to do and rewards for our work. You've blessed us all with health and with second chances."

I looked over at him, thinking about my own second chance, since I got out of jail. Bud was looking at Marylou again. Her head was bowed low and her soft blond hair was hanging toward her hands, which rested, tightly clasped, on the table in front of her.

I glanced around. Nancy Sutton was looking at

Marylou, too. Her eyebrows were pulled together like she was trying to find the answer to a puzzle in Marylou's blond hair. She caught me watching her and quickly ducked her head. That disturbed me. Nancy Sutton was up to something.

Bud said, "But the most important way you've blessed us is in each other. Help us remember that the people we love and who love us, these are our most important blessings. None of the other blessings you've given us in our lives means a thing compared to the people we love."

He stopped abruptly, swallowed hard, and his final sentence came out in a rush. "Bless this food to our use and us to thy service. Amen."

I didn't look up right away. I was blinking back tears. I understood for the first time what grace meant. What it was supposed to do when it was said in the right spirit.

Bud picked up the carving knife. "Now, anybody here want some turkey?"

Everybody had pretty much just grabbed chairs and sat, in no particular order, except that Mike had directed Bud and Marylou to the head and foot of my table, and Mike and Bump sat at the head and foot of the other table. I guess it had something to do with a notion of who were the hosts and hostesses or something. Anyway, I had ended up between Luther and Reginald.

There was a flurry of passing bowls and shit that seemed like it'd never be over. As Luther passed me the asparagus, I said, "So, where's your brother Emmett today?"

He took the yams from Bud and spooned some onto his plate. "Emmett? He's doing Thanksgiving at his fiancée's parents' house, up in Fairfield." He lowered his voice. "What's *she* doing here, anyway?" He jerked his head toward the other table, and I knew he meant Nancy Sutton, who sat to Bump's right with her wineglass lifted to her lips.

I shrugged. "I was wondering that myself."

"Look at her."

I did. She was laughing at something Bump had just said. Danny nudged her from her other side and passed her the cranberries.

Luther said, "Like she didn't have a care in the world. Like her boyfriend *didn't* try to kill himself last night and it was all her fault." He handed me the yams and turned to take the bowl of stuffing from Bud.

Bud said, "You didn't get any wine, didja, Terry? Pass your glass over here and I'll pour you some."

"No. Thanks, Bud. I'm good with my Coke."

He looked at me. "You don't drink, do ya?"

"Not anymore, Bud. Not since jail."

Marylou said, "Except that one night."

I turned to look at her. "Huh?"

She passed the asparagus on to Ray and looked at me. "That one night, when you didn't come home. You must have been drinking that night."

I said, "What are you talking about?"

She shrugged and smiled. "Never mind. It's all water under the bridge now. Forget I said anything."

I stared at her. "No. What night are you talking about?"

She brushed her hair back from her cheek and thought about it. A confused look came into her eyes. "That one night. I waited and waited. Everything was so terrible, and you didn't come home."

She stopped in confusion, realizing that what she was saying didn't make any sense, since she and I hadn't cohabited since before I went to jail. As far as I knew, she didn't even know where I lived. Except that she somehow had known I lived in Chandler's Trailer Park, which was how she happened to go there looking for me one particular night. With Reese Tornow.

It hit me like a fist to the gut. She was talking about the night Reese Tornow had been shot. She had a vague recollection of waiting for me in that trailer and of how she had tried, in her state of confusion, to figure out why I wasn't there, since a truck that looked a lot like mine was parked right outside.

I shot a glance toward the other table, realizing for the first time that I had serious suspicions about Nancy Sutton. But Nancy was deep in conversation with Bump. I turned back to Marylou.

I said quietly. "We'll talk about this later. No more now. Okay? Not another word."

She nodded, still looking confused.

Bud said, "What's this all about? Is it what I think it is?"

I nodded. His eyebrows knotted as he looked from me to Marylou and back again. Then he glanced warily over his shoulder at Nancy.

I said, "Luther." He leaned toward me. I kept my voice low. "You guys said your pool team played Logan's the night Reese Tornow was shot. Right?"

He nodded.

"And the match was at Logan's?"

He nodded.

I said, "What time did Jack Moberly leave the bar that night?"

He chewed on his lip, thinking. He looked past me to Reginald, who had leaned over to hear.

Reginald said, "He was still there when we left, wasn't he?"

Luther said, "I can't really remember."

Reginald said, "Because he was drinking with that guy with the bad leg."

I said, "A guy named Tony?"

Luther said, "That's right. Jack was drinking with Tony Porter and a couple of other guys. That's right. And Missy Logan. Remember, Reginald? Missy Logan came in that night."

Reginald said, "Missy Logan is Rick Logan's wife. She doesn't come in the bar much, but when she does, it's a party. Her and the regulars down there. Sometimes they'll stay there most of the night. Missy closes the place and turns off the lights. Then they sit there drinking and smoking weed."

Luther nodded. "I remember that now. I remember when Missy walked in, Tony said it was a good thing he wasn't sleepy, because her arrival meant it was going to be an all-nighter."

"Wo. An all-nighter? That's what he said?"

They both nodded. Reginald said, "When we left, they were doing shots and playing the instant lottery machine. What time was that? Maybe midnight?"

Reginald nodded. "They were still going strong. Missy, Jack, Tony Porter, and a few others."

"And you're sure that was the night Reese Tornow was shot?"

Reginald nodded.

Luther said, "What time was he shot?"

I said, "Four-thirty."

They looked at each other.

I said, "Can you find out how late Jack Moberly stayed?"

Luther nodded. "I'll call around. I've got all the numbers in the league paperwork."

I reached in my back pocket and pulled out a business card. I wrote my cell-phone number on it and handed it to Luther. "Find out as soon as you can, and call me."

He took the card and nodded.

The gravy was the last thing passed around. I sloshed it all over everything on my plate and went to work. Both tables got pretty quiet. The sounds of logs crackling in the fire and the clicking of flatware took the place of conversation for a while, except for the occasional compliment on the fine food. As the piles of food on the plates diminished, the conversation began to pick up again.

I heard laughter and glanced over toward Bump's

table. He was refilling Nancy Sutton's wineglass and she was laughing a little too loudly. She sure didn't seem like a woman whose boyfriend had tried to kill himself the previous night. Mike got up from the table and walked out to the kitchen to refill the plate of dinner rolls. I picked up my empty glass and followed her out.

She tossed me a smile as she opened the oven and began to pile rolls onto the plate. "More Coke? I'd have gotten it for you."

I said, "I wanted to talk to you, anyway."

She raised her eyebrows and I saw her pause and catch her breath a little. Good sign.

I said, "You got any connections down at Grand County Hospital?"

It wasn't the question she wanted, and that was a good sign, too.

She finished filling the plate, let the oven pop closed, and nodded.

I said, "Can you find out how Jack Moberly's doing?"

"Sure. No problem. I didn't realize—was—*is*—he a friend of yours?"

I had to think about that. "Put it this way. I think he was gonna be."

She said, "I'll call right now," and gave me a wink. She winks good.

She carried the rolls out to the table and headed down the back hall. Could have been five minutes later, she came back out and asked me to help her bring in a few more logs. Reaching past her shoulder, I pulled the sliding-glass door open and we stepped out onto the back porch. I slid the door closed and we looked at each other.

When she spoke, her breath came out like angel hair. "He's hanging in there, but they don't like his chances."

I shook my head and looked out across her big

backyard. It was still snowing steadily. The air was crisp and had a bite to it. In the fading light of dusk, the snow was tinted blue, and there was a lot of purple in the fat snow clouds. From next door I could hear the low purr of Bump's hot-tub motor.

I said, "Shouldn't they send him downtown? Wouldn't he have a better chance if they moved him to, like, Cleveland Clinic or something?"

She said, "I went into a lot of detail. It sounds like they're doing everything possible. The move itself would be a big risk, you know, in a case like this."

I nodded. To our right, a large clump of snow slid off the lower bough of a pine tree and fell to the ground with a soft thud.

She said, "But there's still hope. Every hour he hangs on improves his odds."

I nodded and looked back at her. She was shivering. Even though it was pretty to watch, I handed her a log, pulled the door open for her, and grabbed four more. We stepped back inside, stomping snow off our shoes.

Ray scrambled to take the logs out of my arms, and I went back to my place at the table. Danny caught my eye and bounced his eyebrows at me. I saw he thought I'd used the opportunity to make my move on Mike. Wrong, my boy. I shook my head at him.

Marylou, Mike, and the twins began clearing the tables, and Jackson started taking dessert orders. Everybody groaned at the idea of dessert after the big meal, but everybody but Nancy gave in.

Nancy got louder. Bump was whispering to her, trying to quiet her down, but when she laughed it was a bar laugh, pitched to be heard over a blaring jukebox. She drained the last of her glass and waved it at Bump.

He grinned at her. "Nope. You're cut off, young lady. Iced tea or Coke?"

She was instantly angry. Laughing one second, livid

the next. Head case. She leaned back in her chair, folded her arms across her chest, and fixed Bump with a long, hateful glare. A red burn crept into her cheeks, while a streak of absolute white surrounded her mouth.

She sat there a minute, chewing on her lower lip. Then, in a cold, even voice, she said, "He did it, you know."

There was dead silence. Everybody at both tables froze and stared at her. She ran her defiant green eyes around the tables and back to Bump.

She nodded. "Fuckin' bastard. I hope he's dead."

Bump said, "What are you saying? That Jack Moberly killed Reese Tornow?"

She nodded. "Reese and me were gonna run away together. Someplace warm. Just as soon as Reese got his government check. Jack couldn't stand that. So he killed him."

Danny said, "But how do you know? Were you there? Did you see it?"

She turned toward him. Even from where I sat, I thought I saw a flicker of something in her eyes. Confusion, maybe, or doubt, or even cold calculation. Something. I thought I saw her run down a list of options and then tilt her head when she chose one.

"I don't wanna talk about it."

I said, "Just tell us what happened that night. You and Jack. You were together in your trailer?"

She blinked at me.

Danny said, "You guys saw the Vee Dub drive in?"

She chewed her lip, blinking rapidly.

Bump said, "Or maybe you were home alone. Jack came in after the Vee Dub was already there?"

Danny said, "If Reese was gonna run away with you, why'd he let Amy Grodell move in with him?"

She hooted. "That crusty bitch. I'd like to get my hands on her. But he didn't care a thing for her. He was just using her to get her money."

I said, "Why'd he need her money if he was expecting a big government check?"

She faltered. Then she decided to be insulted. "This is very rude, picking on me at a time like this. My boyfriend's fighting for his life in the hospital, for God's sake."

This chick sure could shift gears in a hurry. I said, "Nancy—"

She said, "Take me home, Bump. I'm not having fun anymore."

Bump said, "Now? We haven't even had dessert."

Danny said, "Couldn't you just answer a few questions?"

She was already pushing away from the table. She reached out a steadying hand as she stood. "No, I could *not*. You're not the cops. You're just a bunch of rude and insensitive jerks."

Bump followed her over to the coat closet.

Bud pushed back from the table and stood up with a casual groan. "I think I'll go along, if you two don't mind. Catch a little fresh air before dessert. In fact, my car's parked out on the street. I'll drive."

Bud looked back at us as Bump helped Nancy on with her jacket. The three of them left without another word being said. Bud pulled the door closed behind them and the rest of us sat there, speechless.

Danny broke the silence. "Well, what crawled up *her* ass?"

Luther was the only one who heard me say it the first time. The rest of them were laughing too hard.

I waited until they were quieter. Then I said it again. "*She* did it."

Danny nodded. "I think so, too."

Marylou said, "Is that why Bud . . ." She turned to look at the front door.

I turned to Danny. "We gotta see a copy of Jack Moberly's suicide note."

"John'll get a copy of it for us."

"He's in Indiana. He won't be back until tomorrow night."

Marylou said, "Ask Bud. He'll be able to get a copy of it. Bud can do anything." The pride in her voice made me smile to myself.

"Yeah. We'll ask Bud." I elbowed Luther. "We gotta confirm that Jack Moberly stayed late at Logan's that night and find out exactly what time he left. Can you get those phone numbers now?"

He was already pushing away from the table. "The paperwork's at home. Be right back."

I stood, dug my keys out of my hip pocket, and flipped them to him. "Take my truck. It's last in line."

During the time we waited for Bump, Bud, and Luther to finish their various running around, we cleared the tables and put away the leftover food. There was a lot of running back and forth between the two houses, fitting everything into the refrigerators. A giant coffeemaker was loaded and started up, and people began to return to the tables. Dessert was served.

Marylou surprised me by pitching in with cleanup. I was beginning to believe in the New and Improved Marylou. When everything was done, she came out with a cup of coffee and a slice of pumpkin pie and sat in her place at the foot of the table. The pie sat untouched in front of her. She sipped on her coffee and watched the front door.

As I set my coffee and pie on the table and pulled out my chair to sit down, she raised her thumb to her mouth and began to chew vigorously on the nail. I brushed it away from her face.

"What are you doing? You're not a nail biter."

She looked like she was ready to cry. "Why aren't they back? Shouldn't they be back by now?"

I patted her hand. "Don't you worry about Bud and Bump. They can take care of themselves."

"But—"

I said, "Listen, I don't wanna forget to tell you this.

I don't want you to move into the town house just
yet. Stay right here where you're safe. For a few more
days. Okay?"

She nodded.

Luther returned with the paperwork. He and Reginald took a minute to split up the phone numbers.
Then they went to work. Reginald began making calls
on his cell phone. Luther used the wall phone in the
kitchen.

Because it was Thanksgiving, nobody was where
they should be. The twins called friends and friends
of friends, trying to figure out where somebody could
be reached who could answer our question. After a
frustratingly long time, Reginald snapped his cell
phone shut and said, "*All right!* Hang up, Luther. I've
got the answer."

Luther spoke briefly into the phone he was using
and fitted the receiver into its slot on the kitchen wall.
Everyone turned to Reginald and waited.

"I tracked down Missy Logan. She was at her
aunt's. She said they definitely stayed after closing that
night. Jack Moberly, too. They were all there until
well past four."

I said, "No shit. How well past four?"

"She wasn't sure."

I lit a smoke. "We gotta pin it down better than
that. If he left at five after, he had time to drive back
to Chandler's and shoot Reese at four-thirty. If he left
at twenty-five past, he didn't."

They went back to their phones. Gruf came in then,
all rosy and merry from his parents' table, and Bud
and Bump came in a few minutes later. Marylou ran
crying into Bud's arms. She almost knocked him over.

The twins kept calling until they'd talked to everyone who could give information, but no one was able
to be any clearer than Missy Logan. They'd left Logan's after four that night, but no one was sure how
long after four.

Everybody had their pie and coffee while we rehashed the facts. After a while, more coffee was made. A while after that, Bud dragged out some leftovers and was able to persuade the twins and Danny to join him. Around eight, Bump brought out the Flinch games and a hand was dealt out at each table, but the cards sat there pretty much ignored while we went over the details of the murder.

I remembered to bring up Jack Moberly's suicide note. Bud said he thought he ought to be able to get a copy. He'd see what he could do.

Finally around ten, the party began to break up. At the front door, Mike took my hands, looked up into my eyes, and listened while I told her how special the day had been to me, how perfect everything had been, and thanked her for inviting me.

I wanted to grab her. I wanted to wrap her up in my arms and gently lay her down right there on the floor. I wanted to drag her down that back hallway by her hair. All those things and more. But by that time I had what I thought was a pretty good strategy mapped out for winning her, so I stood there holding her hands and I even rocked back a little so my chest was in the way of her being able to reach my lips.

I knew she wanted me to kiss her. And that was good. But that wasn't how it was going to happen. The idea that my strategy was based on came from something that'd happened on card night, when I was standing in her kitchen holding that bag of stuff from Petey's. I didn't hand it to her and I didn't set it down in neutral territory where she could peek inside. But she wanted to know what was in it, so she reached out and took it away from me.

She pulled her hands free and ran them lightly up and down my arms.

She said, "I'm glad you came."

I said, "So am I," and I left.

Chapter 21

At Brewster's Friday morning, Bump walked in just as Mary was pouring my coffee. He sat down chewing his lip. "Still no change in Jack Moberly's condition. Mike left a note on my door this morning and told me to tell you."

I said, "Thanks."

He glanced at Alan and said, "I just stopped by Petey's. Nancy Sutton's back at work. Hittin' on all the customers like she hasn't got a care in the world. Smiled at me like I was the man of her dreams."

Gruf looked at him. "Quick recovery."

Bump said, "That's what I thought. That girl's pretty fast on her feet."

Alan had put down his newspaper. "Hitting on customers? Nancy Sutton hits on the customers?"

Bump said, "Fuck yeah. Hitting on 'em. You know how some girls do?"

"Yeah, but that wasn't exactly the picture I had of Nancy Sutton."

Danny said, "Why? What kind of picture of her did you have?"

Alan shrugged. "I don't know. More like a hit*tee,* I guess, rather than a hit*ter.*"

All four of us guffawed. Bump said, "Dude, you better take a closer look at your picture. Now, lemme see, do I want me some ba*con*? Or some sau*saaage*?"

Over at the bar, the work was intense. Danny and I hit the bathrooms hard. Danny went to work building the men's room walls and ceiling while I did the same in the women's room.

Gruf and Jackson were busy up front. He was running between the dining room and kitchen like a track star, and she followed him around with a notebook and pen. Every time he thought of something that needed to get done, he told her and she wrote it down. Also, he kept sending her running off to get this or call that place or do some other thing. He sent her out to pick up the new Smitty's T-shirts, and she stopped off to show them to us on her way back in. They were black and they looked pretty cool. Actually, they looked almost exactly like the old Carlo's T-shirts.

The gang began to drift in for training at a little past ten. A lot of them came in through the back door, and most of them stuck their heads around the corner to say hi on their way up front.

Gruf and Jackson had set up at a table off to the side of the bar where they could sign people in, get the tax paperwork done, and distribute T-shirts. By the time I glanced down the hall around eleven, everybody was standing there in their black Smitty's T-shirts, looking around and asking questions. Gruf rounded them up and herded them out of sight into the new dining room.

I don't exactly know what he did with them after that, but every time I happened to pass by where I could see them, they all seemed to be running around like crazy people. Debby, Princess, one of the twins, and Flute were behind the bar, where Smitty was training them in the bartending arts. Over in the dining room and kitchen, there was a lot of running around and a lot of laughter. Grocery deliveries started arriving. There was a huge delivery from Syscos, and another huge one from Euclid Fish.

At around eleven, Bud stuck his head into the women's room. He looked grim. I put down my hammer and followed him out to the bar. Danny saw us go by and he came out, too. Bud ordered a Corona, drank a thirsty slug, then pulled a folded piece of paper from his jacket pocket. He handed it to me. It was a copy of Jack Moberly's suicide note.

I stared at it. It was heartbreaking to look at the immature scrawl. He'd written it in longhand, but you could see that the words were constructed letter by agonizing letter. The letters were too round and too large.

He'd written it in pencil. I'd have known that even if the copy machine hadn't reproduced the smudged areas where he'd erased. A carpenter might not have an ink pen to his name, but we've always got pencils. We use pencils to figure our measurements. Mark our cutting lines.

He hadn't addressed it to Nancy Sutton, but it was obviously meant for her. It said:

> *Either way I'm going to lose you. I can't see any way we come out of this together.*

That was it. The way the guy summed up all his reasons for wanting to end his life. I passed it to Danny. He read it and handed it back to me.

I said, "Well, shit."

Bud said, "It's so sad. And what does he mean, either way? What does that mean?"

Danny said, "Yeah, that tells us a whole lot of nothin'."

Bud took off and we went back to work until Gruf yelled down the hall that he was breaking for lunch. Danny appeared behind me and stood in my light, watching me unchuck my drill bit. I looked up at him.

"Okay, Boss. I gotta ask. When the fuck are you gonna make your move on Mike?"

I looked around at him. "Don't call me Boss. And I'm not." I fit the bit back into its case and lit a smoke.

He leaned on the unfinished doorjamb. "Why the fuck not? It's obvious she likes you. I know she'd go out with you."

"I'm not looking to go out with her. I'm looking to marry her."

His head jerked back. Then he laughed. "Go large, I always say. But, dude, you gotta start somewhere."

I said, "I already have."

He stared at me. "I don't get it. I mean, I guess you know what you're doing. You've never had any trouble getting the girls. But I think you're—"

I held up my cigarette hand. "Listen. I'll explain it to you. Is she the most beautiful girl you ever saw?"

"Yeah. Definitely."

"Yeah. And where does she work?"

"Cleveland Clinic. Right?"

"Exactly. And what do you have at Cleveland Clinic? Tons of rich doctors, rich patients, ambitious gonna-be-rich whad'ya call 'em. Interns or something. Right?"

"Right. So you're afraid—"

"I'm not afraid of anything. If she wanted a rich guy, she'd have married one by now. Right?"

He nodded. "Okay."

"The way I figure it, there's gotta be guys calling her all the time. Probably got some of 'em sending her flowers, buying her candy, corny stuff like that. Falling all over themselves trying to get her to notice them. Right?"

"Prob-*lee*."

"Yeah. Following her around like puppies, telling her how beautiful she is, how wonderful she is. She knows she can get whoever she wants and he'll come running whenever she snaps her fingers. Right?"

"Right . . ."

"Okay. But she hasn't hooked up with any of 'em. So maybe her mind's on her career right now, and she doesn't want distractions."

"Maybe so."

"Yeah. Then along comes a guy who doesn't call. That'd be me."

Danny laughed.

"I'm sure by now she knows I'm attracted to her. I mean, everybody seems to know, so I'm sure Bump's told her. But I'm not tripping all over my dick every time she's around."

"Oh, jeez. I see where you're going with this. This is just stupid."

I shook my head. "No, it's not. I haven't called her. And I'm not gonna call her."

"Then how are you gonna get together?"

I smiled at him. "Watch and learn, Daniel Ignatius. When she's ready, she's gonna call *me*."

The employees were apparently eating in shifts. Some were sitting at tables in the new dining room and some were still working. Lunch was still being made by Smitty and Benny in the old kitchen, but Gruf told us Hammer was gearing up to be able to prepare supper in the new one, for whoever wanted to try it out.

We waited for our lunches at the bar; then we carried them back to the new dining room. Bump was sitting at the big eight-person table in the middle, so we spread out around it while he spooned some gravy onto his mashed potatoes.

He said, "Nancy Sutton's left me three voice mails so far today. Wantin' to know when we're gonna get together again. Wantin' me to call her back. Each time she sounds more pissed. I think I've got one of those *Fatal Attraction* things on my hands."

Nobody laughed. Especially not me.

Danny drowned his cheeseburger in mustard. Then he looked over at me. "You know what I keep thinking about?"

I had a mouthful. I just waved my cheeseburger at him to proceed.

" 'No visible marks.' "

Bump said, "What's that mean? I don't get it."

"When John was telling us about asking Nancy Sutton how she knew it was Reese Tornow they brought out of that trailer, he said Brian Bell came up with the idea that Jack Moberly was in the habit of hitting her. The phrase they used was, 'no visible marks.' Brian Bell said that's what wife beaters do. Hit 'em where it won't show."

I swallowed so I could talk. "Yeah? So?"

"But then she's well enough to be gone that day you guys went over to her trailer. Remember? When you talked to Jack Moberly? I mean, if she was hurt so bad she couldn't show up for work . . ."

Bump said, "Go on."

"So what I'm thinking, maybe there weren't any visible marks because there *weren't* any marks. Maybe she wasn't hurt at all. No fall down the steps, no getting beaten, no nothing."

Bump said, "Why would she claim to be hurt when she really wasn't?"

Danny said, "Bump, the morning after Reese Tornow was shot, you talked to her. I remember you said she got upset when you asked her questions about it."

Bump said, "Yeah, she did. She said it was because of recognizing him when they brought the body out."

Gruf said, "Only she was lying about that. She didn't see his face then."

Bump said, "Yeah."

Danny said, "Well, what I'm thinking is, maybe she wasn't hurt at all. Maybe she just didn't wanna answer any more questions about it."

Gruf said, "Because, like Terry says, she was the one who did it?"

I said, "By claiming to be hurt, she had an excuse to hide out for a while. Not have to answer as many questions. Maybe even then she was working on the idea of trying to frame Jack Moberly for it."

Bump said, "Huh."

We ate in silence for a while, everybody lost in thought. I finished eating, pushed my plate aside, and lit up. One by one, the rest of the guys did the same. All of a sudden Debby was loading our dirty dishes onto a bus tray. We all yelled at her that we'd clean up our own mess, but she ignored us. Then a twin was at the table giving us all fresh beverages.

When he'd gone away, I said, "Okay. We know Jack Moberly didn't leave Logan's until after four that morning, right?"

Everybody said, "Right."

Just then a sharp rap on the table made everybody jump. I looked up to see Alan with his nightstick in one hand, a can of Coke in the other. He was in uniform, even though he didn't usually start his shift until midnight, if I remembered right. He gave us all the cop scrutiny. Which he was pretty good at it, too. Then he slid his nightstick back where it belonged.

I said, "What's up, Alan? Aren't you on duty kind of early?"

He looked around the room, nodding, then settled himself at the table. He popped the top on the Coke and drank a slug.

He said, "I couldn't sleep. Those remarks you made this morning, Bump, about Nancy Sutton hitting on guys. Those didn't compute with *anything* I have."

We exchanged glances around the table, and Alan saw it. He said, "I think it's time for you guys to tell me everything you know."

I thought it was, too. I told him what we'd been talking about, but I let him draw his own conclusions. I could tell he was doing just that, because he didn't look too happy.

I said, "I was just about to see if we could put it all together. I had just said that we know Jack Moberly was at Logan's Bar in Bagby until after four the morning Reese Tornow got shot."

Alan shook his head. "No. Last call's at one-thirty."

Danny said, "And it probably was. But the owner's wife was there that night. She closed the place. Then she and some of her friends sat around until after four. Jack Moberly was one of 'em."

"Shit."

Just then John walked in. He stared at us with a puzzled look on his face. "What's going on?"

I said, "You back from Indiana already?"

"Yeah. I figured I'd stop here, say hi, get some lunch. What's going on? Alan, why're you here?"

Alan said, "We were just about to have a nice heart-to-heart about the Tornow case. Pull up a chair."

John joined us at the table. Debby and the twin were right there to take his lunch order and hook him up with a Bud.

It took all of us to give him a summary of what he'd missed. He listened while he ate. Alan listened, too. Occasionally, Alan groaned. You could see how shocked he was by everything we had to say about Nancy Sutton's behavior at Logan's, what we'd learned about her at Logan's, and her behavior at Mike's Thanksgiving dinner.

When Danny was finished, Alan said, "Okay. So even supposing Jack Moberly *was* at Logan's until after four. Tornow wasn't shot until four-thirty. Moberly still had plenty of time."

I said, "I was just about to go through that. I was just about to bring up the fight."

Alan said, "What fight?"

Danny said, "There was a loud, long fight in Moberly's trailer right before the shots were fired."

Alan glared at Danny. "How do you know that?"

Danny said, "The neighbors across the street told us. The Abbotts. It woke them up. They were lying there listening to the fight before they heard the gunshots."

I said, "They thought it was Jack and Nancy fighting. The noise was coming from their trailer, and they heard Nancy yelling."

Alan said, "Well, damn it all to hell." He looked at John. "How'd we miss that?"

John said, "We didn't miss it. Danny and Terry asked me if we knew about it. I checked and it was right there in the file."

Alan said, "Well, shit. Go on, Terry."

I said, "But the Abbotts don't remember hearing Jack's voice. Just Nancy's. So what I was about to bring up was, maybe Jack *did* have time to leave Logan's after four and get back here and shoot Tornow at four-thirty, but how did he have time to have a long yelling, throwing-things, screaming war with Nancy Sutton in between?"

Bump said, "Wo."

Danny said, "Holy shit. You're right."

I said, "And even if the fight was between Jack and Nancy, why would he have gone over to the other trailer to shoot Reese Tornow? He couldn't have thought Nancy was with Tornow. Nancy was right there, fighting with him."

Alan said, *"Dammit."*

John said, "Wait a minute. Say Jack Moberly was still driving home from Logan's at the time of the fight. Then who was Nancy Sutton fighting with?"

I said, thinking out loud, "That woman's got a bad temper. She's nuts. Maybe she was alone. Maybe she saw Tornow's car parked there, went over to have a look, saw Marylou and him together, went back to her trailer, and freaked out."

Bump said, "She thought she was gonna run away with Tornow. Remember, she said they were waiting for his government check?"

I said, "And he told Nancy he was waiting for his chance to clean out Amy Grodell."

Bump said, "But then she caught him with *another* woman—Marylou. She freaked out, got her gun, went back to the other trailer, shot Tornow in the head, and took a couple of shots at Marylou.''

I said, "But couldn't stick around to make sure she hit Marylou because Moberly showed up?"

Danny said, "Oh my God. Listen to this. The Vee Dub was found at LaDue Reservoir. It broke down there. Right?"

Alan nodded.

Danny said, "And where does Nancy Sutton's mother live?"

Alan said, "Hartville."

Danny nodded. "Hartville. Straight south of LaDue. So maybe *she* was driving the Vee Dub, trying to run to her mother's after she shot Tornow. But the Vee Dub broke down at LaDue."

Alan said, "Why would she have taken the Vee Dub and not her own car?"

I had that one covered. "Because her car's parked over at the BP station."

Danny smacked his open palm on the table. "And she didn't just grab Jack's truck, because she thought it wasn't there."

We all thought about that for a minute.

Alan said, "If that's the way it happened, then what? You've got Nancy stranded at LaDue Reservoir with a car that won't run. But she was at work at Pete's the next morning. How'd she get back to Spencer?"

Then Bump said, " 'What the fuck. *You're* not Nancy.' "

Chapter 22

Alan's problem was that he'd already gotten two arrest warrants for the perpetrator in the Tornow murder. The first was for Pookie Grodell. Then, after Moberly's suicide attempt, Alan had canceled that one and told Judge Urquhart he wanted a new one for Jack Moberly, if he survived.

Alan explained to us that Judge Urquhart was not generally known as an easygoing guy. In fact, he had been "pretty damn pissy" about the second arrest warrant. So now, in order to go to the judge and get a third one for Nancy Sutton, Alan was going to have to have a shitload of extremely convincing evidence. He sent John home to get into his uniform. Then he and John went to work on it.

We went back to our own work. Danny's a magician with wallpaper, so he hung the paper in the men's room. Then he came over to the women's and papered it while I installed the lighting. By five we were just about done with the men's john.

Also by five, there were some very pleasant aromas coming out of the new kitchen. About the time I didn't think I could stand it anymore, Gruf came back to tell us we were going to be the first guests in the dining room. We brushed the sawdust and plaster from our hair and clothes and followed him to the doorway.

Gruf told us to play it straight and act like honest-to-God customers. We had to wait to be seated at the lectern thing with the long, skinny green library lamp on it. We had to follow four-inch-heeled Cindy to a booth, and we had to study the fancy menus.

Fancy menus, Cindy all dressed up, that enormous brass and crystal chandelier glittering across a significant chunk of the ceiling, the thick carpet, the plush booth benches. I suddenly felt very uncomfortable. I suddenly felt a little sick, thinking Smitty's Bar wasn't gonna be at all like Carlo's. Not at all.

When Danny saw the prices, he about shit. He leaned across the table and whispered, "Dude, I don't want a twenty-six-dollar steak. I'm trying to save some money."

But one of the twins, glorious in his black Smitty's T-shirt and black jeans, was on his way to the booth to take our order, and he overheard Danny's remark. He said, "You silly. There's no charge during training. And anyway, once we're open, food's half-price for the staff."

I happened to glance back toward the kitchen while he was talking, just in time to see Hammer go moon walking past the doorway wearing what looked a lot like a bra wrapped around his spankin' white chef's hat. A second later there was a loud squeal from somewhere in the kitchen, followed by a lot of laughter.

Then Bump came walking in past the pool tables carrying a big box. He had his customary black leather vest pulled on over his black Smitty's T-shirt. He yelled for Gruf, who stuck his head around the kitchen doorway.

Gruf said, "What?"

Bump said, "The rest of the linen," and tossed the box to him. Then he slid in next to me and lit a smoke.

The twin said, "Are we ready to order?"

Bump said, "A Coke and a chef salad." He thumped his chest and let out a long belch. "No onion."

I burst out laughing and said to myself, You silly.

No need to worry. It was gonna be *exactly* like working at Carlo's.

Meanwhile, Gruf walked out to the bar and told all the regulars they were welcome to come into the dining room. Try out the cuisine. Whatever they wanted was on the house. Because they were members.

They began to straggle in and fit themselves into the booths and at the tables like they were afraid they were gonna break something. Tiny stood in the doorway, looking the place over good. He ignored Cindy when she asked him if he'd like to follow her to a booth, walked straight to the big center table for eight underneath the big center nine-thousand-dollar chandelier, and pulled out a chair.

Mule followed him over timidly, glancing around like he thought any minute Cindy would yell at him for sitting at the big table. But when she didn't, he pulled out a chair across from Tiny and sat. A few of the other Members joined them, and Cindy passed out the menus.

I eavesdropped on the guys at Tiny and Mule's table long enough to hear Tiny order the lobster tail. After that I went back to watching everybody on the staff do their thing. It looked like everybody knew what they were doing. It looked like Gruf already had the place running pretty smoothly.

My pork chop, Danny's filet mignon, and Bump's chef salad arrived, and we got busy. After we finished, we lit smokes and Gruf came out to sit with us for a minute. We talked about this and that for a while as the Members finished eating and gradually faded back out to the bar to huddle together and critique the food.

We were the last customers in the dining room. I elbowed Bump. "Okay, it's been fun, but I wanna go home and take a shower."

He picked up his half-empty glass of iced tea and slid from the booth. I followed him. The twin who had been our waiter, at least I think it was the same one, came walking out from the kitchen to ask how everything was.

I turned and was about to answer him when Bump muttered, "Shit. What's *she* doing here?"

I saw he was looking out toward the bar. I turned, and there was Nancy Sutton. She was standing with her hands flat on the front pool table, glaring at us. Bump walked toward her. I followed him.

He said smoothly, "Hey, girl. What're you doing here?"

She rocked back and stuck her hands in the pockets of the white fake fur jacket she wore. "I don't know how many times I've called you, Bump." Her voice was tight and angry. There were deep lines at the corners of her mouth.

She was wearing tight, faded, straight-leg jeans tucked into tall white high-heeled boots. One boot heel bounced angrily, nervously, on the floor. She said, "I've called you and called you and left so many messages. Did you forget how to dial a phone?"

Bump walked past her to set his glass on the bar. She watched him. I stayed where I was. He turned back, smiling, his hands spread palms up. "Easy there, kid. I been kinda busy."

Her anger was building. "Busy, huh? How long does it take to dial a phone?"

He had his mouth open to answer when I caught movement in my peripheral. I turned to see Alan and John walk in the front door. Alan was surprised to see her standing there. He said, "Nancy Sutton?"

I found out later that he had finally gotten the arrest warrant. He and John had gone to Pete's and then Nancy and Jack's trailer, looking for her. Having no luck, they'd decided to stop in the bar and see if Bump had any idea where she might be. Surprise.

She knew right away why they were there. I was watching them, and that was why I didn't see her pull the gun. I saw Alan freeze and John freeze behind him, and then I turned back toward her and saw her standing there pointing that gun at them. Her hand was perfectly steady, and I couldn't see any expression on her face or in her eyes at all.

Alan forced a smile and said, "Hey, now. There's no need for that. Put it away." He moved his shoulders slightly, like he was gonna take another step, but she stopped him.

"Hold it right there." She must have had ice water in her veins. She seemed perfectly calm.

Bump was on her left, a good three steps away, even with his long legs. I was on her right, and closer. One average-length step would do it for me. Alan and John were by the front wall, close enough to get shot, but too far away to do anything to prevent it.

The Members had begun to notice what was going on. They saw the gun and a buzz went up as they began to whisper to each other. I saw Tiny coming toward us around the front of the bar, but I didn't see Mule come around the back. I didn't even notice him until he was just a few steps behind Nancy.

Suddenly everybody got quiet. I don't think anybody was even breathing at that point. Everybody was frozen, staring at that gun.

Mule took a little sideways step and leaned out to peek at Nancy's face. He said, "Hi, Nancy Sutton."

She started. Her eyes skittered toward him and jumped right back to Alan and John.

She said tightly, "Shut up, Mule."

He smiled and took another little step. He nodded. "Nancy Sutton. Remember down at Logan's that one time?"

She was annoyed. She glanced quickly from Alan to Mule and back to Alan. "Shut up, Mule."

But he had something on his mind. He took another little step, smiling, and said, "You're pretty."

She whirled on him, really angry now, and brought

the gun around to point at his chest. "Shut the fuck *up,* Mule." Just as quickly, before Alan could make a move, she brought the gun back around to him.

I looked at Mule. He was still smiling. He caught my eye, and he shocked me by winking at me. I think my mouth probably dropped open, and I thought, I've gotta do something before he gets himself killed.

He took another little step and said, "Can I touch your hair?"

This time her face went red. She swung the gun around to him and screamed, *"No.* Shut the fuck *up."*

I judged where I needed to be standing, stepped in, and said softly, "Can I?"

When she whirled back to me, I was ready with my left hand. I did the patented Bump Bellini move, sweeping my hand across the gun, grabbing the barrel, sweeping it up and away.

I know I did it perfectly. I know I did it exactly the way Bump did it when he took the gun away from Dirt Grodell. And I did end up with the gun backward in my hand and her yelping and grabbing her trigger finger. There was just one little foul-up. As I took it away from her, she got a shot off.

She slunk away from me, sucking her trigger finger, and Alan and John charged us and took hold of her. I turned to look toward the dining room and was relieved to see there wasn't anyone slumping in the doorway. I wondered where the bullet had gone. I looked farther into the dining room and stared. There was a strange quality to the light in there.

I couldn't understand what I was seeing. There seemed to be movement in the very air, like how it would be if there was such a thing as ghosts and there was one moving through the dining room.

Someone had come up behind me. I looked around. Tiny was staring into the dining room, and behind him, Mule. Smitty had come out from behind the bar and he stopped and stared, too.

Tiny said, "Holy shit."

I looked back and I still couldn't understand it. Then the sparkles caught my eye. I looked up. The big chandelier seemed to have lights shooting around it. I shook my head and looked closer. Little beams of reflected light seemed to be shooting off every surface of the brass. The crystal seemed to be quivering. Shivering.

Then the entire massive chandelier gave a sharp lurch. Behind me, Smitty groaned, "Nooo."

There was another sharp lurch. Then, in slow motion, the entire beautiful humongous nine-thousand-dollar brass and crystal chandelier crashed onto the big round oak table beneath it. In one split second there was a crystalline rain, and in another, all that beautiful crystal was shattered and scattered across the table and the thick red carpeting like a glittering nine-thousand-dollar gravel job.

Chapter 23

Nancy Sutton got hauled off to begin her new and exciting life as a permanent guest of the state. Mule got installed on the back side of the bar with a lot of hearty backslaps and a big pile of drink chits in front of him. Smitty got installed in the corner booth of the dining room with a double shot of Old Grand-Dad and my sincere apologies. Gruf got on the phone in the old kitchen and called the insurance man and the chandelier company. The rest of us got down on our hands and knees in a wide perimeter around the dining room and spent the next hour or so picking glass out of the thick carpet.

Are we having fun yet?

It was probably a full five minutes of silence before somebody cracked the first joke. It took nine or ten jokes before Smitty looked around smiling and probably another nine or ten before my own mood lightened, I felt so horrible.

It was well after seven before we'd gotten everything we could get by hand. We all stood in a circle staring at the poor brass carcass sitting on the table. Danny and I inspected the place where the bullet had pierced the brass shaft and the wiring inside it and torn a big enough hole that the weight of the chandelier had pulled it all loose.

Then we wrapped the thing in a tarp, lifted it off the table, and carried it back to a corner of the old kitchen, in case the insurance man needed to inspect it or something. By the time we returned to the dining

room, the troops had the table for eight cleared of
glass and everyone was standing around admiring the
deep gouges the chandelier had left in the brand-
new oak.

Gruf said, "I guess we'll have to order a new table,
too, huh, Dad?"

Bump said, "Uh-uh."

Everybody looked at him.

He said, "No fuckin' way. That table's got character
now. Leave it the way it is. And don't fix that bullet
hole, either."

I said, "Bullet hole?"

Bump pointed, and we all moved over to examine
the hole in the side wall where the bullet had rico-
cheted after it severed the chandelier shaft. It was at
right about eye level if you were sitting in that center
booth, three or four inches above the chair rail.

Gruf and Smitty looked at each other. Then they
started to laugh.

Smitty said, "When he's right, he's right. We'll stick
with this table, and the bullet hole stays, too."

Not long after that, Gruf sent the troops home.
Then Bump, Danny, Gruf, Jackson, and me took turns
with the vacuum cleaner, going over the carpet again
and again to make sure we had all the little slivers out.

We ended up sprawled around the table for eight.
Smitty came out with a tray full of beverages and ev-
erybody but Jackson lit up. Jackson doesn't smoke.
Then Danny sat up straight.

"I gotta go. Deets is expecting me."

I said, "So, when were you gonna tell me about you
and Deets?"

I could see by the crinkle at the corner of his mouth
that he was smiling, even though I was looking at his
profile. That crinkle told me everything.

I said, "Oh yeah? When did all that happen?"

"The day after she told me she finally booted out
the scumbag that was living with her."

He scratched his crotch. He scooched in his chair,

like he might have something else to say on the subject. I waited patiently.

He said, "Uh."

I looked over at him.

"She wants me to move in with her."

"No shit?"

He nodded.

I said, "What did you say?"

He said, "I told her I might start thinking about it."

You gotta understand that I've known Danny since the days when we both thought girls were annoying. The fact that he hadn't told her straight up to forget it was significant. Even his triple-hedging "might start thinking," was a pretty radical commitment for Danny Gillespie.

Jackson said, "Ain't love grand? Listen, I gotta scoot, too. Gruf, can you give me a ride home, or should I call my brother?"

Gruf said, "No problem. Lemme grab my coat."

Bump and I decided to get a refill on our Cokes before we split. I carried our glasses over to the bar and Smitty topped them off. We were just lighting up smokes when Bump got a phone call. He carried his cell phone out into the poolroom to talk. A minute later he came back, smiling.

"That was Mike. Her friend at the hospital says our boy's awake. But he won't talk to anybody."

I said, "Jack Moberly's awake?"

Gruf nodded.

I said, "I gotta go down there. Think one of your friends down there could get me in to see him?"

Bump snorted.

All kinds of machines were blinking and beeping all around Jack Moberly's bed. Ugly little tubes came out of the machines and disappeared up under the sheet that covered him. A bunch of colored wires crept out from under the thick bandages that were wrapped around his head.

I didn't want to be there. I didn't want to look at

any of it or at him. I stood in the doorway with Bump right behind me and watched him for a while. Jack's eyes were open. He was staring straight up at the ceiling.

Bump nudged me from behind and we walked over to his bed. I touched Jack's shoulder. One of the machines started to beep faster, like it was yelling at me, and I jumped back a little. Jack rolled his head and looked at me. His big black eyes blinked in surprise, and a tiny smile broke out through his dry, cracked lips.

His voice was raspy and weak. "Relax. You—didn't—kill—me. The beeping—just means—my brain's—working." He spoke slowly, but his voice was so faint it was hard to understand him.

Bump said, "Dude, after your stupid-ass stunt, you're fuckin' lucky it is."

I elbowed him in the gut and gave him a very stern look, but when I turned back to Jack, I was surprised to see he was smiling again.

He said, "You two—don't—look like—candy stripers."

Bump said, "Fuck."

I could see the two of them were going to head down a side road of mutual ripping and ragging and I'd never get my thing said if I didn't step in right away.

I turned to Bump. "Gimme a minute alone, dude."

He still had his mouth open, and he hesitated a minute. Then he shrugged and left without arguing. Jack watched me. His face slowly sagged and I saw that his eyes were bloodshot.

I waited a minute. Then I said, "You remember me?"

"I—remember you. The—carpenter."

I nodded. "Why didn't you call me?"

He turned his head away. A sudden tear slid out from the inside corner of his eye and rolled across the bridge of his nose. He turned his eyes back to me.

"You can't help. Nobody can. It's all over for me."

I said, "Fuck that." He looked away. "It's all over for Nancy, though. The cops just arrested her."

He squeezed his eyes shut tight. Tears flooded out. He said, "Go away."

I said, "Jack, she killed Reese Tornow. In a way, you woulda been her second victim. Jack. You listening?"

He didn't respond at all.

"She doesn't feel anything for anybody. She's a user. You can't love somebody like that."

His eyes came back to me, blazing with feverish intensity. "You don't understand."

"Yes, I do. You think you shoulda been a hero and saved her ass. What if your aim had been a little better? You think she woulda loved you then? Fuck. She was going right on with her life while you were in here fighting for yours. She'd already written you off."

He shook his head and then winced. He said, "You don't know."

"I know, all right. You've been used, Jack. Wise up."

He turned his head toward the window and stared without seeing for a while. I pulled over a chair and wished for a smoke.

I said, "That night. The night she shot him. Did you hear the shots?"

He acted like he didn't hear me, but I knew he did. I said, "You'd just gotten home from Logan's."

He turned toward me, a look of surprise on his thin, pale face.

I said, "Yeah, I know about that. Come on, man. They've already got her. I wanna know what happened."

He looked away.

I said, "That fucked-up blonde that was in the trailer with Reese Tornow? That was my ex-wife."

He looked back at me, blinking. "Why was she there? Was he—fucking her, too?"

I shook my head. "No. She was looking for me that night. He was trying to help her. Did you hear the shots?"

He let some time go by. Then he said, "I got home—went inside—and the—place looked like a—bomb went off. Trashed."

I nodded. "She must have seen them in the other trailer and went nuts. She thought Tornow was doing Marylou."

"That's your wife's name?"

"Ex-wife."

He said, "Nancy's got a temper."

I thought he was understating it just a tinch, but I let it go.

He said, "She wasn't—in the trailer. I was—worried. I went back out in the—driveway."

"That's when you heard the shots?"

"Yeah. I looked—down the street—saw Reese's VW parked there. Got—scared. Ran to the trailer. The doors were open. Ran—inside. Saw him—lying there. Heard a woman crying in the—can. I thought it was Nancy. I thought she'd been shot, too. Hand me that—glass, would you?"

There was a glass of ice water on the patient tray, with one of those bendy straws sticking up out of it. He didn't lift his hand. I saw I'd have to hold the glass to his chest and put the straw in his mouth. I did.

He sipped, smacked his dry lips, sipped again, pushed the straw away with his tongue.

I said, "That enough?"

He nodded. I set the glass back on the tray. I wondered if he was paralyzed and that was why he didn't reach for the glass. But as I turned back to him, he shifted position in the bed. I was relieved to see both arms and both legs move as he tried to get more comfortable.

I decided maybe he didn't move his hand because it would have made the IV hurt. Never having had an

IV (knock wood) I didn't know whether it would hurt to move your hand or not.

I said, "So you looked in the bathroom."

"And it wasn't Nancy. It was your—Marylou."

"You said, 'What the fuck. *You're* not Nancy.' "

"I don't know what I said. I heard a car—door slam. I ran back—to the door, and the VW was pulling away. I knew it had to be her. I knew—she must have been the one who—shot him. She was hiding—somewhere in the trailer when I went in. I ran—back to my truck. By the time I got up to the highway, she was out of—sight. I didn't know what to do."

I said, "Then you figured out that she was on her way down to Hartville. Going to her mother's."

He gave me a surprised look. Then he nodded. He cleared his throat a couple of times.

I said, "More water?"

He nodded. I brought the glass over for him again. It looked like it was painful for him to swallow. Later, Mike explained that they'd had him on a ventilator, and that makes the throat dry and raw. I set the glass back on the stand.

I said, "You caught up with her at LaDue Reservoir, where the VW broke down."

He nodded. "I drove right—on by before I realized it. She wasn't in it. I got in, thinking—maybe if she was fucked up, maybe she crawled in the backseat—to sleep. But she wasn't—there. I checked the glove box and under the seats, to make sure she didn't leave the gun or—anything—else in the car. Then I drove—on. I caught up with her on that long curve. She was trying to walk to—her mother's."

I said, "Walk from LaDue to Hartville? That's—what? Thirty, forty miles?"

He sighed. "Then she didn't want to get in the truck. Then she didn't want to—come back to Spencer. I told her, you gotta be at—work. If you don't show up for work, you're gonna—gonna—look suspicious."

I nodded.

He said, "I swear, she looked at me like I was the crazy one. She had—no—idea she'd done anything wrong."

I said, "Jack, she tried to pin it on you."

He stared at me. I nodded. Tears rolled freely down his cheeks. I looked out the window and waited for him. The minutes ticked by.

Eventually he sighed and said, "I wanna die. Everything's too—hard."

I touched his shoulder. "Somebody told you it was gonna be easy? They lied. Look at me."

His eyes came back to mine. I smiled at him.

I said, "Sometimes life is tough. Big fuckin' deal. You suck it up and go on. Jack. Look at me."

His wandering, watering eyes came back to mine. I smiled again.

I said, "Guys like you and me, we get up, we go to work, we bust ass all day, we go home, we go to bed. Sometimes it's a good day, sometimes it's a bad day, sometimes it's just a day. But we still get up again."

He closed his eyes and shook his head. "I don't wanna get up."

I gripped his shoulder tighter. I wanted to make a place there on his shoulder that he'd feel and think about after I'd gone.

I said, "Oh, you're *gonna* get up again, one of these days. If I have to drag you out of that bed. Jack. Jack?"

He looked up at me.

I said, "I've got a carpenter job waiting for you if you want it. I've got a place for you to live if you need it. You're gonna get up."

His eyes had slid away again. He shrugged his shoulder, feebly trying to shrug off my grip. I gave it a little more pressure and then I let go. I knew he was exhausted. I knew I needed to leave him alone so he could sleep.

I said, "This right now? This is the worst it's ever gonna be for you. From this point on, it gets better and better. You rest now. I'll be back tomorrow."

I stepped out into the hall and pulled the door closed behind me. Bump was leaning against the wall. He dragged himself upright and watched me rub my scalp through my short puppy-dog hair. I pulled on my black knit cap.

He said, "Well?"

I folded the cap up off my forehead and pulled my jacket collar straight. I said, "He'll be okay. We'll make sure of that."

We turned and started down the hall toward the nurse's station. A cute little blond nurse leaned out across the high desk and peeked our way. When she saw Bump coming, she gave a little squeal and ducked back out of sight.

Bump chuckled.

Turn the page for a preview
of the Working Man's Mystery
featuring Terry Saltz

EARLY EIGHT

Coming soon from Signet

Procol Harum's "Salty Dog" was playing on the juke-box. I could barely hear it over the commotion in the busy kitchen at Smitty's Bar and Eats, but that didn't stop me from singing along while I watched the seconds tick down on the bread timer. My name's Terry Saltz. I'm a carpenter. I also moonlight a few nights a week at Smitty's. Technically I'm a bouncer, but at Smitty's you pitch in where you're needed. That's why I was baking bread.

Suddenly Danny Gillespie was beside me, elbowing me in the ribs. "Boss. Seven thirty. Let's go." His freckled face was all serious. That was an unusual condition for him. He was chewing the inside of his cheek. The chewing action was making his strawberry blond mustache bounce.

I said, "Hang on. I gotta get these loaves out of the oven when the timer goes off. And don't call me Boss."

Danny snickered. Then Hammer spoke up. Which I didn't even think he was paying any attention. He'd been standing there with his hands tucked under his armpits like he was in a hypnotic trance or something, watching the hot new waitress as she tried to reach the take-home cartons that were stacked on a high shelf.

Hammer said, "Go on, Boss. I'll take care of the bread."

I frowned at him for calling me Boss before I lifted down the boxes the new girl was never gonna reach without a stepladder. Then I followed Danny out of the kitchen and across the busy dining room. Sexy-ass dining room with thick burgundy carpeting, dark green wainscoted walls, and sparkling brass chandeliers dimmed down to half-light. Most of the tables were surrounded by happy, chewing customers.

We came to the doorway from the dining room to the pool hall and I stopped and stared. "Holy shit. Where'd all these *people* come from?"

Both of Smitty's teams were shooting at home that first night of pool league. You figure, four pool teams with six to eight players each, okay, that's a lot of people. But that didn't account for the crowd all along the front of the bar. Besides a lot of unfamiliar faces, I saw that Smitty had come out from behind the bar.

Danny threaded his way between the pool tables to where our team, looking tough and menacing in black Smitty's T-shirts and black jeans, was huddled around our scorer's table. I followed him, looking around with my mouth open.

The Elliot twins, Luther and Reginald, were our co-captains. They were sitting at our scorer's table, studying the score sheet. The rest of our team was hovering over them. A fat guy I didn't know was also hovering there. He was talking to the twins. As I walked up, he said, "Well, I guess we oughtta get started. Who you putting up first?"

Luther said, "Saltz. New player. Unranked."

The fat guy bustled back to his team's end of the table.

Bump Bellini was standing behind the twins, screwing a stick together. Some of his long blond hair had gotten loose from his ponytail. He blew it away from his nose. I looked closer at the stick. It was mine. The new one I'd bought two weeks earlier. He saw me and walked over, holding out my stick.

I couldn't stop staring at the crowd. It was a total clusterfuck, all around the pool tables and in front of the bar. People were glancing my way, rubbing their chins, putting their heads together and talking quietly, like they were discussing something important. I didn't like the look of things at all.

I pushed past Bump so I could talk to the twins. We had six players on our team, and only five sets are played in a match, so I was thinking I could sit out this first week. You know? Get a feel from the sidelines for what these matches were like.

I said to Reginald Elliot, "Due. Play somebody else first. And where the *fuck* did all these people come from?"

Reginald grinned up at me. "Believe me, Precious. It's better to go first when you're new. If you wait, your jitters will only get worse."

Don't get the wrong idea about that Precious thing. The twins are gay. They call everybody Precious.

"But Danny, Bump, and Gruf are all new, too. Seriously, I'm not ready."

The twins were shaking their blond heads. Reginald said, "Danny, Bump, and Gruf have all played in leagues before. You're the inexperienced one, so you're up. You'll have a five-minute practice session and then it's a race to three. That means, whoever wins three games first."

"I *know* what it means."

I stole a glance across the pool table toward the other team's end. We were playing the team for Four Corners Tavern in Woodcrest. The team that called themselves the Terminators. The fat guy was waddling toward us. He said, "We're playing Tiffany," and jerked this thumb to indicate a fat, messy girl who had stepped up to the table and was beginning to rack the balls.

Tiffany was wearing a school buy yellow T-shirt that said I'M WITH STUPID and had a big red pointing arrow. I watched the arrow, but no matter which way she turned, I didn't see Stupid anywhere. I wondered if maybe Stupid had gotten a load of her T-shirt and decided she wasn't with him after all.

A voice close to my ear said, "Wouldja?"

Danny was standing beside me. I saw he was watching Tiffany, too. I said, "Not even with *your* dick." Then I turned back to tell Reginald that I wasn't shooting first, but he wasn't there anymore. He was over at the bar getting his gin and tonic refreshed. Gruf Ridolfi straightened up from the score book. He ran his fingers through his long black DA, grinned at me, and gave me the thumbs-up.

I said, "No. Dude. Somebody else has to go first. I—"

"New guy always goes first," Gruf said firmly. "It's easier on the nerves that way."

"*Whose* nerves?"

Tiffany's five-minute practice session seemed like it was over before it started. Then it was my turn to practice. There was nothing I could do but suck it up. I racked the balls, positioned the cue ball, lined up to break, and totally biffed. My stick glanced over the top of the cue ball and the cue ball rolled sideways about two inches. I'd forgotten to chalk the tip of my stick.

Tiffany snickered. Behind me, people groaned. Somebody said, "Noonan." It sounded like Gruf. I turned around. Gruf was scratching his head and looking up at the ceiling. I turned back to the table and found the chalk. Somehow I got through my practice session, even though my bridge hand seemed to have developed a slight tremor. Then it was time to shoot for the break.

Tiffany won the break. I racked the balls and stepped back out of the way. Reginald came to stand beside me. He reached over and brushed bread flour off the front of my black Smitty's T-shirt. Tiffany broke, and the thirteen ball dropped into the corner pocket. She walked around the table, decided to try a rail shot on the eleven, and missed. I started for the table.

Danny said, "Boss. Don't forget to chalk up."

Which was irritating, because I would've forgotten.

I decided to go for the four in the side, but just as I was lining up on it, Reginald stopped me. "Time out."

I stood up and turned around. *"What."*

Reginald stepped close beside me, cocked his hip, frowned, cupped his chin, and stared at the table. "Let's talk about your strategy."

I said, "My strategy is: Sink all the solids and then drop the eight." Like, What the fuck?

He allowed a tight smile. "Well, yes. In a perfect world."

Across the way, Tiffany said loudly, "Tick tock, there, Shitty's. In this lifetime, huh?"

The Terminators all snickered.

Reginald ignored her and gave me my first four shots, telling me what English to use and where to leave the cue ball. I paid attention. The Elliot twins are far and away the two best shots in the entire bar league.

I lined up on the one ball to the corner like he'd said. The one dropped, but I shot a little too hard and ended up with the cue ball behind two stripes and no good shots on a solid. I'd only managed to get one lousy ball down and I was already screwed. I stood up from the table, baffled.

Reginald said, "Time out."

Tiffany yelled. *"Foul.* He already had a time out."

Reginald looked over with his mouth open, but her fat captain was already telling her that I was a new, unranked player and was entitled to unlimited time-outs in my first two matches.

Reginald said, "We'll call a Safety. Remember, to make it a legal shot, you have to hit one of your own balls first. Then something has to hit a rail." He showed me what to do by sketching lines in the air above the green felt surface with his finger.

I nodded and lined up for the shot. Reginald said, "Call the Safety, Precious."

Tiffany said, "Yeah. Call the Safety, Precious."

I straightened. "Safety." I stood there breathing for a few seconds. *Jeez.* Up until the last ten minutes or so, I'd been pretty good at pool. Now I felt like I'd never played the game in my life.

I chalked my stick and managed to do what he'd told me. My team and most of the people standing in front of the bar nodded and clapped. The Safety worked like it was supposed to and Tiffany scratched. I sank a couple of balls and then blew an easy shot. Then she blew an easy shot, and then I managed to run out the table. One, zip.

Tiffany racked the balls, swearing to herself. I chalked my stick. I broke, and the four ball dropped. I lined up on the three ball to the corner pocket. Tiffany suddenly appeared in my line of vision, twirling her stick. Distracted, I glanced at her, and in that glance I caught sight of a face in the crowd just over her shoulder. I went back to lining up my shot before I realized whose face it was. I stood up and looked again, but he had disappeared.

I took a few steps toward the bar, craning my neck, trying to find him. I took a few more steps so that I could see down the back hall, but there was no sign of him. Danny, looking puzzled, had stepped up beside me. I said, "I thought I saw my brother. Berk. Did you see him?"

He shook his head. "What would Berk be doing here? Are you sure it was him?"

I wasn't. It'd been yeas since I'd seen Berk, and it's been only a split-second glance. I shrugged it off and went back to the table, but I couldn't get my head clear. My shot went wide, and my cue ball didn't end up where I meant for it too, either. It was lined up to give Tiffany a bunny shot, eleven to the side. She made her shot, and three more, before she blew a bank shot and scratched.

I shook out the cobwebs and settled myself down.

Then I ran the table. Two, zip. The fans went wild. Gruf and Bump stood on either side of me, pounding me on the back.

Bump said, "One more game, dude."

Gruf said, "Bring it on home now."

I laughed at them. I broke, sinking the two ball, and missed a rail shot to the corner. Tiffany sank two but missed a bank shot into the side pocket. As I stepped up, I noticed for the first time that the eight ball was sitting on the side rail, dangerously close to the near corner pocket. I dropped four balls, but then I hesitated. I looked back to the scorer's table to see if Reginald was going to come out to talk to me. He nodded at me to go ahead and see what I could do.

I thought I could maybe clip the six ball into the side pocket, but then the cue ball would be heading up toward that eight ball. You never want to risk an Early Eight. Early Eight is instant death. Sink that bad-ass black eight ball before it's time and it's insta-matic Game Over. I looked for a Safety, found one, and made it. My team applauded.

Tiffany stepped up, called the nine in the side, and made a tough bank shot. But the cue ball kept going. It banked around to make a perfect rail shot on the eight. The eight dropped into the corner pocket with a thud. Early Eight. My team and most of the bar erupted into cheers. I'd won my first ever bar league set, three-zip. I was suddenly swallowed up by laughing, black-slapping teammates.

Then the other end of the room erupted in cheers. A bunch of people from Lo-Lites Bar in Ladonia were cheering for the tall, slender blonde who had just won her set. She strutted back to her table, laughing, pumping the air with her hands in that "raise the roof" gesture. I heard her say, "That's me. Red-Hot. Just like my license plate says."

None of us knew it on that frigid January night, of course, but that blond girl didn't have much longer to

be red-hot. In just a few hours, she was going to be
ice-cold. The long, tall blonde from Lo-Lites in Ladonia was about to experience the ultimate Early
Eight.